T0278676

SOUND
THE
GONG

PRAISE FOR *STRIKE THE ZITHER*

★ "Military stratagems, qi-infused zither duets, and divine interference
come together in this tightly crafted reimagining of the Chinese classic
Three Kingdoms . . . A riveting series opener."
—*Kirkus*, starred review

★ "The protagonist's clever narration and boundless ambition, coupled
with He's powerful, action-packed prose, quick pacing, anticipatory
atmosphere, and immersive worldbuilding, exemplify the origins of the
source material while developing a distinct and evocative adventure."
—*Publishers Weekly*, starred review

"A fierce reimagining of the Chinese classic . . . This riveting read is full
of twists and surprises that shock and delight, building up to the epic
conclusion that left me gasping."
—Judy I. Lin, #1 *New York Times*–bestselling author of
The Book of Tea duology

"Joan He takes no prisoners, and this is her latest triumph. An
intricate, expansive epic . . . this book is as ambitious as its
scheming, ruthless cast—and just like its narrator, delivers above
and beyond."
—Margaret Owen, *New York Times*–bestselling author of *Painted Devils*

"Filled with twists and turns, *Strike the Zither* is a meticulously plotted,
supremely satisfying story that explores identity, legacy, and loyalty in
unexpected ways. This is Joan He's best yet."
—Hannah Whitten, *New York Times*–bestselling author of *For the Wolf*

"*Strike the Zither* reimagines the Chinese classic *Romance of the Three
Kingdoms* in a way never seen before, with intense twists and turns that
pay homage to its inspiration while being refreshingly different. A brilliant
exploration of destiny and identity!"
—Xiran Jay Zhao, #1 *New York Times*–bestselling author of *Iron Widow*

"*Strike the Zither* is a page-turner, full of unexpected twists, with an expansive, intricate world of sisterhood and subterfuge. He's smooth, economical style is the perfect vehicle for this gripping political fantasy, marrying cat-and-mouse intrigue with a tenderness and emotional depth that heightens the stakes of every new reveal. A standout work from a remarkable author."
—Olivie Blake, *New York Times*–bestselling author of *The Atlas Six*

"Rich with intrigue and epic in scale. *Strike the Zither* grows tall on the heroic classics it draws from, yet beats powerfully with a heart of its own."
—Chloe Gong, #1 *New York Times*–bestselling author of the These Violent Delights Duet

"Richly layered and highly creative, *Strike the Zither* offers a world brimming with war, love, and unforgettable characters. A truly magnificent book."
—June Hur, bestselling author of *The Red Palace*

"In this tautly plotted, vividly reimagined tale of a beloved Chinese classic, He orchestrates an epic page-turner . . . *Strike the Zither* will keep you guessing—and gasping for more."
—June CL Tan, internationally bestselling author of *Jade Fire Gold*

"This soaring, masterful retelling becomes an epic all of its own . . . Readers will get lost in this rich, gorgeous, and dangerous world."
—Emily Suvada, author of *This Mortal Coil*

"A twisty, body-snatching, gender-flipped retelling of *The Romance of the Three Kingdoms*. Prepare to be transported."
—Rebecca Lim, award-winning author of *Tiger Daughter*

BOOKS BY JOAN HE

Descendant of the Crane
The Ones We're Meant to Find

The Kingdom of Three duology
Strike the Zither
Sound the Gong

SOUND THE GONG

THE KINGDOM OF THREE DUOLOGY
BOOK TWO

JOAN HE

ROARING BROOK PRESS
NEW YORK

Published by Roaring Brook Press
Roaring Brook Press is a division of Holtzbrinck Publishing Holdings
Limited Partnership
120 Broadway, New York, NY 10271 • fiercereads.com

Copyright © 2024 by Joan He
Map copyright © 2022 by Anna Frohmann
Portrait illustrations copyright © 2024 by Tida Kietsungden
All rights reserved.

Our books may be purchased in bulk for promotional, educational, or
business use. Please contact your local bookseller or the Macmillan Corporate
and Premium Sales Department at (800) 221-7945 ext. 5442 or by email at
MacmillanSpecialMarkets@macmillan.com.

Library of Congress Cataloging-in-Publication Data is available.

First edition, 2024
Book design by Aurora Parlagreco
Printed in the United States of America

ISBN 978-1-250-85536-7 (hardcover)
1 3 5 7 9 10 8 6 4 2

To William, my 知音

MAJOR FIGURES

North / Capital of the Xin Empire / Kingdom of Miracles
Empress: Xin Bao*
Prime Ministress: Miasma
Strategist: Crow
Advisor: Plum
Notable Generals: Viper, Talon, Leopard

Southlands / Kingdom of Knowledge
Lordess: Cicada
Strategist: November

Westlands / Kingdom of Humanity
Lordess: Xin Ren*
Swornsisters: Cloud, Lotus
Notable Generals: Tourmaline, Aster, Bracken
Advisor: Sikou Hai
Strategist: Unfilled

*Surname precedes given name. For example, Xin Bao and Xin Ren both share the surname "Xin."

CONTENTS

孟靡梦

Miasma (Meng Mimeng), empire prime ministress, regent to
Empress Xin Bao, commander of the North

岳蝉

Cicada (Yue Chan), sister to Cricket, queen of the Southlands

马白山

Tourmaline (Ma Baishan), general to Xin Ren

周森入

Crow (Zhou Senru), strategist to Miasma

Please note that this is a work of fantasy. The Xin Dynasty as depicted does not exist in history, and the story is neither set in China nor a true-to-times portrayal of social orders and demographics. Furthermore, Sound the Gong *should not be used as an educational reference for Chinese philosophy and spirituality; the metaphysics of qì; the mythology of gods; the techniques of the gǔqín; or the rules of wéiqí beyond white going first, an ancient Chinese tradition that has faded from relevancy. The reality of war, conversely, remains relevant to this day and is therefore preserved wherever necessitated by the story. For more content warnings, please visit joanhewrites.com/stg.*

SOUND

THE

GONG

STANZA THREE

To the north, a miasma
held her army at Dasan.
This would be no repeat of the Scarp.

To the south, a cicada,
allied with a foe,
prepared to reclaim the marsh.

To the west, a lordess
had inherited her uncle's stronghold
with no will to ascend his throne.

And in the skies above,
the heavens remained one god short.

The air is moist. It smells of earth.

It tastes of blood.

"The empire wasn't behind the ambush, Cloud."

"But the survivors said they were." Cloud joins me at my shrine's entrance. "The soldiers wore empire uniforms and carried empire weapons."

Of course they did. As the cicadas begin to sing, I clench the arrow. "That's what the South wanted you to believe."

"You're saying Cicada betrayed us."

"And allied with Miasma."

"How do you know that?" Cloud demands, but the better question is how did I *not* know? Even if I didn't have evidence, I have a strategist's common sense. Cicada wouldn't have betrayed us unless Miasma had more to offer . . . such as the return of the Marshlands. The arrow shaft digs into my palm. *There's something else.* A revelation just beyond my grasp. The cicadas screech like crows as I rack my thoughts. *Why do I feel so slow?*

Is it this body's fault?

"We need to tell Ren," Cloud says, and I come back to myself.

"No. Absolutely not." I grab her arm. "Tell Ren the Southlands betrayed us, and we'll never fight alongside them again."

"You *still* want them for allies?" Cloud tries to shake me off, but I hold on. "The people who shot you?"

"I don't care if they skinned me alive. You want Ren to beat Miasma, do you not? To unite the three kingdoms?"

"Do I? Why, yes," Cloud drawls. "Enough"—she rips her arm free—"to be exiled for *your* coup, *Zephyr*, just so *you* can stay and help her."

"Then never forget." I grab her again. "We need to follow the Rising Zephyr Objective to win. We *need* the South on our side before we can march on the empire. I won't have Ren chasing vengeance like a peasant."

I search Cloud's face, waiting for this nonnegotiable to sink in. *Don't make me regret trusting you.*

And she won't. In a few days, without breathing a word to Ren about Cicada, Cloud will leave for the Marshlands and monitor the South for me from its capital. I have faith in these events as if I've already lived them. My fingers uncurl, releasing Cloud. She won't run to Ren—

But she tears off.

"*Cloud!*"

No. This shouldn't be happening. I rush after her, into the banyans. I swear I've had this conversation with Cloud before. She never tells Ren. That means—

I'm dreaming. The ground pulses under my feet, and I sink. *Don't fight it.* Quicksand closes over my head. *If I die—*

I'll wake up.

I break the surface, gasping for air. The bed is squishy and wet beneath me—and no bed at all.

I'm in a swamp of corpses.

Soldiers march past me, carrying Ren's banners.

"For Zephyr!"

No. I'm right here. "Stop!" I shout. "*Sto—*"

I gurgle, an arrow shot through my throat.

My spirit detaches, and powerless, I can only watch as an enemy horde swarms Cloud, spears stabbing down.

Watch as Ren dies avenging her swornsister.

No. No, no, no. I float over the killing fields, beating my head with my fists. I must still be dreaming. It's the only explanation. *Wake up. Wake up.*

Wake—up—

‡ ‡ ‡

My eye flies open to the beams of the barracks.

二十五

A NAME BEFITTING

Some think the gods walk this realm.

For once, the peasants are not wrong.

Gods do exist, in forms from bees to children. Many dynasties ago, I preferred floating through the skies as a cloud myself. Those days feel like a distant dream as I groan on the ground, biting dust.

"Aiya, Lotus! I know you have more fight left in you!"

Above me is the face of Xin Ren. My lordess, swornsister, and current sparring partner who just knocked me on my back.

Ren offers me a hand. I grab it and—grunting—pull myself up. Around us in the training field, our soldiers are supposed to be drilling, *supposed to* being the key words. Hard not to watch your lordess fight her second-in-command, especially when said second-in-command is losing as badly as I am.

"Is it the eye?" asks Ren, passing me my pole.

If only. Two working eyes wouldn't solve my biggest problem: I'm not really Lotus, slayer of tigers, nightmare of men. My name is Zephyr, god of weather, and I'm ashamed to report that

SOUND THE GONG ‡ 5

I never thought to master the art of pole fighting in my forty thousand years of existence.

"Just tired," I reply, hoping Ren is too. She's already dueled three other soldiers, her way of reminding the camp that we're all equals, united in our mission to free Empress Xin Bao from Miasma.

And I, impostor of a warrior, am not exempt. My hopes are dashed as Ren steps back. "Again."

Again, we duel.

Again, I lose.

"Again," Ren says, and for a second I'm whisked back to Master Yao's porch, his fan smacking my shoulder as I pluck the zither.

Again! Play again!

But Ren is nothing like my former mentor. Even as I miss easy parries, she doesn't berate me, giving tips instead—*Sweep. Hands apart. Stab.* But some causes are lost from the start, and on the eighth bout, I'm too slow. Ren's pole whacks into my side—left, right, left. I back up. I can't block.

Then don't. Find the pattern. The pattern Ren created on purpose. To onlookers, it's not obvious.

It is to Lotus. *No cheating, Peacock!* I can almost hear her shout, her blood boiling at the insult. *No cheat—*

I fall left after Ren's rightward attack, levering her pole down. *Now finish it.* I surge at her—and trip. *Ugh—!*

By fate or luck, I flail into Ren.

I smash my lordess into the ground.

Everything spins. Cheers of Lotus's name. My elbows—are crushing Ren's ribs. I scramble off. "Ren. Are you okay?"

No answer.

"Ren."

She opens her eyes and crosses them.

"Not funny!"

"I know, I know." Ren sits up. "I'm sorry. Though I did feel my life flash before my eyes. But I'm fine!" Her gaze is alight with laughter. Then it sobers. "And you, Lotus?" I sweat harder as she says, "You seem more than tired."

Is this it? Has Ren finally seen me for who I am?

"Have you been getting enough sleep?"

It'd certainly make my life easier, to be exposed as Zephyr.

It just wouldn't be worth Ren losing a swornsister.

"Six hours a day," I lie.

It's a respectable amount for a soldier, but Ren looks aghast. "No wonder. Remember what happened the last time I woke you up before dawn?"

Something mortifying, I'm sure. "Lotus will sleep more."

"Good. I order you to, as your lordess."

I help Ren to her feet, frowning as she pats her chest. If she's hurt, she won't say so, would brush it off if I pressed. She threw the fight because she knows the power of appearances. "Sorry about that too," she says, gesturing to her pole, but no apology is required. I understand. We're *not* all equal. Lose too many duels as Ren's swornsister, and the soldiers won't follow me into battle.

SOUND THE GONG ‡ 7

The same applies to Ren. Her position in the Westlands should be beyond dispute, down to her title.

That is the battle I must win before any other.

As Ren and I leave the training field, I catch Tourmaline's eye across it. She makes quick work of her opponent and walks over.

"Lordess," she greets, falling into step beside Ren.

"Tourmaline. How's Awl formation coming along?"

"We've perfected it."

"Good. And Flying Geese?"

While Tourmaline details our training progress, I watch Ren. The truth is I haven't been sleeping much at all. The nightmares keep me up—of Ren, dying, sometimes to Miasma, sometimes to Cicada. But it won't happen. I'm still Ren's strategist, even if I can't advise her directly. I glance over Ren's head and nod at Tourmaline.

Now.

"Lordess," the warrior begins as Ren observes the soldiers sparring in training field two. "About the coronation . . ."

Silence descends, heavier than the noon sun.

"My answer is the same," Ren at last says. "I will not assume my uncle's throne. I will only govern the people, as I have for the last two months, so that their lives aren't disrupted. Isn't that sufficient?"

It should be. The title of governor is a formality. The coronation? Worthless ritual and ceremony, if you ask me. Did Master Shencius? No. *Order won't flow through the world unless a person's name befits their role,* he wrote. Three centuries later, people still live by his words. It's why so many follow Ren: She has the surname Xin.

It must be why Ren, a traditionalist to her core, can't see past the name "Lotus" and to my soul underneath.

When Tourmaline doesn't answer, Ren turns from the training field and walks away.

We hurry after her.

"The people are nervous." Tourmaline does the talking, as we discussed. She's known more for her . . . sensibilities compared to Lotus. "Since marching down to Dasan, Miasma hasn't moved from it."

A shrewd play by the prime ministress, no doubt still burned by her loss at the Scarp. Rather than march into the mountainous, unfavorable terrain of the Westlands, she dallies in Dasan, trying to lure us out—

"Then we march on Dasan," Ren says.

"*No!*" I yell even as Lotus's blood spikes. *Battle! Battle!*

"No," Tourmaline repeats, blessedly calm. "Not yet. That's just what Miasma wants. A coronation would reassert your authority in the eyes of the populace without the need for battle. Your officialdom ought to match Miasma's."

Please, I think as Ren stops by the palisades of training field three. *Assume the proper title.*

"You forget something, Tourmaline." Ren's gaze swings to the warrior, then to me. "I never wanted this. I never wanted any of this." Her eyes burn into mine, and I swallow. I know. Asking Ren to celebrate her new office is like asking her to celebrate the bloody coup, Xin Gong's death, and the prophecy that's haunted her since childhood:

Xin Ren—she will betray her clan.

But what was portended has come to pass, and if Ren can justify filling in as governor for the people's good, she can justify a coronation. As she stalks into training field three—alone, Tourmaline and I not invited to follow—my mouth opens. *Reason with her.* My lungs expand.

"Even the cockroaches are calling themselves king!"

Ren marches faster.

I start after her—and am held back by Tourmaline. She catches my fist before I can register cocking it.

Maybe I really do need more sleep. I mumble some excuse about that and the heat, and Tourmaline gives my knuckles a sympathetic squeeze.

"All is not lost." Out in the field, the soldiers bow to Ren. "She's training the troops," Tourmaline says. "She *could* still be camping out at your shrine."

"Don't remind me."

"She wants to fight. Morale is high." Tourmaline tugs me away from the field and with her, through the rest of camp. "We can still march north"—I glare at her—"when the time is right. We still have our allies."

Ah, our "allies," who kindly repaid my diplomacy with an arrow to the back—not that Tourmaline knows, or Ren. It's like I told Cloud: Vengeance is for peasants. Strategists don't let yesterday's blood poison tomorrow's well. Why declare the alliance broken when I can repair it?

Can you repair it, though? goes a voice in my head, and I wish it were just the voice of doubt. *You haven't been able to convince Ren to call herself "governor" when she's practically acting as one. Are you even still her strat—*

"Shut up!"

"Zephyr?" Tourmaline blinks, and I kick myself for actually shouting my thoughts.

"Lotus," I remind her. "And it's nothing." Tourmaline looks unconvinced. "It was Cloud. I imagined her harping just now." *Sorry, Cloud.* "What do you think she's even doing in the Marshlands these days?" I ask as we take the path to the stables.

The clamor of camp fades, the air quiet like Tourmaline's voice. "If not dueling their generals, then challenging the magistrates to chess."

"Chess."

"She once mentioned beating everyone in her village."

Is that so? I smile. Cloud would be pleased to hear Tourmaline recounting her feats, but she shouldn't boast until she's beaten *me*.

"You're lucky she didn't see you today," Tourmaline goes on. "It reflects badly on me when you lose four duels in a row."

My smile capsizes to a scowl. *Three, not four*—but Tourmaline *would* notice Ren's throw, as my mentor behind the scenes. "It's Ren. She's too good."

"She trained hard."

"For years," I retort. Experience wins fights, not brute strength, and my experience is but months old. It wasn't too long ago that I ordered Tourmaline to poison Ren's cavalry, I think sulkily as we enter the stables—then guiltily when the horses whinny.

Tourmaline checks over them—"my daily penance"—while I go to Rice Cake. He stares at me. Unlike most humans, he knows I'm not Lotus.

He has my respect for it. "You could look happier," I mutter, flicking his nose. He blows a snot bubble. "Point taken. You miss her, not me."

His answer is unspoken, like the words in my heart.

I miss her too. I miss Lotus's spirit despite all the dirt I've eaten for it. I even miss Cloud. The empty stall next to Rice Cake's, where her mare would be, drives home her absence.

Would Cloud have better luck convincing Ren? I don't know, don't know how she is. She writes sparingly, sending only military updates to our camp. I should be glad. No additional word means no movement from the South.

Still, when a scout rushes into the stables, shouting, "Report!" I nearly seize him. *Tell me it's from Cloud.*

Then I realize it's the soldier I tasked with watching over our infirmary.

Come to me and me first, I told him, *if anything changes.*

Naïve of me, to speak of change as an *if* and not a *when*.

"He's awake, General Lotus."

‡ ‡ ‡

"*Awake*, you said." I whirl on the soldier. "Not *gone*."

Behind us is the infirmary bed, devoid of one masked, comatose Sikou Hai.

The soldier quakes. "H-he was just here."

Useless. My hand flies to my ax and the soldier thuds to his knees, pleading mercy. Lotus's reputation outlives her, but right now that's useless too. As Tourmaline and I stare at the pallet, we're both thinking the same grim thing. Ren despises the coup enough as is. What will she do if Xin Gong's surviving son reminds her that he *wasn't* collateral damage? As for Aster, Bracken, and all the other Westlands generals loyal to us because of Sikou Hai? Who would blame them for switching sides if they learned the truth of how their liege was brutally used to instigate the coup, then discarded?

Not I, the mastermind behind it.

"I'll handle it," I say to Tourmaline, and stride out. I spin, eye roving over our surroundings.

Where is he? I wonder—and not just to myself.

I thought you told me to shut up.

I take it back. I'm deeply, sorely repentant. Now, where is he?

No idea. Dewdrop's yawn vibrates through my skull. She flies out from my collar, stretching her wings, and I frown.

Find out.

Don't feel like it. She dodges my swat. *Do that again, and I'll sting you.*

Why are you being so difficult? Rhetorical. While I can't read minds like my bee god-sister, I can guess at hers. She's worried. The Masked Mother, empress of all deities, knows I'm here and enmeshed with the humans. One of these days, she'll punish me, but less severely for less meddling, or so goes the logic.

And I get it. I don't *want* to suffer a hundred lightning strikes over fifty. But if I'm going to suffer regardless, then let my time here count for something. Let me win, and if—gods forbid—I must lose, let it be to one person.

My true rival.

No offense to Sikou Hai, but he's not it. Now, where could he be? Where could he even *reach*? His study, all the way over in Xin City, is out of the question. As for the camp—the outhouse, the barracks, and the armory all yield nothing. Only the banyan path is left.

I stomp into the fig trees, clenching my ax.

You said we wouldn't be here for long, buzzes Dewdrop. *Before you took this body, you said you were less than two steps from realizing your so-called Rising Zephyr Objective. But it seems like more. Your alliance with the South is not repaired. Here in the West, your lordess refuses to legitimize herself. As for the North—*

March on them now, and we'd play right into Miasma's hand.

So?

We'd lose!

Dewdrop bobs, a bee's shrug. *It's been a long time since you cared about winning.*

I've always cared.

Not in heaven.

There was nothing to win there. And no one to win it for.

So Nadir and myself are "no ones" now.

You said that, not me. Point is, you don't need *me.*

Your Ren doesn't either. She isn't made for winning any more than you're made for pole fighting. I smart, but Dewdrop's not done. *You could all but carry her to the top, and she still wouldn't take the empress's throne.*

I never wanted her to take the empress's throne.

"Even the cockroaches—"

That was Lotus's temper speaking. But my aim is Ren's, liberate Xin Bao, and it hasn't changed since—since Ren beseeched me at Thistlegate to help her. But why am I defending myself to Dewdrop?

I never asked you for your assessment on Xin Ren, I think at my god-sister. *I asked you to find out more information on the South since they betrayed us.*

That would be interfering with fate.

Fate. Fate. Fate. I'm tired of hearing about it, tired of the sun—blinding me again—as I emerge from the banyans. My shrine lies just ahead. In and out I step.

No Sikou Hai.

I growl, and birds flee the nearest tree. Cowards, all of them.

Except for one. A bird that's not a bird, I see as my eye focuses, but a shred of white fabric caught on a branch.

Infirmary robe.

More shreds dangle from branches, deeper into the woods.

I follow the shreds, through the trees and eventually up the basin, cursing the guard soldier with every step. *He's awake.* Clearly, and has been for ages. I scan the ground as it rises, not sure if I should be searching for a person or a corpse. *Will you at least tell me if he's alive?* I think to Dewdrop.

She buzzes.

Fine. Be that way. I tear through a clump of brush with my bare hands, then cut through the next clump with my ax. It feels nice, chopping things, and too soon, the brush clears. The sky is a bright, bright blue over the cliff.

A figure in infirmary white sits at the edge.

I approach. Sunlight glitters off the river below. The current is quiet, this high up. Higher fly the birds, their conversations inaudible to us. It's the silence of a slingshot fitted with a stone, mine to release and control—

My boot lands on a pebble and it *clucks*.

"Took you long enough."

His voice is scratchy, unused for two months.

"Thought you'd be more careful," I say, closing the distance.

"Just to face death at your hand again, General Lotus?" Sikou Hai has eyes only for the tan stretch of Marshlands beyond the river.

I have an eye only for the back of his head.

Not my hand, I should correct. *Your brother's.* It was Sikou Dun who stabbed Sikou Hai at the wedding. Everyone saw. What they didn't see was how Sikou Hai's brother danced from *my* strings. He discovered the coup, flew into a rage, and drove a scim into Sikou Hai's chest because of *my* involvement—which I left no evidence of. I should tell Sikou Hai he's mistaken in his assumptions.

But a literati like Sikou Hai trusts his mind. He suspects me and always will.

It's gratifying, frankly, to be credited for my machinations.

"Let's settle this, General," Sikou Hai says, eyes still on the river. "Does my being alive help you?"

"I don't know." Sikou Hai is a loose end. I don't usually deal with loose ends. "Are you going to tell Ren?"

"About your role in the coup? Would you kill me if I did?"

"Depends." Cloud claimed to be the coup's mastermind so that Ren would send her, not me, to the Marshlands. I can't squander her sacrifice. "Maybe."

"I'd respect you more if you said yes."

I'm baffled by his words, then inflamed. "Why?" It's like this is all a game to him, and I'm the beast he baited with a trail of shreds. "Could *you* kill someone?" *Don't yell*—but I can't keep my voice down. "Actually drive a knife into them? Watch the life leave their eyes?" *Close your mouth.* "I didn't think so. Why should *I* be respected for bloodletting, then? Is it because I look the way I do? Well, let me tell you something, Sikou Hai: We're the same. I'm you. A—"

A strategist.

I bite down, sense finally damming the flood.

"I know." Sikou Hai's head turns. Away from the river. To me. His face is unmasked, his scars bare to the sun.

"I've *known*," he says, with emphasis, "ever since you spoke up at our meetings, planning the coup against my uncle. No—earlier. When you played the zither. From that alone, I knew you were more than a warrior.

"Of course, knowing is one thing. Admitting is another. I knew you were more, but I couldn't admit what that 'more' was. I couldn't see your plans as tactics, until you dumped me in the forest." His voice turns sardonic. "Then I had plenty of time to come to terms with what you were."

Will he say *monster* or *murderer*?

"You're Xin Ren's strategist." Sikou Hai's gaze meets mine, and I can't move. He's sitting, pale and frail, and I'm standing like a boulder, but even boulders can fall off cliffs, and my heart teeters as he says, "I see that now. But I haven't heard of you." He breathes in and grimaces. "What is your sobriquet?"

Sobriquet. I don't know which to pick. Words. I seem to have forgotten how to speak them.

Then Lotus's temper flares, quick and decisive. "Zephyr."

My name is Zephyr.

I've seen two people react to my true identity. Tourmaline, despite believing in reincarnation, didn't know what to think. Cloud wanted to strangle me for taking Lotus's body.

Sikou Hai—he stands. "Zephyr," he repeats. "Disciple of Yao Mengqi. Master of the zither. Predictor of the weather. The wisest among us." His voice rasps, pained, reverent, awed. "You're a god among strategists."

At first, the only word I can hear is *god*. Then I realize.

He acknowledged me as Zephyr.

Sikou Hai kneels.

"Rising Zephyr." He stares up at me, eyes sunken but bright. "I've been a follower of yours for a long time. Please accept me as your disciple."

The wind stirs. Birds fly. I could too—I'm that light.

I've been seen.

It's the most powerful feeling.

Reality returns in the next moment. "Wait. Don't you want

to know how"—*I'm alive?*—"or why"—*I look like this?* Does he believe in reincarnation? In deities?

"The impossible is possible with you," Sikou Hai says, resolute, offering nothing else by way of explanation.

Well.

I won't say no to worship.

Slowly, I lower my ax. A disciple. I've never had one. My own mentors—Master Yao, the poet, the chess master, the ex-imperial cosmologist—trained me so well, I've surpassed them. I'd sooner step in oxshit than have Sikou Hai surpass me.

But.

Sikou Hai is the only adopted son of Xin Gong's left. Ren will listen to him out of guilt if nothing else. I will finally have a mouthpiece for my plans.

"Rise," I say to Sikou Hai.

"Accept me first."

"Accepted. Now *rise*."

He bows, touching his head three times to the ground before rising—and staggering. I steady him. "We're going back." How is he still conscious? "No more leaving the infirmary without my permission."

Sikou Hai pulls free. "Tell me what I've missed."

"Later."

"No, now," Sikou Hai insists, and my eye twitches. "I've been incapacitated for too long."

"I'll tell you as we—"

—*walk.*

I walk, past Sikou Hai, gaze drawn to the river as something flows down it like a leaf, tiny from our elevation.

It's a skiff.

On it is a person, clad in black.

Crow. His smile slices through my mind. His bandaged hand, covering mine. I blink, and the memories vanish, leaving only the person on the river. The skiff comes ashore, our troops surrounding the lone passenger as he disembarks.

He bears something gilded in his arms.

A messenger.

"Come," I say to Sikou Hai, and he does, without argument. The pieces on the chessboard have changed, and I don't need to explain myself when I hoist him over my back like a sack of rice for expediency's sake. To advise Ren, we must stay abreast of every development.

It's imperative that we get back to camp.

And we do, just in time to see the messenger marched in by our soldiers. He's ushered before Ren as our generals and officials gather around.

"A gift from the North," he says, presenting a gilded box.

Ren accepts it.

She lifts the lid.

The camp goes silent.

二十六

KILL THE MESSENGER

A gift from the North.

For a long time after opening the box, Ren stares down at it. She doesn't move, but her qì grows violent with emotion. A darkness wells between her lips, then drips out the corner of her mouth.

Blood.

"Lordess!" Aster and Tourmaline support her while I seize the box—dropping it when I see the contents.

Gods be damned. I dive for it, but it's too late. The box hits the ground and out bounces the head. It rolls, and everyone scrambles back, myself included. *Ten hells.* That *thing* must be diseased, with its shriveled skin and stringy hair clasped back—

—by *my* hair clasp. I recognize it before I can recognize my head in its abject state. My nose wrinkles.

To think I used to be fond of it.

Then a moan from Ren throws everything into focus. "Call the physician," I order one soldier. I turn to another, unluckier one. "You—collect the head."

The rest of us flock to Ren. Officials and generals—ours and the Westlands'—throng around her and start moving her toward the command tent.

I fall to the back of the retinue, where Tourmaline is.

"I thought we recovered the body," I whisper. Qilin's body, specifically, killed by an arrow that definitely *was* recovered; it's resting in my shrine as we speak.

"We did," Tourmaline whispers back.

"Without a *head*. You could have mentioned it."

"It seemed irrelevant."

Until now. Who sent it? Was it really Miasma, or is the messenger actually one of Cicada's and the South wants us to pin the head on the empire as well?

It was Miasma, Dewdrop thinks.

Oh, now *you decide to help.*

It's not helping if the answer makes no difference. It just proves my point from before. You're surrounded by enemies . . .

So, it was Miasma, I think to myself as Dewdrop drones on. How very like her.

At least it was my head she sent and not our empress's.

Inside the command tent, we sit Ren down. The physician arrives and reads her pulse. "The disturbance to your qì activated an existing injury—"

"Injury?" pipes up an official.

"Bruising at the chest from a blunt force," says the physician, and *my* chest pangs. That would be me. "It'll heal in time, but I'll write a prescription."

A servant delivers tea. Ren doesn't touch it. Her eyes are

sheened, and my chest pangs again. *I'm right here*, I wish I could tell her. *The head? It's rotted meat.*

But that's not how the mortals see it. Warriors sever the heads of their enemies in this life to deny them peace in the next; even the aunties at Qilin's orphanage avoided burning corpses when they could to keep the body intact.

And Ren is painfully mortal. "I'll kill her." She looks up at us, and I'm reliving my nightmare as she says, "We'll march on the North by the week's end."

No one objects. Have they all fallen asleep? *Miasma couldn't have sent a more obvious provocation!* I could scream.

But I'm Lotus. Lotus would never question her lordess, and it's Sikou Hai who says, "You mustn't," his voice turning heads. Shock ripples through the ranks.

"Young Master Sikou!"

"Young Master Sikou! You're awake!"

He's masked now, but still unsteady as he walks forward. Aster rushes to him; he brushes her aside, proceeding alone toward the parting crowd.

He stops before Ren and bows. "Lordess."

"Please, at ease." Sikou Hai rises, and so does Ren, out of her seat. "Sikou Hai." A pregnant pause. "Forgive me."

She bows to him, and every breath stops.

"Your father and your brother." Ren's voice is pained. "We didn't manage to save them."

"Lordess, please," Tourmaline murmurs, causing the tent to parrot her. A superior bowing to her subordinate? It's improper, and Sikou Hai's silence is appropriately strained, the unmasked half of his face paler than when I approached him on the cliff.

"If you feel like you owe me," he finally says, "then listen. You mustn't march on the North."

At last, a voice of reason!

"The mountain routes that make it so hard to invade the Westlands also make it hard to transport supplies out of it. If we march to Miasma from here, she'll defeat us by stalling confrontation and starving out our soldiers."

Yes! Exactly as I'd have said it!

"I'm aware," says Ren. "But Miasma's message is an insult. A challenge. The realm will soon know if I rose to meet it or backed down."

"We won't back down." Sikou Hai goes to the map hanging at the rear of the tent. "We'll respond by taking Bikong."

What? No!

Sikou Hai taps the fort, then draws two fingers southward. "Your other swornsister, Cloud. She's stationed in the Marshlands capital right now. She'll have no issue transporting her troops up the Mica." He sweeps his hand back north, following the Mica River's eastern offshoot until it nearly converges with the Gypsum. Bikong sits under the pincer. Nominally a Marshlands fort, Miasma's outpost in reality. Sikou Hai knows this like any statesman would. "We will seize Bikong from Miasma without abandoning our position here," he declares, radiating confidence—until he sees my expression.

You fool! Bikong is a great prize—and a great risk. Miasma is no longer our only enemy. Cicada is set on reclaiming the Marshlands, the heart of which Cloud will leave unguarded to carry out this attack. Sikou Hai doesn't yet know the peril of that, but he *should* have known better than to strategize without me. I glare at him, and his gaze wavers, but the plan has been shared and Ren has latched on.

"It's decided." She strides to the front of the tent and stops, her back toward us. "We'll do as Young Master Sikou says. Send word of the objective to Cloud."

"Yes, lordess," answers an official, ledger already out.

"Send Lotus." Eyes turn to me, but not Ren's. Her gaze remains fixed forward as I say, "I'll carry the message."

"No."

"But—"

"Would you refuse an order from your queen?"

A beat.

We fall to our knees.

Queen. A title to match Miasma's, a title that seemed so out of reach just hours earlier. Perhaps I should *thank* my head for appearing, because something feels changed. The air is sharper, cooler, the day outside turned to dusk when Ren parts the tent flaps. "And send a message to Miasma."

The official looks up, brush poised, but Ren walks out and speaks to the waiting soldiers.

"Kill the messenger."

‡ ‡ ‡

People change, Crow once said as he'd sat beside me, skipping stones over the lake.

People change.

I thought nothing could startle me more than my head today, but Ren, lordess of the commoners, killing innocent messengers? Is this the change Crow spoke of? No—she's rattled. It's like the blood—a one-time eruption. No permanent damage has been done to her or anyone.

And no damage will. I race into the training field just as the chopping block is carried in by a group of soldiers. The other group, tasked with preparing the messenger for his beheading, is still on its way. Thank heavens. I wasn't sure if I'd beat them.

They can't witness what I'm about to say.

"New orders," I bark at the soldiers. "When the messenger arrives, put him into the prison barracks."

The soldiers blink.

"*Do it!*" I bellow.

"Yes, General Lotus!"

I leave the field before Miasma's minion can see me. Let him think the order has come from Ren. Let him think—

"What are you doing?"

Sikou Hai walks in behind me.

"I heard what you just said." He nears, and I see red. "We can't disregard Queen Xin's orders—"

I lift him off his feet by his neck. "*You ruined everything!*"

Sikou Hai gags.

Good, gag! Teach him a lesson, Peacock!

Zephyr!

Peacock!

"*Zephyr, no!*" Tourmaline yells, and I recoil. The haze of red scatters. Sikou Hai falls from my grasp.

"I—I'm sorry." My hands shake. "I—I don't know—"

—*what got into me.* Shamefaced, I glance to Tourmaline, but there's no judgment in her eyes. If anything, *she* looks contrite. She crouches by Sikou Hai as he coughs and says, "The name you heard was a mistake. I was confused—"

"He knows," I interrupt. "He knows I'm Zephyr."

"Yes, I'm her disciple," Sikou Hai chokes out.

Tourmaline looks to me; my silence confirms the partnership. She notably doesn't congratulate it. "Did you stop the execution?" she asks me, and nods when I nod. "Ren's not being herself."

"You can't always shield her," Sikou Hai says between gasps. "Eventually, you have to trust her."

"*Eventually,*" I growl, "when I also trust her advisors. The advice you gave on the Marshlands—"

"Is better than marching on the North."

Is it? When we do march on the North, it must be with the assurance we can win. Defeat is not an option. From this perspective, sending Cloud to take Bikong *would* seem like the lesser evil.

It could also doom our entire mission.

"The Marshlands are vital to us," I say. Between the coup and the governorship, Ren seems to have forgotten Cicada ever asked for them back, and I have no intentions of reminding her. Until we can trust the South again—"We need them as both a buffer from the South and a launch point for our eventual northbound campaign."

"I know," says Sikou Hai.

"Losing the marsh would be akin to losing a limb."

"Why—" Sikou coughs. "Why would we lose . . ."

The marsh.

I watch as comprehension dawns, slow then quick. "Cicada wants the Marshlands," Sikou Hai says. "But she's our ally. She wouldn't take it by force. Unless . . ." His eyes probe mine. "The alliance has broken."

Is that true, Zephyr? ask Tourmaline's eyes, on me as well.

Sikou Hai, you really have ruined everything. This is *not* how I wanted to debrief everyone, but my disciple leaves me with no choice.

"Tourmaline. Ask Ren to send you to the Marshlands capital with a legion. Say it's to replace Cloud's forces, nothing else. Disguise yourselves as merchants." Stratagem Twenty-Two: Open the Door to Catch the Thief. "Let the Southlands come for the Marshlands thinking we've left it unguarded, then close in on them." *Crush them!* Lotus would say, but I force my fists to loosen. "Do it with minimal bloodshed."

We'll see who Cicada wants to ally with when *we* control her forces.

"One legion won't be enough to bring the South to heel," Sikou Hai says, sounding skeptical.

"That's why Cloud will fall back from Bikong to reinforce Tourmaline."

"She won't leave Bikong until she wins." Tourmaline's skepticism feels more like a betrayal.

"Sieges take time," Sikou Hai adds. "Why not tell Ren that the South has betrayed us and have more forces sent to the Marsh—"

"She'll want evidence!" I snap. "She'd trust an ally until we shattered that trust with evidence."

"You have such evidence," Sikou Hai infers, and I close my tired, aching eye, hating that he can be so right *and* so blind. Crow would never need the obvious stated.

He'd know my deepest fears with a single glance.

"If you want to tell Ren about the South, then do it," I say to Sikou Hai. "Force a confession out of the messenger. Have him say *Cicada* sent the head. See how Ren reacts."

No one argues with me after that.

‡ ‡ ‡

Over the next week, the reports trickle in.

Cloud has moved her troops up the Mica.

Cloud has marched on Bikong.

Cloud has laid siege to the fort.

The mood in our camp lifts, and Ren approves Tourmaline's request to travel to the Marshlands capital. Only I remain tense. It takes six days for Cloud's messages to reach us from Bikong. As we rejoice, Cloud could be facing a fresh attack. Could be losing. Could be dying.

Is it not exhausting? asks Dewdrop when I pester after Cloud's status for the umpteenth time on my way to the barracks. *To be worried over so many fickle humans?*

Status.

Dewdrop sighs. *Alive.*

And Miasma's reinforcements? They could come from Dasan, or the empire capital, or both directions. That would spell disaster for Cloud. *How many are on their way to Bikong?*

You're a god too, you know.

Yes, I am. I draw up short of the barracks.

Why rely on Dewdrop when I have myself?

That's not what I meant. Dewdrop flies after me as I go to the cliffs where I found Sikou Hai. *What are you doing?*

I sit on the rock. *You said we could bend the rules in small ways.*

The Masked Mother—

Has known I'm here since the coup. She hasn't called me back yet.

But when she does—

Lightning strikes. A hundred. A thousand.

No, Zephyr. You could be banished—for good this time, Dewdrop adds, and that silences me. It's true. Some banished gods are never heard from again.

No one knows what becomes of them.

If, in exchange for one more heartbeat on earth, I lose Dewdrop and Nadir forever . . .

A chill goes down my spine.

But *is* it forever if I don't die? Because gods can't, whereas Cloud can. *Ren* can.

They always die one after another in my nightmares.

I can't let that happen.

I raise my hands. I've summoned fog, according to Dewdrop, as Qilin. Manifested rain. Created winds. I've tried so hard to master Lotus's strength that I've neglected the strength I already have.

Closing my eye, I go within myself, mentally reaching for the well of power stored in my core. I reach deeper when I don't find it, past the memories—

—*of being as light as a feather*—

—*everything at my fingertips yet to be mastered*—

—*I find a board among Nadir's things, a replica of a mortal's game. I don't care about the mortals, but I like this game, the rush of winning—by five points, eleven, nineteen. Other gods come to Aurora Nest, just to play me, and I beat them all*—

—*god after god*—

—*until they start to beat me, their losses turned to wins through the centuries. Everyone has an eternity to surpass and be surpassed. No mark I make lasts*—

—*"Why try so hard?" a god asks as we drink together on the terraces above the clouds, and I begin to wonder it myself*—

—*Why indeed*—

—*if everything I do can be redone, undone, outdone*—

—*why not rest*—

No. I won't rest. I reach even deeper, until I find my power. I channel it between my palms. An orb qì forms. I pull my hands apart, growing the orb, then send it out. It zooms over the Marshlands, and for a breath, I can see the plains, the rivers, the villages as if I'm also flying over them, as if I could soar straight to Cloud—

The sights vanish. The orb is still traveling; I just can't use it to see beyond ten lǐ. An annoying limitation, but I don't need eyes to make a storm.

I send the orb shooting into the clouds over Dasan, a thousand five hundred lǐ to the northeast.

Seconds later, the qì takes effect—over there, and back in me. I sway forward, hands splayed upon the stone. Sweat falls from my face, landing between my spread fingers the same way rain must be landing in the Mica River. I pant. Was it always this hard?

Doesn't matter; it's done. The rain won't let up. By tomorrow, the Mica will flood, pinning down any reinforcements Miasma tries to send from Dasan.

The rain has another use, if Cloud can see it. If she's any good at chess, she'd know the importance of terrain. Rivers give life.

They can also take.

End it quickly, I think to Cloud, wishing I could speak into her mind like Dewdrop. *Don't let it become a war of attrition.*

The moment it does will be the moment Cicada moves in on the marsh.

‡ ‡ ‡

Six more days pass before Cloud's next report: Empire reinforcements from Dasan had their supply wagons trapped in the mud, halting their march. Meanwhile, forces led by Talon from the capital reached Bikong in the night and set up camp across the river from Cloud's tents; by dawn, both camps were swept away, Cloud's tents mere decoys, Cloud herself breaking the dams of the Mica upriver to unleash the flood. Army lost, Talon escaped behind the walls of Bikong, joining Miasma's other forces under siege.

In response, our camp throws a feast. As the revelry rises, I clench my wine goblet. Bikong hasn't yet surrendered. That means more reinforcements are to come. If only I knew the conditions on the ground. I turn to Ren. "Lotus wants to join Cloud at Bikong."

"Why? To steal all the glory from Cloud?" Ren teases.

Glory. I barely remember her. "Miasma is crafty," I push. "Cloud has no strategist."

"That's true. Sikou Hai's been asking to go—"

"*No!*"

Ren smiles at the outburst. "I told him he's not well enough for the journey."

And I'm going to tell him a thing or two about knowing his station. *Since when did a disciple go in place of his mentor?* I think darkly as an official steals Ren and her seat is overtaken by a drumstick-eating contest. I excuse myself and walk off to the barracks, dodging drunken soldiers, only to stop for one, slumped against a tree.

In the branches floats her dazed spirit.

Rat-livers. I squat before her, about to smack her cheeks when I remember how touching an unconscious Lotus and Sikou Hai almost sucked in *my* spirit. I rise, step back, and kick her leg. She snorts.

The tree is spiritless, when I glance back to it.

Warriors! I shake my head, resuming my walk. *Drinking themselves silly, to the point of detachment—*

Detachment.

That's it.

Zephyr . . . , warns Dewdrop, reading my intentions as I stride into my shrine, kneel before the altar, and fish under its fabric skirt, feeling past the box of Zephyr's last possessions, to the cloth bundle.

It unties to everything I've collected since becoming Lotus, starting with Crow's cloak. My face warms as I remember waking up to it settled over my shoulders. *Focus.* I move aside the cloak, then the sheets of calligraphy—all of the same phrase, my most recent attempts nearly indistinguishable from my old brushmanship—until I've uncovered the jugs of wine. Cloud gifted them to me before riding for the Marshlands.

What's the occasion? I'd asked, brow raised.

Lotus's birthday. It's in two months.

Now in two weeks. What have I accomplished in this time? Not nearly enough.

I uncork a jug, releasing the aroma of peaches. If Lotus could smell this, she'd be remembering the day she swore sisterhood with Ren and Cloud under the peach trees, her mind transported by the scent.

My mind stays in the shrine. I don't have Lotus's memories. I don't have anything at all, no prowess or influence. I thought I needed this body to help Ren, but it's become a prison. I take a glug, scrunch my face, then down the rest.

One jug empty.

A second joins it.

Soon, my body is heavy, warm, numb. This dulling of sensation and thought . . . how I relied on it in the heavens. *Ping.* The final jug falls out of my hand. I slump. The ceiling of the shrine spins and shrinks, a sliver between my closing eyelids.

When they reopen, I see myself from above.

Lotus's body, all sprawled out.

The wine spreads like blood on the ground.

I extend a hand. *My hand.* Fingers long and dexterous, immaterial and translucent. The form I favor as a god. My qì is so light, unburdened by matter.

It worked.

I drift out the shrine's entrance.

Zephyr! Dewdrop buzzes in agitation as I hover in the night, reacclimating to my spirit. *Remember the consequences of a spirit straying too far from its body?*

You said that regarding human spirits. I'm a god.

Still—

I summon a cloud and we soar.

Out of the Westlands, the basin flattens to marsh. The Mica snakes north, its banks lined with watchtowers, villages and cities asleep at this hour.

But a battle never sleeps, and I see the fires of Cloud's war camp first. Her tents are pitched half a lǐ from Bikong itself.

The fort walls tower into the night, the battlements lit with torches.

When I joined Ren, she was a lordess on the run. We hid behind such ramparts. We never could have laid siege to them. That we now can is a feat to be proud of. But unease skitters through me. *Never underestimate the defense*, my chess master would say as she played the black stone, destined to go after white like night after day. *Do so, and you'll lose.*

Bikong is not unbreachable; there's just a cost to doing so. I see that cost already in the bloodstained field where Cloud led her charge. A graveyard of boulders and arrows extends from the walls. Ladders, crushed by the defenders, lie like blackened skeletons. A bigger skeleton burns—an assault tower that would have carried our soldiers. I hope everyone got out, but in Cloud's camp, stretchers are draped with people who look barely human. I avert my gaze from their faces. I made my most costly mistake when I saw a person instead of a pawn. I went back for Lotus, in Pumice Pass.

I failed to save her or myself.

Girding my heart, I float past the wounded, through the soldiers. Some shiver. A torch flickers. A tent flap moves. A horse whinnies, spooked. But otherwise, the camp carries on, as do I, in my search for Cloud.

I find her by her voice, strong and proud.

"Why should I believe you?"

She stands before a command tent at the edge of camp.

Before her kneels a man. "Because Miasma passed me over and gave the promotion to him," he answers.

A holler rises somewhere in the night past Cloud's cordon. "Ma Ying, you defector! Come out and fight me! Take the position of lieutenant fair and square!"

Defector. Or so he says. I've feigned defection too; I know an act when I see one. The man knelt before Cloud is an empire spy. The other person just outside camp? An accomplice to bolster the façade.

But Cloud nods, permitting the man to rise, mount, and ride out to face his challenger. In front of the tents, under the eye of Cloud's soldiers, the two men charge. A single bout later, the challenger's head is dangling from the man's fist. He rides back with it and offers it to Cloud. "For you."

Cloud reaches out.

"Don't," I say reflexively, knowing very well that Cloud can't hear me. No mortal can when I'm a spirit, and any "exception" has boiled down to coincidence—the entrance of something or someone else causing a behavioral shift or, in Cloud's case, a lowered arm. She closes her hand around the pole of her glaive instead.

She sends the blade into the man's heart.

The soldiers stare. I stare too, queasily. *Coincidence?*

Unaffected, Cloud pulls out her blade, letting the man and his booty tumble to the ground.

"Dispose of them," she orders, departing with a sweep of her blue cloak.

I follow her, the glaive she calls Blue Serpent dripping blood as she walks past tent after tent, into one that's empty. Unlit.

Just coincidence.

The flaps fall shut, ensconcing us in darkness.

Cloud stands there, unmoving.

She pivots and thrusts, as if she can see me.

二十七

SIEGE OF BIKONG

She can . . . see me?

I look down at the crescent blade, slit through my chest. I look up at Cloud.

"What do you see?" I whisper, and cringe. Surely she can't—

"Dust. Less than, really."

—hear me.

Cloud can hear me.

"Why did you have me kill the defector?" Cloud asks, and I step back from her glaive.

"I only told you to decline the head, not to kill him."

Cloud waves a hand, as if it's all the same.

Warriors. Sometimes I still can't believe I am one. "He claimed that Miasma had given the role of lieutenant to the person he killed," I say. "But Miasma has an eye for talent. And the accomplice—from the way he fought—had no talent."

"So you're a judge of fighters now? How well do *you* fight?" Cloud's glaive hurtles in before I can reply.

"Will you *stop* that?"

"Why should I?" Cloud cuts through my waist, ribboning me like a radish. "I can't kill you. What are you anyway? A spirit?"

Divine spirit, thank you very much. But yes, a spirit who, up until now, has been unable to interact with the living world in this form. Neither Ren, Tourmaline, Miasma, Crow, nor Cloud could see me before, let alone hear me. *What changed?* I wonder as Dewdrop thinks, *How strange*, which isn't comforting, coming from a seventy-thousand-year-old deity.

"Let me guess why you're here." Cloud gives my spirit one final slice, then strides to the middle of the tent. She sits behind a low table. "You don't trust me to wage this war."

The Cloud of old would have said it hatefully. We didn't always see eye to eye. We still don't. But Cloud didn't tell Ren about Cicada. She's been monitoring the South at my request. Maybe it's foolish to hope she'll listen again.

Or maybe we've made progress. "You need to withdraw from Bikong."

"Withdraw?" Cloud laughs, then sees that I'm serious. "Did you not read my reports on how I broke the dams?" *I did. I sent the rain.* But I let Cloud go on. "You should have seen it—how Talon and all his empire soldiers ran from the waters! Now he's holed up in that fort like a rat. Just wait. He'll come scuttling out once I break the walls."

My heart sinks with every word of Cloud's. Arrogance was my downfall. I didn't think anyone could outsmart me.

Cicada of the Southlands did.

"Have you forgotten, Cloud? The North is now allied with

the South. While you fight Miasma's forces here, you leave the Marshlands capital open for Cicada's taking."

Cloud crosses her arms. "You still don't have evidence of their alliance."

Not this again. "I don't *need* evidence."

"What about Cicada's feud with Miasma? I did some digging of my own; I know Cicada thinks the empire sponsored the pirates who killed her sister Cricket."

Old news. "Vengeance is—"

"—for peasants. Hear me out," says Cloud as I bristle. "Cicada and Miasma are only allies of convenience. If things go badly here at Bikong for Miasma's forces, Cicada won't swoop in to help them. Likewise, if I fall back to the Marshlands capital before Cicada can secure it, Miasma won't send them assistance. So long as I've crushed the empire's fighting spirit *here*"—Cloud slams two fingers down on the table like it's a chessboard—"Cicada won't move. And I have them crushed."

"Even so—"

"And don't downplay yourself. I know your snakelike ways." I frown, but Cloud grins. "You must've sent forces to replace mine in the Marshlands. Well?"

"Only a few," I grumble. *And Tourmaline leads them.* But mentioning her is a weapon I should save, for when Cloud is one push from being convinced. "Our soldiers need your help."

"And I will help, *after* I win. Have a little faith in me. Lotus would." The moonlight is diffuse in the tent, but in Cloud's gaze, it seems concentrated. Her eyes sparkle, then grow shadowed.

"Lotus." Her gaze rises to an approximation of mine. "If you're here, where's Lotus's body?"

I hesitate.

My undoing. Cloud is on her feet, advancing on me. "What happened? Answer me, Zephyr."

Lie. Lie. Lie. "I-it was the peach wine." I bite my lip, look aside. "I drank it and . . . separated from the body."

"You left her unguarded."

"Cloud . . ." She speaks of the body as if it's more than a vessel that will never again house Lotus's spirit. "Cloud," I say more firmly. "She's gone."

"You don't know for certain. You didn't search for her spirit. I will."

Ask her how, says the voice of reason in my head. *Force her to face reality. Kill her hope. Reveal to her that you're a god; you know what you're talking about.*

In the past, I'd have done just that. When Cloud orders me to go back "or I never want to see your face again," it shouldn't feel like a threat. *The feeling is mutual,* past-me would have said, instead of actually listening to Cloud, like I do now.

As I drift away, the camp disappearing below, Dewdrop finally speaks.

I have a very bad feeling about this. The way she could see you . . .

"Ku saw Qilin's spirit." My mind winces as I say it. Qilin's spirit, which departed as I was banished into her body, robbing me of my two real sisters and Ku of her one.

That's different, Dewdrop argues. *Humans can sometimes*

see the ghosts of relatives. But gods cannot be detected by mortals until we adopt a fleshly form, or until they depart theirs as spirits or ghosts. The Marshlands rush by beneath us. *I have a theory, but Nadir would know better.*

Nadir would, as the god-sister of mine who made the first mortals. I thought she'd understand my connection to them, but she doesn't. I can already feel her disappointment, waiting for me back at home. It can't be helped. All I can do now is win. Then, at least, I won't disappoint myself.

The night is a shade lighter by the time I return to the Westlands, over a thousand lǐ covered in half an hour. The shrine is undisturbed; Lotus's body is as I left it. I descend into it, but my fingers don't move when I make a fist. My spirit is like the wine, puddled and unabsorbed.

I rise out of the body. Descend into it once more.

Still no adherence.

I warned you, Dewdrop thinks as I float back out.

"It's the alcohol. It'll wear off."

What makes you so certain?

"The other soldier's spirit returned."

They were human. You're a god masquerading as one. Dewdrop looks over the body. *What if she vomits? What if she chokes to death?*

I . . . didn't consider that. Lotus's heartbeat feels strong when I check it, but Dewdrop has a point. Even the sturdiest humans are frail compared to us gods.

"Stay here," I say at last, "and stand guard." Dewdrop is silent. "Please, Dewdrop. Do this one thing for me."

How am I to stand guard? What shall you have me do if something happens?

"Just—alert me!" With that, I soar, escaping the scene.

"Gods!" Cloud curses and spins on me when I say her name, back in the tent. "I told you to leave!"

"I did. I asked"—*a bee*—"Tourmaline to guard the body."

I omit the rest. Cloud never did approve of me assuming Lotus's form. For all I know, she'll be happy to hear of this . . . complication. I'm alone in my anxiety, an anxiety I didn't have to unlock. I could have lied to Cloud from the start, then returned to the body a few hours later, when it was more sober. But protecting Cloud's hope was easier than telling her the truth. And right now, there are more pressing truths she needs to face.

"Cloud, you *have* to withdraw from Bikong."

"Hells, I thought you were done."

I would be if Cloud weren't so mule-headed. "Make an excuse to Ren, or lose on purpose."

"Do you hear yourself?"

"Withdraw."

"No."

"Do it!"

"Never." A drumbeat pulses through the camp, percussed by shouts. *Reinforcements! Miasma's!* "Perfect timing," says Cloud. "I'll show you how silly you sound." She dons her helmet, focused but unharried, and holds up a hand when I open my mouth. "No. Shush. You're a soldier in my tent. Report to me. How is Ren?" I keep my silence. "I saw the title of queen on her missives. What changed?"

Nothing significant, just the return of my four-month-old head. "We convinced her," I snap as Cloud checks over her armor. Then I sigh. "She's well. So is Tourmaline."

Cloud's shoulders stiffen. "Did I ask about Tourmaline?"

"She's been helping me with my fighting."

"Then come! Fight with us." Cloud grabs her glaive and twirls it, smirking as I shy away. "Watch and learn, Zephyr. I don't know when you became such a defeatist, but I'll show you how sieges are won."

"Cloud—"

She strides out of the tent. Fuming, I follow, floating in her mare's wake after she mounts, my spirit apparent to no one else.

The drums beat on. Before our camp, our soldiers are already in formation, rectangular shields overlapping like gills. Cloud rides through their ranks. The walls of Bikong loom to our right, overlooking the Mica. The river is swollen, the banks overrun, Talon's camp reduced to flotsam in the mud.

At our final line of soldiers, Cloud stops.

Troops from the empire stand ahead of her, at least ten rows deep, but their ranks are thin. It speaks to Miasma's pride: The battle-wise don't need numbers to lift a siege.

They will rely on strategy.

I reexamine the walls of Bikong on our right. Talon and his company are behind them. Charging out would be suicidal; they'd be bottlenecked by the gates and our garrison. Even so, I ask Cloud, "How broken did you say their fighting spirits are?"

"In smithereens," Cloud says under her breath. "Trust me."

Trust doesn't come easily to me. But neither does pole fighting or delegating my ideas. Nothing has been easy as Lotus. *What is one more thing*, I tell myself, even as I hear phantom screams. The enemy ranks swim. The stillness is an illusion. The lines will break, as they do in my nightmares, and I will be powerless in the bedlam.

But when our line finally breaks, it's for Cloud. Alone, she rides into the plain.

"Well?" she asks, voice lifted. "Who dares challenge me?"

Wind. Whinnies. The creak of armor.

"I," says a voice in reply.

A warrior, cloaked in leopard skin, eye patched in black, rides out of Miasma's front line. She stops a hundred strides from Cloud, and recognition lights my mind. I've met her. General Leopard. It was she who greeted me when I defected to Miasma.

"Where is your prime ministress?" Cloud hollers.

"Not here to waste time on the likes of you."

Miasma isn't here. Then who did she send in command?

"*The likes of me.*" Cloud scoffs. "The likes of me, whom she released *after* I shot you in the eye. How does it feel to be so treasured?" As she speaks, two empire soldiers carry something oblong to Leopard. "What's that? Your coffin?"

"Yours." The coffin is set down, and Leopard draws her broadsword. "By order of the prime ministress, I'm to take you alive if you surrender and dead if you resist!"

Cloud looks to her glaive. "Blue Serpent, I'm sorry. You will have to suffer the blood of a rodent today."

I palm my face.

"Come at me!" roars Leopard.

"With pleasure!" Cloud roars back, whirling her glaive overhead.

"Cloud, wait—"

She's beside me, and then she's not. I'm left in a cloud of dust as steel meets steel in a terrifying, brilliant chorus. On the far side of the plain, Cloud and her mare twist around.

Near me, Leopard does the same.

Glaive and broadsword cross again.

Seven bouts. Fifteen. At twenty, Leopard tears off her armor. Cloud copies her. *Why, Cloud?* For range of motion? Or some other warrior reason? Only Cloud would know. As she said, I have to trust her. I just don't trust the enemy soldiers. For what it's worth, they're watching this display of might as raptly as ours while I watch *them*, gaze scouring their ranks.

Stilling on him.

He cuts a slender figure atop his horse amid the cavalry, his long hair astream, his eyes on the duel unfolding in the plain. Just like the others, he doesn't see me.

Some ill, addled part of me wishes he could.

It's cured by Cloud's roar. She's hot on Leopard's hooves as the other warrior retreats—pulling Cloud with her, toward the enemy. My eyes widen. *Careful!* I mean to shout, before I've even seen the metal glint between Leopard's arm and torso.

"Careful" becomes "*Crossbolt!*"

Backward Cloud snaps in her saddle. The crossbolt clears the air over her face and strikes the ground.

The ground. Not Cloud. My heart resumes beating as Cloud rights herself. Her eyes narrow to slits. She jabs her glaive at Leopard.

"*Milk-dribbling coward!*" she screams as the warrior reaches her own lines. "*Teat-sucking rat!*"

Leopard wheels her steed around, refacing Cloud.

"Let it go, General."

My heart stops for a second time.

His voice. In real life. I'm not dreaming it.

"Master Crow—"

"We'll fight her another day." The gong sounds, ordering Leopard's retreat. Shields lift to let her back in. Before the line can close, he rides out.

He trots into the plain in nothing more than his black robes and cloak, painfully exposed to the elements—and to Cloud's wrath.

"Interloper! I wasn't done with her!"

"Cloud," Crow acknowledges. "It's good to see you well."

"*You*—"

I float to Cloud; she glares at me as if *I'm* to blame for the Northern strategist's conduct.

If it helps, I'm just as vexed by it. *Do you have a death wish?* I think furiously to Crow as Cloud shouts, "Tomorrow! I will fight you, and I will drown your minions like I did Talon's!"

Crow bows from atop his mount. "I look forward to it."

Death wish confirmed.

"Don't," I warn Cloud as her face reddens.

"Don't this, don't that." A muscle jumps in her jaw. She squeezes Blue Serpent, and my throat feels like it's in her vise grip too before she turns her mare, rear to Crow.

I exhale.

Our soldiers retreat, respectively, under the drone of gongs. As the empire withdraws to its camp along the riverbank, I linger, watching them. Watching *him*. He winds to his tent; I float higher to mark its spot. As a spirit, I could easily go to him. Tap his shoulder.

Whisper in his ear a reprimand.

Don't you dare die to anyone else.

I shake my head, clearing it, and catch up to Cloud, who's muttering expletives.

"Coward. Rat. That slimy, asslicking strategist." She's talking about Crow—at least, I think she is. We pass before Bikong's walls, dawn fanning over the top. The light is soft—

Sharpening to a point between the battlements.

This time, Cloud doesn't react fast enough.

The crossbolt flies down.

I don't see where it hits her. I just see a mist of blood.

And then I see nothing at all. The walls of Bikong vanish as my spirit flies, falls, and thuds. My hair is matted with sweat. Wine—it soaks my back.

I'm in Lotus's body again.

二十八
WEAPON OF CHOICE

Cloud. Head aching, I stumble to my feet, out of my shrine, into the dawn.

I race to Ren's quarters.

Her doors open just as I reach them, Ren seemingly seconds from striding out herself. "Lotus." Her face is pale, her expression gaunt. "I was about to find you. I . . . I had a dream."

"Of what?"

"Cloud. She was standing in my room, drenched in blood."

The bottom of my stomach falls out. *Cloud, gone.*

No—I don't believe in premonitions.

But I also didn't believe in gods.

I coax Ren back into the room, sit her on the bed, and kneel before it.

"I sent her away, thinking it'd protect her," Ren whispers. "I knew if she stayed here after the coup, people would wonder why the martial law hadn't been applied to her. I thought she'd safer, out of mind and sight. But I was wrong."

I'm silent. Even if Ren hadn't exiled Cloud to protect her,

I'd tell her that it's no crime to have guarded her reputation. "Perhaps Qilin would have advised differently," Ren says, and on this, I'm less certain. Perhaps I wouldn't have staged the coup at all as Qilin.

By then, I was already a different strategist.

What I do know is this: "Ren. Let me ride to Cloud. With me, we can take Bikong faster."

Her eyes rise to mine, and for a heartbeat, I feel like Zephyr. Like I could have spoken the words as Zephyr.

Like I could be Ren's Qilin *and* call her and Cloud my swornsisters.

Then Ren nods, and I remember my place. "Go," she says. "Go and protect our sister."

"Lotus will."

‡ ‡ ‡

Please be okay.

The thought pounds through me, harder than even the gallop. The others in the convoy, insisted on by Ren, refresh their mounts halfway. I keep Rice Cake. Lotus wouldn't want him handed off, and he shows no signs of flagging. It's as if he knows we're racing toward his owner's swornsister.

Ren's only surviving one.

Please be okay.

She's alive, Dewdrop finally gives up on day three when she realizes that no matter what she withholds, I'm riding to Bikong. *For now.*

What do you mean? Where was Cloud hit?

Inconsequential, is Dewdrop's maddening answer. *You see weather patterns in the stars' configurations. I see the streams of human life. This Cloud of yours has not long for this world.*

"You're wrong." I speak out loud in my adamancy, the wind swallowing my words before they can reach the other riders. "I will save her."

Cloud, *and* our Southlands alliance.

In two moves, I will turn the conditions in our favor.

Luring the enemy out is half the battle. Now that Cloud's been struck, Cicada will be advancing on the Marshlands, where Tourmaline is ready and waiting. I *will* convince Cloud to reinforce her.

Assuming she's conscious enough to be convinced.

Please be okay.

The river winds up the plain.

Please be okay.

Another day.

We arrive at Bikong in the wee hours of the sixth. The empire has set up camp, and Cloud's camp—is still standing. It's not until I see her tents that I realize I hadn't allowed myself to imagine the alternative. Now it floods my mind: a waking nightmare of empire soldiers falling on Cloud. Our camp, routed. Our cause lost right here at Bikong to Miasma. Talon. Crow.

I'll kill him. I'll kill them all. I urge Rice Cake faster, pulling ahead.

"Halt!" cry our soldiers on guard before the camp.

Rice Cake rears.

"*Who dares stop me!*" I roar from atop him, brandishing my ax.

"General Lotus!" The soldiers fall back.

"Where's Cloud?"

"In her tent—"

I plow forward. The dawn is still young.

In the dark, Cloud's tent glows orange.

I dismount and stride in before I can process thought or emotion.

Cloud sits at the low table, left arm bare and stretched over a bowl. Blood oozes from a puncture wound below her elbow. The injury seems mild, but I'm no physician. I search the tent for one of ours. There's only a woman in tan, grinding herbs in a mortar, and a soldier, sitting opposite Cloud, a chessboard between them. His gaze lifts from the game at my entrance. "General Lotus . . ."

"Out," Cloud barks—at me, I'm thinking, before she says, "I want to play my swornsister."

The soldier shoots to his feet, bows, and scurries.

I take his place, ignoring the game. "How bad is it?"

"Nasty little vermin poisoned the bolt."

Poisoned. It explains Cloud's sickly pallor, her under-eyes bruised purple.

After five nights on horseback, I doubt I look much better. "Why are you just getting treated?" I glance to the woman, then back to Cloud. My voice lowers to a hiss. "*It's been six days.*"

"Blame our physicians," Cloud says. "They extracted the bolt, but it took three days of the wound not closing before they realized it was poisoned. And then none of them had any ideas as to how to remove it without removing the arm. Until this one here." Cloud nods at the woman. "She said the treatment is straightforward."

The physician neither denies nor affirms it. She only asks Cloud if she'd like wine to endure the procedure.

"None needed," says Cloud.

"Wait—" My eye whirls to the physician. "State your name."

"Jin Hua, General."

"What are your credentials?"

"I trained under the late Chen Ling."

"Who do you serve?"

"Forgive my swornsister," Cloud cuts in, then turns to me. "You're being rude."

"And you're being brainless. This is your life at stake."

"My life, which means I get to decide the treatment." *Ugh.* "All physicians swear an oath to do no harm when they complete their training. As Master Shencius would say—"

Listen to me, not him!

"—they are second only to monks in benevolence. I trust them."

Good for Cloud. I used to judge by role alone too. I can no longer. I may look like a warrior, but I still hate gore.

"What does the procedure entail?" I ask, brows hiking when Cloud doesn't answer. "You don't know."

How, oh how, has Cloud lived to be twenty-some years old?

"Well?" I prompt the physician.

"I'll need to part the skin and flesh," she explains, "to get to the bone itself. Then I'll scrape it."

"The bone."

"Yes. I know the properties of this poison well. It comes from a plant native to the South." *Well there you go, Cloud.* Evidence of Cicada's alliance with Miasma. "If any trace of it remains, she'll lose use of the arm."

"Poison is the weapon of cowards," Cloud spits.

And of bugs. Who's to say the physician isn't working under Cicada? Or Miasma? "May I proceed?" asks the woman, lifting a small knife, and my stomach turns at the risk of letting a stranger, affiliations unknown, slice into Cloud. But if it *is* poison, and none of our physicians can remove it—

"Yes," says Cloud.

That reckless, obstinate warrior. My lips purse as she clears her game with the previous soldier and resets the board. "Must we?"

"Did you not hear the physician?" asks Cloud, placing two white and two black stones in the opening formation. "I intend to keep my arm."

I meant the chess. Cloud hands me white before I can ask for black, the color traditionally offered to the stronger player to offset the disadvantage of starting second. Reluctantly, I take the white pot of stones, and Cloud smirks. "You're not the only one with brains."

Tourmaline was right about Cloud's hobbies. She was right about Cloud staying on Bikong too. But Cloud is poisoned, about to be cut open.

If I fail to convince her under these conditions, I am no strategist.

"The siege must end." I place a white stone, beginning the game.

"It will, tomorrow, with our victory." The physician starts to cut. Cloud is soundless; with her other hand, she plays her piece.

Fighting nausea, I force myself to speak.

"The cicadas are still singing." May Cloud understand the message in the poem. "Their numbers gather nearby. Soon, to the reeds they will fly."

"And before then"—Cloud builds out a diagonal—"these walls will fall."

I ignore her play, establishing territory in a different part of the board. "Stratagem Eleven, Cloud," I croak. "Cede the Hill for the Mountain. One day, we *will* take Bikong, but it doesn't have to be now. The greater Marshlands are more crucial to us. Without them, our future offensives against Miasma will face steep odds."

Cloud lifts a stone, but doesn't place it. A *scritch-scratching* fills the tent.

The sound of metal filing bone.

My eye stings as I swallow the acid in my throat. Cloud is quiet, but her own eyes shine, and there's the faintest gleam of moisture at her hairline.

Now's my chance to dig in *my* knife. "Tourmaline is in the Marshlands. She needs your help." *Surely, this will move Cloud,* I think as blood streams into the bowl.

Cloud remains quiet.

Then: "I'm here for a purpose." Her voice betrays no pain. "To send a message to Miasma, and one message only: Victory for my queen." She places her stone, mindless of my forays. "Would you abandon Ren for that Crow of yours? No," she says, silencing my protests. "Then don't think less of me by using my heart against me. I know my priorities, and I know the risks. I'll go to Tourmaline *after* I report the win."

"Cloud—"

"Play."

I do, making sure to slam my pieces.

"General Cloud," the physician says at long last. "I've scraped the bone and drained the blood tainted by poison."

Cloud closes her fist and flexes. "Thank you. I feel better than ever." And I feel faint. "Will you not consider serving Ren?" Cloud asks the woman, who bows.

"I'm a wandering physician, loyal to all in the realm."

Cloud's gaze softens, and despite myself, so do my misgivings. We both must be thinking of Ren's mother.

"I came by your camp because I'd heard legends of your divine feats," the physician adds, and Cloud snorts.

"Me, divine? Blasphemy."

As the resident god, I'm inclined to agree.

The physician smiles. "I'll allow my senses to be the judge. Many a human would have screamed, undergoing what you did." She rises and bows again. "But even so, I do not wish to bind myself to one person or place."

"I respect your wishes." Cloud rises too. "Let me see you safely out of the camp, at the very least."

I stay in the tent as they exit, studying the chessboard dotted with Cloud's and my pieces.

I would have won, but by fewer than seven points.

The margin is slimmer than I'd like.

Maybe Cloud is right. Maybe Bikong is a day away from falling. Maybe we can secure both objectives, and I've grown too wary to see it.

But the tides of war can also change without warning. As I step out of the tent, a soldier finds me. "From the Westlands, General," she says, delivering a reed tube.

Inside is a message from Sikou Hai.

Watchtower after watchtower has lit up on the banks of the Mica. It's Tourmaline's signal. I'm writing to you so that you may receive this faster than a missive from the Marshlands capital, which sees the arrival of the thief.

Send Cloud quickly.

Just as I forecasted. Cicada's moved in. The hour to withdraw from Bikong is *now*. But Cloud won't, so long as she believes she can take the fort—a belief that will stand, untested, until the Northern relief force overwhelms or outmaneuvers us.

Why haven't they? It's strange, after all this time. I look out to the empire camp. The river remains high. But with each day, the danger of another flood recedes with the water levels.

Something else that's strange: Miasma's generosity toward the South. Yes, they're allied, and yes, Miasma sent my head partly to create an opening for Cicada in the Marshlands. But if I were Miasma, I wouldn't allow Cicada the element of surprise for long. I'd leak her movements to Cloud to hasten our abandonment of Bikong. So why hasn't the empire spread news of Cicada infiltrating the Marshlands?

You're frowning, thinks Dewdrop, buzzing by my shoulder. *What are you thinking about now?*

My gaze drifts from the chessboard to the bowl of blood.

I'm thinking about him. The empire strategist who knows exactly what he is—or isn't—doing.

He holds the answers.

I'll pry them out of him, strategist to strategist.

‡ ‡ ‡

"Leave. Master Crow won't see anyone."

These words. They take me back, to the junk. I'm outside his cabin doors, clueless as to how he's faring behind them. He could be dying or already dead, killed by the arrow on course for me. My heart constricts. I shouldn't care. Shouldn't care. Shouldn't care.

He's the enemy, and I'm standing in front of the enemy camp.

The memory fades, the soldiers before me bleeding back in. Their spears are pointed—have been since they saw me approaching from across the plain.

"I come not as a warrior," I explain, "but as a negotiator."

The soldiers don't move or speak.

If that's how they want to do this, fine. I have a way of *making* Crow want to see me.

I reach under my breastplate and withdraw the letter I wrote, as Qilin.

About time, thinks Dewdrop.

I saved it for a reason. "Deliver this to him."

I hold out the letter, but the spears only press closer.

Melon-brains. Crow too. *Just what are you planning?* I think, stalking back into our camp. Something stubs my toe and I curse, then slow. It's an arrow, stuck in the ground.

I pull it out.

Minutes later, I've tied my letter to the shaft and found a bow. I walk back to the front of our camp.

Fit arrow to bowstring.

Careful now, lest you kill him, thinks Dewdrop, reminding me of all the targets I've missed. All the duels I've lost. My frustration sparks against the frustration of not being able to convince Cloud. *Mortals!*

Thankfully, I'm not them. I'm definitely not a real warrior. I can't hold my own in a duel like Cloud did against Leopard.

But I can guide this arrow as a god.

I let go.

二十九
DUET

*G*o.

I close my eye, sensing the air as it's sliced open.

Focusing, I bend the currents.

The arrow curves around a soldier's shoulder and flies past the whipping post, through the flaps of Crow's tent. It thuds into the main pillar, and as my qì quivers, I catch sight of his head, turning toward the tent's entrance.

Then the air around the arrow stills, breaking my qì's connection. The scene disintegrates before I can glimpse his face.

His cheek, almost grazed.

I release a breath.

And double over, pain clawing my chest. My powers exact their toll, just like when I summoned the rain, and memories of heaven flood me, ending with my final game as a god. I'd lost to a deity I'd once beaten.

After they'd left, I'd thrown the board.

Now, catching my breath, I sneer at the person I was.

I'd never leave a game on a loss.

This time, I cross the plain with just the bow. The enemy soldiers point their spears again, but soon, a general gallops up on a stallion.

"You! Did you shoot that arrow?"

"Yes." I hold up the bow—visual proof is more impactful— and the general's gaze cuts to the soldiers.

"Check her for weapons, then take her to him."

Done and about to be done. The front lines part. Finally. I stride for the opening.

"Ze-Lotus!"

Cloud. She's behind me when I turn, my false name stilted in her mouth.

There's nothing stilted about her glare. *Just what in the hells are you doing?* it says. *Get back here!* She voices none of it, not wanting to alert the enemy that I've come without orders.

Let's keep it that way. "Wait for me," I call to her, then walk forward, past the shields.

Trust me, for a turn.

‡ ‡ ‡

Soldiers escort me through the camp, into the tent.

In the center, he stands.

"Hello, Lotus. We meet again."

I saw him from above, as a spirit, but it's different, so different, confronting him in the flesh. Firelight from the braziers falls over us both. His face is underlit, the planes of his cheeks and forehead shadowed. If only I could clear the shadows like I would a mask. I'm suddenly seized with the urge to do just that—to draw him into the light, out of these pretenses, and put my lips to his ear. *Yes and no, Crow.*

We meet again, but not as Crow and Lotus.

But I don't act on whims, and neither does Crow. "Any particular reason for sending this?" He holds up the letter, and though I've been waiting for him to ask, I'm caught off guard. It's his manner. His tone, so blasé, as if the letter is just a piece of paper. I expected . . . more.

Fool of me to. He's a strategist, like myself. Emotions are a liability. Of course he'd hide them. I should look to his actions. They speak more than his words. I'm in his tent.

I have his attention.

"I wanted to meet with you," I say, lightening my own tone. "I seem to have succeeded."

Crow regards me carefully. It's nothing like the last time we met face-to-face, by the lake. Why would it be? Crow's forces are here to break the siege. This can only end with one victor, one loser.

"Indeed you have," he at last grants. "Did Zephyr give this letter to you too?"

Too. What else did I, as Zephyr, supposedly give to Lotus? Then I remember another time I felt this pinned. In the dark of the stables, cornered by Crow, I'd claimed that Zephyr had told me his name. He doubted me then—still doubts me, by the lilt of his voice—and I untense. He cares, enough to have an opinion on what Zephyr would or would not share.

I have more than an opinion. "No. She didn't."

"I didn't think so," Crow murmurs.

"We found it with her body." The head of which Miasma collected first. Surely Crow knew of her revolting actions. He is her strategist. An enemy who holds a secret pertinent to this siege. *Ask him—*

"Tell me, then." Crow speaks before I can. "To what do I owe the pleasure of your visit?"

"I challenge you to a duet."

"Still two on one zither?"

Mmm, Dewdrop thinks, as if the prospect is delicious.

I'll squash her right after I squash my rival. "One zither each," I say to Crow, willing my face to cool.

"A proper duet." Crow lets the words hang for an uncomfortably long second. "If my memory isn't failing me, you weren't eager to play during our last encounter."

"I've been practicing since. I liked it."

His stare is cryptic.

I was cryptic too, the night I sat at his zither as Lotus. I left him wanting, left him wondering how a warrior like myself could unlock the instrument's qì with just one note.

Now's your chance to find out, I think to Crow. *Can you resist it?*

I know I wouldn't.

"Bring them," he finally says, eyes never leaving mine as the guards depart, carrying out his order. They return with two zithers. I recognize the first as Crow's. Midnight wood. Strings white as snow. He takes it to a table at one end of the tent. I take the second zither to the opposite.

We sit.

Since we last played, I've been thinking over a dilemma.

Zithers are a conduit for the truth in one's heart. Why would a strategist agree to a duet if they're at risk of leaking secrets that could end wars or incite them?

The answer I arrived at solidifies when I meet the challenge in Crow's gaze. We each have secrets, and he's betting on his skill that he can access mine first. A strategist's duet is no different from a warrior's duel in this respect. Both parties stand to injure themselves.

Neither backs down.

Crow raises his arms, black sleeves cascading. "What topic shall we play about?"

"This siege."

"Hmm." My heart tremors at the syllable. "I'd like to play about *you*," Crow says, and plucks. The open note travels through me, and I with it. Back in time and place. My hands—Lotus's— are under Crow's.

We played this very note, by the lake.

Focus. This scene is safe. I play as well, and the space between us swirls, air gone to water. Mist curls—fronds of qì, taking on color. The night appears. The two of us, bent over the same zither. The lake shines behind us, liquid moonlight, as the music rises.

An image within an image.

It changes as we play on. Crow and Lotus disappear, replaced by a hut. My breath stops. *Thistlegate?*

It's not. The image clarifies, and I see the pig carcasses, strung from the thatched roof. What—?

Lotus. She's from a family of butchers, Cloud once told me.

Relief—I haven't leaked my identity—turns into bewilderment. I shouldn't have these memories. I don't *remember* these memories.

How, then, can my music be conveying my thoughts?

Something's wrong, Dewdrop thinks. *Stop playing. This—*

Crow plucks another note—two. They vibrate, like rubbed stones. A question sings in the resulting harmonic.

Zephyr—

I can't leave empty-handed.

I play my response, throwing my notes. The image ripples. Changes. I see Lotus and myself—as Zephyr, in Qilin's body—crossing a river together. Cloud is up ahead. Tourmaline brings up the rear, and Ren—she's beside me, between Lotus and Zephyr, just like the old times—

Before my eyes, Zephyr starts to fade.

Quickly I play louder, faster. The image changes to the siege. I strike the zither and Bikong ignites. Arrows soar and our soldiers rush the walls. Smoke blooms and blood spills—enemy blood. *Fight back*, my music says, *or we will slaughter you.*

Crow's hands fall to the strings, his notes aggressive, so unlike his previous play. His music dominates mine, and in the siege I've painted, empire reinforcements pour in.

So they're on their way. What's taking so long? I play more troops of our own onto the field, play in Cloud's determination to take Bikong, my notes high and taunting. Crow responds with an equally taunting trill, strings aggravated under his nails. The music crescendos—

A cough.

From Crow. He coughs again, his bottom lip glossed with blood, and my focus fractures. The sieges between us melts. Another night replaces it, lit not by warfare, but by the moon. It shines silver on the dried riverbed—and on us. My hair is down and loose, my white robes exchanged for black to match Crow's. We come together, my hands on his face, my mouth on his. A memory of mine, and not Lotus's.

It's also a memory of Crow's. It's unclear, in fact, whose heart it's stemming from, and for a beat, it matters not. My transitions soften as the Crow of that night, played to life, pulls me closer, and my stomach clenches, recalling how it felt to lose my balance. My incisors, sinking in. The taste of blood and—

In the scene, Crow pulls away.

Our hands still on the strings, in the present.

Firelight flickers. Movement, in a tent absent of it. Our zithers are silent.

I remember that night. I remember everything we played into existence, except for the last scene. It wasn't Crow who pulled away, breaking the kiss.

It was me. Lotus wouldn't know this, but I do.

Why did the memory change? I think to the other scenes we played. The siege. The troops. Not memories, but wishes, still true and from the heart, just not yet happened. Perhaps Crow wishes he'd been the one to retreat from me, that night in the riverbed—

Retreat.

My gaze hits his. His thoughts are as unknowable as ever. But his actions—his *lack* of action, it speaks. The lack of a decisive attack. The lack of more reinforcements. The siege goes on when they could relieve it.

They don't intend to.

They will retreat. They will retreat, and Cloud won't be able to resist pursuing them north, just like she couldn't resist pursuing Leopard. She will abandon the Marshlands. Tourmaline.

Her own safety.

I rise from my zither. Step back from it. Crow stands too. He senses something amiss. A dissonance. His eyes see Lotus; his mind says it's fine to let me walk out of here; I wouldn't know the discrepancy between the played memory and the real one. But his intuition disagrees, and whereas an ordinary strategist would default to reason, Crow has never been ordinary.

He listens to intuition. "Seize her."

三十

ASH IN HAND

Seize her.

As guards flood the tent, my gaze thunders to Crow's. I asked for a duet. He agreed. Now he admits he can't win with skill alone.

I don't know whether to scorn or applaud him.

Lotus knows only scorn. *"Worm!"* I spit.

Unmoved, Crow raises a hand.

The guards launch at me.

Ren's voice is in my ear: *Duck. Dodge. Sidestep.* But then Lotus takes over: I hurl one guard, headbutt another, flip the table, zither and all, into the mass before the entrance. More guards blockade it. Can't escape, so I won't. I round on a guard behind me and snap his arm. A howl. Sword on the ground. I dive for the weapon, through legs and feet, shoving back up to my own. The soldiers spin—and freeze.

Against my chest I hold Crow, snatched by his cloak.

I press my blade to his throat.

"Disarm. *Now.*"

Swords fall, until only mine is lifted. My hand hums around the hilt. My other hand, clapped on Crow's shoulder, is all too aware of the bone underneath. He seems to be carved from it, statue-still as my blood races. Am I hurting him? My hand trembles, and Crow murmurs, "Steady now. You need me alive."

"*Quiet.*"

I start to move.

The guards stay put.

We emerge from the tent, and conversation quiets. Hands slide to weapons. I press my sword closer—reducing the pressure when Dewdrop thinks, *Your lover is bleeding.*

Hostage, I correct her. A hostage who thankfully cooperates all the way to the final cordon of soldiers. The shields rise up, revealing the plain between our two camps. It should be desolate.

Would be, if not for Cloud. "Lotus!" she shouts, and my thoughts seize.

What's she—

You told her to wait for you, thinks Dewdrop.

Not *in the plain.* My mind spins, and Crow's chest inflates under my arm.

"*Fire!*" he yells.

The fool—!

I whirl and see Cloud, rushing for me. Whirl again, and I see archers among the enemy cordon. *Think.* I still have Crow. My human shield. He's my obvious recourse, and the cause for the split-second delay from his own archers.

A second is all I need. "Their retreat!" I scream to Cloud. My words must make it to her, even if I don't. "You mustn't—"

The arrow hits—
Follow their retreat.
—me. Back of my right shoulder. We fall—together, apart, Crow and I decoupled by the force. Then suddenly, I'm looking down at myself, my spirit in the air as Cloud reaches my body on the ground, retrieving me as Crow's soldiers retrieve him. Some go for Cloud—only to meet our soldiers, surging past her. The two sides crash like floodwaters.

I shout, but no one can hear me.

The world below vanishes.

‡ ‡ ‡

High up in a sea of gray clouds, I awaken. Chains lash me upright to a cold, hard surface.

My frustration is a tighter bond. "What do you want?" Because surely she's here. My captor. The Masked Mother. The arrow wasn't fatal. She took me, ripped me away from the mortal realm.

"Answer me!" I yell over the rumble of thunder. "Where did you take me?"

"The Obelisk of Souls."

That's—

Not the Masked Mother's voice.

I don't quite believe my ears until I see her, walking out of the clouds ahead, a snake in her braid, another around her shoulders.

"Nadir?" I stare at my second sister. Or *could* it be the Masked Mother? She stops before me, and I wait for her face to change. When it doesn't, I stammer, "What—how did—"

She holds out her palm, filled with shards. *From a clay figurine.* The last time she shattered one in my likeness, my memories returned. This time she must have shattered one to make *me* return. But why *now*, at the worst possible moment, when I'm most needed on earth? My glare lands on Dewdrop, hovering by Nadir's ear. *Were you reporting on me?*

Dewdrop buzzes, her non-answer as good as a guilty one, but Nadir says, "Please, Zephyr. Everyone knows you've been in the mortal realm. Including her."

Her. There's only one person Nadir would refer to with such deference and fear.

All gods fear her.

"Is that why you've recalled me?" I hiss, straining against my bonds. "To deliver me to the Masked Mother?"

Nadir's expression chills. "We're *saving* you, Zephyr."

"I don't understand—"

Lightning strikes the Obelisk at my back. One moment, I want to scream but can't. The next, I'm gasping, aftershocks crackling through the nebula of qì I've emitted. It glows, an unearthly blue, like the tail of a comet. But every comet has another tail, a white one of solid matter, and as I catch my breath, I notice the second intermingled substance, more opaque than the first.

The qì of another.

Lotus's. It's all around me. The tang of sweat. A pig's squeal, as it's killed by an ax.

This is Lotus's qì, and it's mixed with mine.

"Do you see now?" asks Nadir. "I'm saving your life."

"Gods can't die."

Nadir doesn't reply. Instead, she waits.

I look at the cloud of qì again.

Mine. Lotus's. So well blended.

It bleeds through me, Nadir's implication.

"When you were banished into Qilin, you had a seal placed on you by the Masked Mother. You didn't this time. *Her*"—Nadir refers to Lotus with the opposite of deference—"qì has been contaminating yours for months. Haven't you noticed? The way you act more like her, and less like yourself?" Nadir steps in, eyes on my face. "Every day, you lose more of your godhood, starting with your powers."

No. You're wrong.

The words catch in my mouth.

Is this why Cloud could see my spirit? Why my qì created those zither scenes of the butchered pigs? *Haven't* I been succumbing to Lotus's temper more, recently?

No, it's just Nadir's theory. *There's no proof*, I think, as Nadir bends down, the clouds around her feet turning to mud. She scoops up a chunk and shapes it into an effigy of Lotus. Easy. Summoning some rain should be easy for me too. Bending an air current shouldn't leave me writhing. Has my power really been fading? Doubts cloud my mind, then clear as Nadir's snake twines down her arm and opens its mouth over the clay Lotus. "No. Wait—"

A jet of flame shoots out, bathing the figurine in white fire. Slowly, Lotus's qì drifts to it. Nadir's brow furrows, and I almost call out again. *Wait!*

That's the last of Lotus's spirit.

So? asks another voice of mine. *It's not yours. It's mortal weakness. Temper and chaos.*

It won't help you win.

The rest of Lotus's qì vanishes into the figurine.

Only mine glows in the nebula now.

"You're always like this, Zephyr." Nadir's voice is quiet. Frayed. As if she too was struck by lightning. "Doing things without thought or consideration for others."

"And have you considered me?" My words surprise me. My anger is cold and true and strictly my own. "I want to help *them*."

"Why? They'll never be worthy. If they act like they cherish you, it's because of what you can do for them. We love you for who you *are*," Nadir says, and I know. I haven't forgotten how Dewdrop would heist back wines from the celestial vineyard for me, how Nadir knew all my drinking buddies by name and would clean up after our messes. "*We're* your family," my sister says, and I can't refute it, but I also want to say *it's different*.

Somehow, it's different.

"I just need time, Nadir. Just a little longer."

"Longer? Any longer, and you wouldn't have been able to return to the heavens at all!" Nadir's eyes shine, damp like her next intake of breath. "Don't you understand?" she asks, and her voice is closer to the mothering tone I'm used to. "The people you serve are bound by fate, and they're fated to fail. Haven't the dreams shown you that by now?"

"How do you know . . ." *My dreams.* My gaze whips to Dewdrop. "You *have* been reporting on me."

"No, Zephyr." I look back to Nadir. "*I* sent the dreams to you," says my sister. "They're glimpses of fate as it'll happen."

We thought that if you felt doomed to fail, you'd give up, Dewdrop thinks to me. *You may like winning, but you hate losing more.*

"You don't know me at all, then. Yes, maybe I was like that. But I don't ever want to be that person again."

"That person is *you*," Nadir insists.

"No." *Heaven makes me that person.* You *make me that person by expecting nothing more of me.* But even hurt, I can't bring myself to hurt Nadir back. "I will change the fates."

"You can't."

"*I can!*"

Thunder claps. Lightning flashes, bleaching Nadir's face.

She snaps her fingers.

The clouds vanish, the Obelisk too. I collapse on a stone-tiled floor. A scroll joins me on the ground, a stretch unfurled. I see Ren's name.

I grope for the scroll.

Her fate stares up at me in black ink.

No.

"Who, then?" I croak.

Who, if not Ren?

"It doesn't matter." Nadir gazes down at me. "You shouldn't care," she says, and we're so far apart. She is heaven, above.

And I am earth. Unyielding as the stone beneath me, I spit, "*You* cared about humans, enough to make them," and Nadir stiffens. I rise. "Why can't I?"

I go through the many shelves, one by one. Scrolls tumble

and fall, my qì yanking them out when my hands can't move fast enough.

"Look all you want!" Nadir cries.

I intend to, with or without permission. But there are too many scrolls. I could be here for days. Dewdrop's bees fly the scrolls I've dislodged back into place, striking an idea in my mind. I pick up Ren's scroll and throw it at the bees. They take it to a shelf. I follow them, and finally find the fates of the people I know, starting with Cloud's.

The siege fails; Cloud is tricked north and killed. Ren will march against Miasma, only to be outflanked by Cicada from the rear. Her fate ends there.

Decades later, Cicada, middle-aged, dies to illness.

The scroll shakes in my grip.

Who, then? Who prevails? Who unites the empire?

I tear Miasma's scroll open.

Death finds her too, just not on the battlefield. It starts from within her skull. A growth, is the physician's diagnosis. She'll offer to remove it, and be executed on suspicion of being an assassin. But not long after the physician's head falls, Miasma will fall herself. She'll never wake up. As the kingdoms continue to war, Xin Bao, empress without heirs, will land under the control of Plum.

Plum. I read on, searching for another name, for Crow's or anyone else's, anyone more relevant, less random.

There is none.

Plum. A senior registrar. Advisor. General, at the peak of her late career, as the fates have recorded. But still—*Plum*. All our efforts, all this bloodshed, and it's *Plum* who ascends the throne when she eventually deposes Xin Bao?

Plum's descendants who unite the three kingdoms?

No. It must be Ren. This scroll—it's but paper. I'll destroy it.

Clenching it shut, I walk. I dispel the damper qì in the air in one step, concentrate the dry in my next. It's as second nature as breathing, now that I'm unhindered by Lotus's qì, and in three steps, the conditions are perfect.

All that's missing is the spark.

I close in on Nadir; she frowns. "What are you—"

I grab the neck of one of her snakes and *squeeze* out a flame-forked tongue.

The library combusts.

Fates burn like kindling. We burn too, our clothes char, then soot. In my hand, the scroll becomes ash. Nadir stares at me, the firestorm reflected in her pitch-black irises.

"You—" Shock flattens her voice. "The Masked Mother—"

"I know." *Do no harm. Do no good.* I'd already broken the fundamental rule of noninterference between mortals and gods. Now I've burned an entire library of destinies.

I know the repercussions will be beyond my fathom.

"What did I tell you, Nadir?"

The voice rings from everywhere and nowhere at once.

Then, out of the flames, steps a qilin.

"For her to accept fate," says the Masked Mother, "she'll have to taste it."

She clops over to my sister, but Nadir doesn't acknowledge her. Her eyes haven't left my face.

"You would go this far for them?" she finally asks, and I clench the ash in my fist.

"I would."

"*Why?* You're not them. You're not human."

I want to be. The words spear through me, wild and sudden. *If we could all choose who to be, I'd want to be them.*

三十一

A CLOUDLESS NIGHT

I want to be . . .

Darkness. Dampness. Something rocks beneath me, like a boat. I'm back in Lotus's body.

Stars glimmer beyond the treetops, the sky cloudless.

More of my mind returns. Nighttime, in a forest, and I—I'm trussed belly-up to a horse. I tug on my binds. Secure. My heart sprints. Have I been captured? The last thing I remember is the arrow—Crow—Cloud—

"Cloud." Silence. "*Cloud,*" I repeat, voice hoarse.

And like a miracle, I hear hers.

"*Yuu.*" At the coaxing note, her mare falls back, bringing her to my side. "About time," she says gruffly.

"What happened?" The trees rustle; rainwater dusts my face.

"The arrow knocked you out. It was poisoned, just like my crossbolt."

Poisoned, like Cloud's crossbolt. The detail strikes me as important, but I can't pinpoint how. My head is foggy, my senses dull.

Will it kill me? I wonder to Dewdrop as my struck shoulder burns. No reply. "Where are we?"

Heartbeats pass. No word from Cloud. No thoughts from Dewdrop. The silence is like one I haven't experienced in months. I'm still a god, in the mortal realm.

And right now, something tells me I'm the only one.

Dewdrop is gone.

"North," Cloud finally answers. "Somewhere north of Hewan."

Too far north. Behind us, the Marshlands have surely fallen to Cicada. Ahead? How much time before we run into Miasma?

"They retreated," Cloud continues, and it's as I warned. "They gave up Bikong hours after you fell, and I thought—well, I thought this was our chance to defeat the empire. So I chased—but they ambushed my flank." We ride through a slant of moonlight, and I see the blood on Cloud's cloak. Her armor is battered and torn. "They surrounded us, but my soldiers broke us out." Deep in the forest, water drips. "It's just us now."

The branches above us sway, casting down a second rain.

Our forces, captured or dead.

The two of us, on the run in empire land.

"Rice Cake?" I rasp, unable to identify my horse.

Dread buries me alive when Cloud doesn't immediately answer. "We were separated while breaking through the enemy lines," she replies at last, and I tell myself that separated doesn't mean dead. Rice Cake fled to safety. I'm sure of it. I say so to Cloud, and she looks away, teeth punishing her bottom lip.

"Hey." My voice cracks. "It's okay."

"It's not, and you know it." A breath, as if Cloud means to say more. *I'm sorry, Zephyr. I should have listened to you.* The apology doesn't come. Cloud's waiting, I realize, for me to speak. To admonish her, then tell her the strategy. Fear rules her silence, not pride.

Her fear is also mine. I have no plans, no tricks. My head throbs from the poison. "Let me think," I say, trying to buy time, but time is what we have the least of. Minutes later, the trees rustle with more than wind. The enemy emerges from the branches.

Their nets fall over us.

‡ ‡ ‡

At first, everything is sharp. The ropes slicing into my arms. The bleak glare of the sun. Panic stabs my mind, memories bleeding from the cuts—

—the Battle of the Scarp—

—the coup against Xin Gong—

—the siege of Bikong—

—the blood I've spilled, the hearts I've shunned—

—will be for naught. They'll die—Cloud, Ren—like they do in my nightmares. *Or is this a nightmare?* I bite my tongue; blood runs down my throat, but I don't wake up.

Then the poison deadens the panic. Days blur. Locations. Out of the forest, we're taken. Through yellow, fallow fields.

Into the capital.

Into the palace.

Polearms whack our legs from standing to kneeling.

Dawn streams through the pillars at our backs, and despite my delirium, I force myself to place us. Dawn means east. East means throne hall, where the empress holds court, but this court holds no officials, or Xin Bao for that matter. The only souls here, it seems, are those of the ghosts, more plentiful than when I was last in the capital. Maybe this is all just a fever dream . . .

Then from behind the screens backdropping the throne, a shadow appears. It stalks through the clustered ghosts. Another shadow follows on its heels, and my delusions flee.

My gaze sinks to my knees as Miasma's voice chimes through the hall.

"Well, well, well. When Crow reported on our gains, I hardly dared to believe it. The mighty Cloud! Our paths seem destined to cross. It must be in our stars, to be lordess and retainer."

"Keep dreaming," Cloud bites out, arms bulging against her restraints.

"What do you say, Crow?" Miasma muses. "Shall I kill them both?"

I recognized his presence the second I saw his shadow. I know the shape he casts. The cadence of his speech.

I was once between his lips like a word, spoken.

But it's high time I remembered: He is no lovesick boy. I am not his weakness.

He will not have sympathy for my lordess's generals.

His answer to Miasma is as expected.

"Gao Yun freed you once. You freed her. Nothing is owed anymore. Free her again, and she will only ride back to Ren."

"What about this one?" Miasma's shadow-head nods at me. "I freed her too, and she ran right back to Ren."

"That is true," Crow concedes. "But if I may request a favor, Mi-Mi."

"Request away."

"I would like to keep her alive, as a prisoner."

My breathing slows.

"Oh?" A question followed by an observation: "You see something in that one."

"She calculated our retreat," says Crow.

"How curious," says Miasma, and my shock wanes. Crow *would* request that I be pardoned. I'm a riddle of a warrior; he won't rest until he's solved me.

Too bad for Crow, I doubt his lordess will grant the favor. She'll either kill us both, or kill me and spare Cloud. *Miasma has always wanted to recruit her*, I'm thinking, as Miasma waves a hand. Sound of soldiers, walking toward us.

Veering toward Cloud.

No. My gaze shoots up. *I burned her fate.* I stare at Cloud as she glares down Miasma, unflinching as the soldiers enclose her. Warriors don't fear death. But it's not cowardly to fight fate, and I will fight Cloud's with everything I have.

I *will* change it.

"You shouldn't have retreated," I blurt to Miasma as the soldiers reach for Cloud. "It harmed you more than it helped."

The prime ministress smiles at that. "Harmed? I don't see the harm in having not one, but two of Ren's swornsisters kneeling before me."

"You could have defeated us *at* Bikong. Instead you retreated.

You benefited by capturing us, yes. But someone else benefited more." I pause for effect. "More than an ally should."

Yes, I know about the alliance with Cicada.

Ask me how.

Armor scrapes, as Cloud is seized. Is dragged on her knees.

Ask me anything at all.

Miasma holds up a hand, and the horrible sound ceases. "Do you know why Cicada broke off her alliance with you and turned to me? Because Charity Ren did not deliver what she promised."

"She never promised the return of the Marshlands." Couldn't, at the time, because the land was still Xin Gong's. And thank heavens it was; by then Cicada had already betrayed us. "You've given Cicada a new base from which to aim straight at the empire's heart," I say, eye boring into Miasma's. "You were a fool this time." I smirk despite my nausea. "Just like the time you trusted the Rising Zephyr."

Blink, and Miasma's kneeling, grabbing my face.

"An animal could not know me. And you, my dear, are nothing more than an animal." She wrenches my head to the side, and I see Cloud again. *What are you doing?* her eyes demand, and I remember the game of chess we played. I can still win.

It just won't be by a great margin.

"Frankly, I can't see what Ren sees in you," Miasma says, and I laugh, causing Cloud's brows to slash down in confusion, then rise.

Zephyr.

No.

I know, on the surface, we're both Ren's swornsisters. In the short term, losing either of us will hurt her. But it's not the same. Cloud is Ren's real family. Cloud is human.

Only one of us can afford to die today.

"Then kill me. Kill me, because I'd rather be Ren's animal than yours." I jerk away from the hand on my face and back to it, teeth crunching into bone. Miasma shoots to her feet, and I spit at her. "Daughter of eunuchs! You needed to declare yourself a *god* just to be legitimate! You're cursed, and you know it! Ghosts haunt you because you're *scared* of the people you've killed. I bet you're *so* scared, you wet your bed from the nightmares."

Miasma stares at me, unblinking. Silent. Blood drips from her hand. I wish I'd taken off her fingers. It'd be fair, considering the finger she took from Crow, who's also silent—gravely so. My actions don't bode well for the favor he asked of his lordess.

"Mi-Mi—" he starts.

"I'm sorry, Crow." Miasma doesn't sound sorry, only dangerous. "I've had a change of heart. Guards."

"No!" Cloud shouts as the guards grab my arms. "Kill me! Kill me instead!"

Miasma sighs. "Call me a fool, but I do believe there will come a day when I recruit you. Besides, I'll need another messenger to deliver the head." The guards start to drag me out but Miasma flicks her injured hand. "Right here will do."

I'm pushed onto all fours, the floor before me speckled with Miasma's blood.

It's nothing compared to the blood I'm about to pour. *What am I doing? Have I lost my mind?* No—I know exactly what I'm doing. If the Masked Mother won't let me come back—if this is to be my final earthly act—I'll set Ren up for success. So long as Cloud lives through losing Bikong, she'll defy her fated death, and Ren won't die either. I won't get to see them march on the North, but Sikou Hai will complete my mission. Hilarious to think I almost sacrificed him, pitting him against his brother in my stratagem to kill Xin Gong with a Borrowed Knife—

A borrowed knife.

If I were Crow, a strategist of the North, I'd advise Miasma to kill *neither* Lotus nor Cloud. I'd deliver them alive to Cicada. A gift to seal the alliance. Let *her* kill Ren's swornsisters.

Let Cicada be Miasma's borrowed knife.

Instead, Miasma will catch the flames of Ren's ire by killing Lotus. It doesn't make sense. The empire feeds off the discord between Cicada and Ren.

So who stands to benefit from Lotus's death by the North's hand?

The same ones who benefited from Crow's retreat at Bikong, allowing Cicada to secure the Marshlands without facing Cloud's reinforcements. The same ones who benefited from the Battle of the Scarp that saw the destruction of the empire's navy—only possible because Crow failed to stop me from tricking Miasma.

If he ever meant to stop me.

Crow has never harmed the Southlands in his schemes. The Southlands, who now supply the empire with their signature poison. It coats their crossbolts. Their arrows. Struck myself, I feel what Cloud must have felt. Only difference? I have more experience at being poisoned than Cloud.

My symptoms now match my symptoms then, back when Crow drugged my tea.

His weapon of choice was this very poison, native to the South, even *before* the Cicada-Miasma alliance.

"Cloud—" I gasp as a soldier lifts his sword, metal blade reflected in the varnish of the floor. Last time I didn't get to finish. This time I *will* speak before I'm silenced.

"*Cloud*—" But my words are also for Miasma, and I look straight at Crow as I say them. If he's to be my final sight in this world, I will make myself his. "He's of the South."

The blade falls.

HEAVEN DECIDES

He's of the South.

Just like when I died in Pumice Pass, my consciousness flees into a memory.

Memories.

I'm standing in Cicada's court on behalf of the North, and Crow is beside me.

I'm at the bottom of the boat; he's on top of me.

We face each other, across zithers; I'm Zephyr, then Lotus. The arrow strikes my shoulder, and it's not an accident.

At the very last second, I turned, covered for Crow, paid back the debt I owed him.

I should have let it hit him.

The memories come quicker, blurring, then focus on one moment. Crow—I'm watching him as he steps into my shrine. In it, he'll leave a peacock fan.

He steps out, and I'm following him up the mountain. Ordering him to turn around. He does, and I know what happens next.

I'll ask him the question eating me alive:

"Why are you really here?"

"I already explained to your lordess," he says, and I know that too; I was beside Ren when he said, *I'm here to pay my respects to your strategist.* I didn't believe him. Not fully. That couldn't be his only motive.

And it wasn't. He'd come west to help Cicada, his true lordess, testify that I was killed by the South, thus spawning their alliance with Miasma. My doubts have been proved right. I was always right.

Why, then, do I feel so wronged?

I turn away from Crow, eyes hot. *Because I wanted to believe it.* To be a fool, and have Crow be one with me. But had Crow actually been a fool—had he visited my shrine *just* to pay his respects—I wouldn't have been compelled to follow him this far up the mountain. He wouldn't bother me like a game I haven't won—*can't* win now that my time on earth has ended.

Well played, Crow. Well played. Except it doesn't feel well played at all. I want to see Crow one more time, and not just to watch Miasma kill him for being a Southern spy.

With my own two hands, I want to destroy him.

‡ ‡ ‡

I come to prone on the floor, cheek pressed to an expanse of peach-and-turquoise agate.

Someone sits before me, cross-legged.

"Do you see now?" *Crow.* I scrabble up and surge for him— but then it's Cloud. Cloud, who was just kneeling with me, who will have to watch her swornsister die before her eyes. Her voice deepens, becomes the voice of twenty. The words echo through the hall as if spoken by a congregation.

"Humans may devise, but heaven decides."

"No." I shake my head. "I saved you. I saved her. Cloud. I took her place. I changed her fate."

"You changed nothing, Qilin." The Masked Mother transforms into Ren. "A swornsister of mine has been killed. I will still die—only now, it'll be in a war of vengeance against Cicada instead of Miasma."

"No. You—Cloud wouldn't let that happen."

"Are you so certain?" Ren becomes Miasma, and the prime ministress tsks. She leans close, bell tinkling. "*He's of the South.*" Her whisper sears my face. "Did you think *I* would act on this intel?"

She pulls back, and cold air floods in. "I won't, but Cloud will. She'll carry your last words to Ren along with Lotus's head. She'll tell her lordess that it was Cicada and her spy who collaborated with Miasma to kill Lotus and, worse, that it was also Cicada who killed her little strategist, Qilin."

Cloud wouldn't. She knows we must have the South as allies. I told her. She listened to me before—

Barely, says a voice, stronger than my pride. *Her first instinct will always be to tell Ren, and now you're not alive to stop her.*

Zephyr. Lotus. They both died because of the South's deception, Cloud will say in a fit of emotion.

Miasma was just the executioner.

"Now, what were the names of the others again? Tourmaline and Sikou Hai? They will corroborate each of Cloud's claims.

Ren will bring to Cicada a war like none other." Miasma grins, pale teeth in pale gums. "She'll die in it. No matter which way the river flows, it will always empty into the ocean."

She waves a hand, and her palace vanishes. A red sky looms above us.

A war cry rises in the distance.

"For Lotus!"

Even before I see the corpses, I know I'm back in my nightmares. But somehow, it's worse. The smell of viscera is more putrid. Blood dyes the mud—lǐ and lǐ of it.

We're in the Marshlands.

I look up and see Cloud and Ren, fighting. *Winning.* Southern banners fall and gongs sound, as Cicada orders her army to retreat and Ren regains the lost territory.

But then—fire. I don't see where it starts, just the chaos ignited by it. Cloud, when I spot her again, is downed. Killed. Ren is next—killed by the enemy and then—the scene pulses, resetting—killed by *our* soldiers as they defect to Cicada.

The scene pulses once more before I can recover, the marshes becoming a misty, forted city with the name Taohui on the walls. There, I see Ren on a bed, wounded but alive. "I'm sorry, Qilin," she whispers. "I couldn't finish our mission." She rises and orders our remaining soldiers out. When they're gone, she picks up one of her double swords.

She brings it to her neck.

"No—!"

Her blood sprays through my spirit.

And then I'm in the Library of Destinies again. A Scribe is

rewriting all the scrolls I burned, the contents changing, but not the ending: Ren's mission dead from the moment Cloud lost Bikong.

This is how it was, how it is, how it will be forevermore. I hear the Masked Mother's voice in my head like Dewdrop's.

Fate will prevail, and you can't stop it.

"Or rather, fate will prevail, and you will have *helped* it," the Masked Mother says, out loud, the two of us back in her palace. I can no longer see her; I can only see the floor, my nose pressed to it. My head is buried under my arms; my breath leaves my mouth in small, wet bursts.

I doomed them.

I doomed them all to die.

I may not have told Ren about Cicada's betrayal, but I did tell the others. I feared the Rising Zephyr Objective would again be left without a successor, but no one knows better than I, its maker, that Ren *can't* win without the Southlands. My murderers or not, they must be our allies.

I should have taken their betrayal to my grave.

But then, my heart whispers, *Crow would always think you were none the wiser to his deception.*

He still does. Crow, who outsmarted me. Standing right there beside me, in Cicada's court.

Pretending, like I was, to be sided with the North.

Miasma doesn't kill him for it?

How can that be?

There must be a mistake. I uncover my head and raise my eyes to the Masked Mother's—hers now set in Nadir's face. "Send me back," I say to the facsimile of my sister.

I hate that the facsimile also has her voice. "Why should I, Zephyr?"

"Why do you do anything? You *knew* I was among the mortals, and yet you let me stay, unpunished. Why? Why haven't you banished me from the heavens for good already?"

"Do you want to be banished for good?" asks the Masked Mother, and it's cruel that she uses Nadir's voice to ask it—

Not cruel. *She possesses no concept of hate or love*, Nadir told me back when I had to reclaim my powers. *She knows no emotion but that of others.*

Whatever you hide, she will see.

Whatever you feel, she will use to test you.

This question feels like a test.

Do you want to be banished for good?

"Yes," I say, meeting the Masked Mother's gaze.

"What do you think permanent banishment is?" she asks, and I don't bother hiding my fear of the unknown, the vastness of all that I can't control.

"It's when you send gods to a place they can't return from."

In answer, the ground beneath my feet falls away. My stomach lurches, braced for more carnage, but a sea of clouds appears instead, the Obelisk of Souls the only structure in its midst.

"It's a great mystery, isn't it? Where the banished gods go." The Masked Mother turns her gaze to the Obelisk and I do too, seeing it anew from my unbound angle.

"Of course, none of these gods return to speak of the new world they call home," the Masked Mother says as qì skims up and down the structure's sides. Up go the souls of mortals released from the mortal realm. Down go the souls washed of their memories and stripped back to their primordial forms, to be repurposed or, in mortal terms, reincarnated. "Like mortals rinsed clean of their previous lives, none of them remember that they were gods at all."

Does that mean what I think it means?

The banished gods . . . are reincarnated into mortals?

"Yes, Zephyr. That is why your sisters fear this fate for you so. But it is what you want, isn't it? To be them?"

The Masked Mother eyes me knowingly, and I balk.

Y-yes. That's what I said. But when I try to visualize it—Ren and her camp marching victorious in the streets and I, a mere mortal without my memories, celebrating a victory I had no part in—my soul flinches. *No.* I don't want to be human. I want—I *want*—

"I want to be *with* them. With Ren's camp. If I'm human, I can't help them."

"Fascinating," muses the Masked Mother, "how you've made Qilin's fate your very own." She cocks her head. "Enlighten me, then, Zephyr: How will you change the mortal fates when you've failed to so far?"

"*You* are the heavens. *You* control the Scribes. *You* decide. So make an exception for me. Let me go back as I am, a god. I'll find my own body. Just give me a chance—a fair chance—to change fate, without the Scribes' interference."

"You ask for much."

"You can do whatever you want with me when I'm done."

"All for a chance to help these humans."

Save Ren; undo my mistake; win. "Yes."

"Even if it costs you the ability to return to the heavens?" asks the Masked Mother.

I don't want to be in the heavens. But this time, I don't blurt out the words. My sisters are in the heavens, and when I hear Nadir's voice next, it's real and hers, the memory wafting through my mind like incense.

Why don't you come cultivate with me, Zephyr?

I'd been pooled on the bed, the sun warm on my back. "Don't feel like it." Cultivation was for strengthening one's powers, but I had no use for stronger powers.

Nadir stroked my hair. "I saw Nebula the other day. He's looking for apprentices."

"That old fart?"

"Zephyr!"

"I don't want to be his apprentice." His blacksmithing was pointless. A celestial weapon strike might strip a god of their powers, but powers could be recultivated, as it so often happened after the heavenly wars. The losers would reappear after a thousand years, powers restored, and rehash the same five conflicts. Suffice to say, I knew better than to bother with godly politics.

Chess was different. A game was a game. A win was a win.

Or had been.

"What about wéiqí?" Nadir asked, and I recalled how she'd

found me the previous week: drunk, the board overturned on the floor, pieces scattered. Nadir had quietly picked up the white and black stones.

"Why don't we play?" she now asked, and I'd pushed my face into my pillow. Couldn't I languish in peace? Couldn't Nadir go away?

My memory of her does, as I face the Masked Mother.

Nadir and Dewdrop will miss me, but there was nothing to miss. I had no purpose. What good is an eternity with them if nothing I do makes a difference?

"If leaving the heavens is what it takes, I'll pay."

"And if it takes your existence?"

"Whatever the price, I'll pay it."

STANZA FOUR

To the north, a miasma
head throbbing, heard a banging
at her doors: "Rebels in the city!"

To the south, a cicada
learned of a queen's loss and smiled.
"Miasma just started a war."

To the west, a queen
received a sister on her knees.
"Kill me for failing her, and kill the South."

And in the skies above,
a deal between gods was struck.

三十三

BETTER TO BETRAY

The deal has been made, the terms set.

Keep this from my sisters. My final request of the Masked Mother.

I cannot promise that, was her answer. *I can only promise you won't be stopped by them.*

Good, because if they knew what I'd agreed to, they wouldn't understand. No price is too great for success, and if I fail—

I'd rather perish.

‡ ‡ ‡

I reappear in the throne hall where I lost my head. The blood is gone. Servants polish the floor, murmuring as they work. From their conversation I glean that Xin Bao is on a pilgrimage to the Northern temples.

At the temple, or here, the empress is of no importance to me. I saw as much of her fate as I needed to when I saw Plum's. Xin Bao will remain oppressed by her regents, heirless to the end. She's not destined to be anything more than a figurehead.

But she is Ren's world, and Ren needs to live to save her and her empire.

I start to drift out of the throne hall, slowing as a ghost flows in, then a second. The influx becomes a river. I flow opposite its current, one river leading me to another: the Mica. From afar, its banks appeared fogged. With ghosts, I see as I drift closer. Some stand on the shore, others in the water.

More join their ranks as the executioners carry on.

"What happened?" I ask the ghost beside me as rows of kneeling people are felled. Dewdrop mentioned that the spirits of humans should be able to see and hear me if freed from their body, but no one answers. I turn to the others. "Anyone?"

Silence, but for the pleas of the living before they're cut short. Some require two blows to kill. Their screams would curdle blood if I had any, but I don't. Don't have time to be distracted. Ren will march on Cicada soon, if she hasn't already. I need to find a body, prevent her death, and repair the alliance.

I drift past the ghosts, careful not to touch their degenerate forms.

"T-there was a rebellion against Miasma."

My head turns.

The ghost who spoke wears the robes of the empire court. "Last night," she continues, "in the name of Lotus, Xin loyalists set fire to the armory. Miasma executed them and their relatives. Then this morning, she had the court follow her here." Her gaze guides mine to the field beyond the river. Two flags fly in the gray sky. One white, one red. "If we'd stayed at home that night, we were ordered to stand under the white flag. If we'd gone to the armory to help put out the fires, we were ordered under the red."

"You went to the red."

The ghost nods, lip wobbling. "Truth is, I was asleep, the whole night. I didn't even hear about the rebels until this morning. But I figured it was a test, that the prime ministress would reward the retainers who'd tried to help . . ."

She was right about it being a test. She was wrong about Miasma. To the prime ministress, anyone at the scene could *also* be a rebel. She'd rather spare those who slept sound in their beds and execute the rest. She's suspicious like that. A scream rends the air, and I grow suspicious myself. "Why are you talking to me, and not the others?"

"I—I don't know," stammers the ghost. She looks down, and I notice the body that's floated toward us, more blood weeping out with the current. "You feel familiar to me. Like we've met."

Have we? Doubtful, I study the body in the water. The river flows, buoying a pale hand to the surface. Caught around the fingers is a string of praying beads, trailing to a worship plaque.

NADIR, GODDESS OF CREATION

"Were you executed too?" asks the ghost, and I glance up into her face, see the fearful uncertainty in it. Nadir would have a comforting word for one of her followers.

I am not Nadir.

"No." I turn away from the girl. "Let go of this world. The Obelisk of Souls will take you and wash you of all these memories. You'll be reincarnated." I draw a breath. "Don't serve a lordess like Miasma, in your next life."

"Wait—"

But I'm already drifting away.

The bodies stretch down the bank. So many bodies—none of which I can take. As a god, I may heal injuries faster, but I can't close fatal wounds. I can lift someone out of a coma; I can't revive someone chopped in half.

Besides, I think, floating to the field, *becoming a Northern official wouldn't be much of an asset.* The surviving ones are amassed under the white flag, like the ghost described. They shake while Miasma watches the executions from upfield.

She is not alone.

My heart chills at the sight of him, standing beside her. Still alive, just as the Masked Mother said.

Not for much longer.

"It's a shame that so much life must end today," Miasma says as I float to her and Crow. "But better to betray the world than have it betray me. Wouldn't you agree, Crow?"

Whatever Crow says in reply, I don't hear. His mouth moves without sound, its shape so lovely. Even lovelier is the bob of his throat as he swallows. The wind rises, carrying his scent to me. In my memories, he smells like herbs and silk.

Now all I can smell is blood.

Crow. It has to be him. Stratagem Nineteen: Remove the Firewood Under the Cauldron. Crow is the source of the South's strength, their secret weapon. He's behind every loss Ren has faced and will face, culminating with the loss of her life at Taohui.

I must remove him.

And I know just how. My eyes go to Miasma. If she turns against Crow, the Southern-Northern alliance will end. Cicada will remember who the real enemy is. She'll seek Ren's aid again. As to whether or not Ren will forgive Cicada ... I'll work on that. I just need a body first—and not any.

His.

I choose him.

In this life and every other I forfeited, I choose him.

You once said we don't have to explain ourselves to each other, I think as night falls over our shared memories, my mind a palace of ice. *Do you remember? It was the final night I pretended to be on your side. You and I are both strategists. We both know.*

It really, really isn't personal.

‡ ‡ ‡

That night, I follow Miasma into her rooms. The seed of suspicion did not take root for whatever reason, but no matter.

I will plant it as many times as I need to.

I stand by as Miasma gets ready for bed. She undoes her lop-sided ponytail and lies down, fully clothed, boots on. The candles flicker—harder, as the ghosts enter. They gather by the bed; one ghost kneels, palms raised as if to deliver a tray. She might be the servant Miasma stabbed mid-dream, inspiring the rumor of Miasma being able to kill assassins in her sleep. I'm among those who believe Miasma was playacting at sleep so she could create a rumor to serve her. But in every rumor is a kernel of truth.

Miasma has many enemies.

Here I am, one of them.

I sit on the bed and stare at her, this woman just two years Ren's senior. Her skin is waxy, her bones prominent. Does she dream of the atrocities she's committed? Does she have nightmares, like I guessed?

She will, after tonight.

If Nadir can send dreams, so can I.

I place my hands over Miasma's eyes and close mine.

The times I touched Lotus and Sikou Hai, I met no resistance. They were empty vessels; I was the liquid that would fill them. Miasma's spirit, on the other hand, is still in her body. At first there's nowhere for me to go. I'm like water poured onto glazed porcelain. I push and shove and—

A great vibration.

If I were focused on Miasma, I'd notice her brow knotting, her jaw tensing, her face in the strictures of a migraine.

But I'm already gone, seeped through the cracks and into Miasma's mind, where all is dark and silent.

Nadir's nightmares worked on me because they pulled at my fears. What are Miasma's?

Show me. I send my qì out into the darkness like the notes of a harmony.

Show me why you don't trust your subordinates.

Why you'd rather betray than be betrayed.

The darkness in front of me shivers, resolving to a scene:

Two young soldiers. One with a royal surname, the other without—but they have something in common.

A shared vision for the future.

At a birthday feast for the court's oldest minister, a Xin loy-
alist like all the others, he asks the assembled officials the question of the hour: "Who dares kill the tyrant who calls himself
regent?"

And a person rises—not the one named Xin, but the one sitting beside her. A recently minted cavalry general, the title so new
that most still see a teenage soldier. Others see a charlatan, aspiring
for more than what someone of her lineage should desire.

"I, Miasma," says the young general. The sobriquet isn't recognized, and murmurs down the table invoke another name,
bestowed by a eunuch.

Mimeng? Her?

She'll fail.

True to their word, she does fail, and in a palace storeroom
she hides as the guards outside race by. *After the assassin!*

And what was anger—they didn't believe in her?—turns
to fear. Black-spots-in-vision and pounding heart. Our heart.
Before I can stop it, my mind merges with Miasma's, and from
her eyes, I watch as the storeroom door slides open. A boot steps
in, and our hand tightens around our only weapon—a hairpin
with a red bell.

We launch up and forward—but it's her.

Xin Ren tugs us out, down the small palace paths used by
servants, through a back door, to a tethered horse. She hands us
the reins. "Leave, and don't look back."

Xin Ren is righteous. Xin Ren is good-hearted.

Xin Ren is a fool, for she doesn't understand that no matter
where we go, the world won't welcome us like it does her. We

have to *carve* ourselves a place, all because we weren't born with the right surname. So we return, not long after.

We finish the job we failed.

And suddenly, we have on our hands a young empress without a regent, and a realm full of tyrants vying to be the next. If they are flies, then the empress is the rot attracting them. She ruins our vision for the future, a continent united, without war, under one strong ruler.

Kill her, we tell Xin Ren, the only person qualified, in the opinion of most commoners, to assume the throne. *If you don't, then I will.*

And before our eyes, Xin Ren's expression grows cold. *You've become the evil you ended.*

Anger, fear, and now betrayal. How childish, that we should feel it. Nothing is unconditional in this dog-eat-dog world. Bonds wither. Trust decays.

All seasons end in winter.

Ren vanishes, and we get up. Step out of the pavilion we met in, into the courtyard. It's snowing. The tree branches are dressed like nobles with their white rabbit-fur muffs. We stare at the snowy branches of a tree . . .

. . . that buds two plums.

They want to kill us.

On the branch land three birds . . .

. . . that become crows.

The people who once saved us.

The candlelit room returns. My breathing is uneven, like I've woken from the dream myself, and as I stare at Miasma—sat upright in the bed—I feel unsettled. Did I regain control at the end? Did Miasma see the same things I did? She calls for a servant to get Plum, and I'm forced to wait too, for the senior registrar, who strides in and bows.

"I had a dream, Plum," says Miasma without preamble. "An odd little dream . . ." Her gaze sweeps through the room and returns to me. I hold my breath. She can't see me. She can't.

When Miasma says nothing else, Plum clears her throat. "I'll summon the imperial cosmologist—"

"Will you, Plum? Do me the honors of interpreting it?"

The senior registrar bows deeper, expression obscured, but I can hear her gulp. "As you wish, Prime Ministress."

Miasma gestures for Plum to pull up a chair, sighing when the older woman stays as is. She begins.

"I dreamed I was in the palace gardens. It was summer, but it was snowing. I heard a caw, and looked up. Do you know what I saw?" A thrill goes through me as Miasma says, "Three crows. They were perched on a tree, pecking at two plums." Miasma rests her chin on her knuckles. "What does that mean?"

Plum's bow deepens. "Forgive any misinterpretations—this is not my usual purview—but snow in summer seems unusual. Perhaps you are under stress or change is imminent. The number three is significant too. I assume it must mean you, Ren, and Cicada. The three kingdoms of this empire."

"Hmm . . . I see. I see. That all makes a lot of sense, Plum." But Miasma isn't done. "What of the crows? What of the plums? How would you interpret those?"

"Those . . ." Plum's waist folds to nearly ninety degrees.

"You dreamed of them because you are used to seeing me and Crow."

"Three crows . . . two plums." I urge Miasma to make the connection. "You have no children, do you, Plum?"

There it is.

"No," says Plum. "No children, Prime Ministress."

"That's right," Miasma murmurs. "You entered this court when you were only a child yourself. Then the two plums . . ."

Miasma ruminates while I study the senior registrar. I suppose she still has years left to birth a descendant.

"Prime Ministress . . ." Plum lifts her gaze ever so slightly, peering over her clasped hands, arms suspended in a perfect bow. "Might I be so bold as to hedge that these dreams started after the warrior's execution?"

Slowly, Miasma nods.

"Her spirit must be to blame. Throw a feast to appease it. Our enemy or not, we ought to honor the life of a swornsister."

An intrepid suggestion. Will Miasma agree with it? Or will she be insulted?

In the ensuing silence, the ghosts watch Miasma closely, perhaps reliving their last moments before the execution order was handed down. Risk or reward.

Which will it be?

"Why didn't you say so earlier?" Miasma waves her hand. "See that the feast is arranged—"

She breaks off, clutching her head with a grimace.

"I also know of a physician, Prime Ministress," Plum murmurs. "I can have her come see you."

"Physicians." Miasma's voice is contemptuous. "Since when have they helped?"

"She's very good, I assure you."

"Send for her, then." With that, Miasma relieves Plum. I follow the senior registrar out. She shuts the door behind her and sags. She's outlived her peers because she has a sixth sense for danger. She knows it was a close call.

Not close enough for my liking. In the fates, Plum deposes Xin Bao after Ren dies. But if Ren lives and makes it to Xin Bao's side? Plum's fate may still bite us. I must end Plum as well, before she ever births a child.

"Bad dream, was it?"

At the voice, Plum stiffens while I straighten. He's here. My other target.

In the shadows down the hall, he waits patiently for Plum to go to him, speaking only when she draws into his earshot and out of Miasma's. "Does she suspect you now?"

"Don't spew nonsense," Plum snaps. "Worry about your own neck." Her eyes dart once to the right, once to the left; her whisper is minced and harsh. "We all heard what that warrior said."

"And what of it? Everyone knows I was born in the South." Plum *hmphs* as I frown. So that's what saved him, a preestablished fact to blunt Miasma's suspicion. Unruffled, Crow presses on. "What did she dream of?"

"Crows and plums."

"Ah."

"Have you nothing else to say?"

"I'm sure you've already provided her with an actionable solution."

The lighter Crow's mood, the more Plum's darkens. "There are times I've wondered myself, if you *really* have the empire's best interests at heart. The Battle of the Scarp—"

"My mistake, and I've paid for it."

"This was a mistake too," Plum hisses. "We should have sent the warrior to Cicada as a gift. Let the Southlands execute her! But what have we done? Nothing but give Xin Ren more motive to come at us."

"She won't," says Crow. "She'll attack the Southlands."

"And why in the heavens would she?"

Crow holds Plum's gaze for a long, cool second. He smiles. "What is a strategist without secrets?"

"You—"

"Good night, Plum." Crow turns, starting down the red dim of the corridor. "And relax. Haven't we all fallen under Miasma's suspicion at one point or another? You yourself are no stranger to having your mail read by her. I'm sure in a few weeks, I'll be sent a test of loyalty to clear my name. So don't lose sleep over me."

"Children!" Plum spits, her disgruntlement a satisfying thing to witness. Then my satisfaction wilts.

Yet again, the seed of suspicion against Crow failed to grow.

I tail him to his room. He sits at his desk, touches a brush to ink, then ink to paper.

Stroke by stroke, words emerge.

Do not let down your guard.

The head may have fallen, but the wind may not blow in the direction we thought.

His brushmanship is neater than when I last visited him as a spirit. His music too was barely affected during our duet. In four short months, he's adapted to losing his finger. He has a soul of steel.

But even steel melts to fire.

Write more, I urge. *Create hard evidence of your betrayal with every black-and-white word.*

When he's finished, he considers the letter. He's surely sent messages like it to Cicada before, just encoded. *Anything is better than nothing,* I think as he lifts the letter off the desk. If he doesn't send it, then Cicada will think Ren is set to march against Miasma as intended. But if he sends it while *his* mail is being monitored . . .

He takes the letter to the brazier and feeds it in.

He does not write a coded version.

Ever so careful, my rival.

It will take more than a nightmare to damn him.

‡ ‡ ‡

Crow is my foe. Plum is my foe. But I have one more—fate— and when the physician Plum vouched for arrives two mornings later, I see that fate is even more heartless than I am.

Because it's the same physician who treated Cloud.

If the scrolls are to be believed, she will tell Miasma she has a mass growing in her head.

She will be executed for it.

"Well, what is it?" asks Miasma after the physician concludes her examination.

Don't, I will her, hoping that she can feel the weight of my stare. *Don't say it.*

Don't.

"You have a mass growing in your head," says the physician and I look away, unable to watch on as she signs her own death edict. "Eventually, it will kill you." A tremor goes through the officials assembled. Plum herself is as pale as the ghosts by the throne. "But I can help."

Miasma leans forward in her seat. "Do say how."

"I will put you to sleep, open your skull, remove the mass, repair the bone, and finish by sewing up the scalp."

Even to me, a god, the words sound out of this realm. It's never been done—certainly not by mortals.

"And how will I trust you not to murder me in my sleep?" asks Miasma.

"That is a question only you can answer."

By now, the officials have distanced themselves from Plum. The court is so quiet, one could hear a bead of sweat fall.

"Prime Ministress—" the senior registrar starts.

"Guards!" Everyone kneels. Soldiers rush in, and Miasma points at the physician. "Take her to the dungeons. Interrogate her. Find out who sent this assassin." She sits back. "Take her associate too."

"Mercy!" cries Plum. "Mercy, Prime Ministress! I'm also a victim of trickery! I'd only heard of her legendary feats. I have no idea what devilry she spouts now!"

The physician keeps quiet.

The ghosts crowd around her as she's towed out, then Plum.

I float after them, to the dungeons, watching from the corner of the stone cell as the physician is roped to the interrogation rack. If only I could do more to help. She did save Cloud.

Then Plum screams from the abutting cell, and I remember I'm here for one purpose.

Stratagem Twelve: Pilfer the Goat from the Passing Herd. I didn't cause the physician's predicament, but I can capitalize on it. With a confession, I can take out Crow and Plum. No— Crow *or* Plum. To have both implicated is too suspect even for Miasma. I must choose. Crow is my greatest rival—

But Plum is Xin Bao's fated deposer. She can't be allowed to live one day longer into Ren's future, and I close my eyes to the physician's blood as it pools on the ground.

It has to be Plum.

Jangle of keys; creak of the door.

A voice from the prison hall. "You've worked hard."

"Master Crow." My eyes open to the interrogators bowing— and narrow as Crow steps in.

What is *he* doing here?

If he's disturbed by the interrogators' handiwork, he doesn't show it. "Take a rest," he says to them. "I'm here to ask the prisoner a few questions on behalf of our prime ministress." When the guards vacillate, he paces deeper into the cell, arms crossed loosely behind his back. "The chefs just finished roasting a boar," he says, his gaze on the ceiling, conspiratorially avoiding the guards'. "Be quick. I'll hold the fort."

"Yes, Master Crow!"

The interrogators leave. Crow maneuvered them so easily.

He did the same to me.

I like you.

A lie.

You deserve to live.

An act.

He steps before the physician, and my thoughts blacken.

He came into this cell sharing my intentions.

"Jin Hua. You, who last treated Gao Yun, otherwise known as Cloud." Crow allows the physician a breath to process that yes, he knows this. The power is his. "Confess," he says, and it sounds like a spell. *Confess.* "Who sent you?"

"I—already said—no one."

"I know. I believe you." He leans in, mouth near the ruins of her ear. "But you know the human body best. How long it'll hold on, even in the face of certain death. Confess and end this needless suffering. Was it Ren or Plum?" His voice softens. "One, you're already guilty of abetting by saving her swornsister. The other is a suspect in the cell next door."

Crow, oh, Crow. I'd expect nothing less from my rival, also trying to kill two birds. Now that Plum has begun to suspect him, eliminating her is only sensible. *You're as ruthless as me*, I think as the physician coughs, but then in Crow's eyes, I glimpse a glimmer of . . . empathy. No. Wrong. She's only a chess piece to him. When he brings out a flask from his robes, it's all calculated. She just can't see it as she shakes her head, declining the drink.

"You—may have your machinations—but I sense a kindness." Her gaze rolls up to Crow. "I must—ask you a favor."

Silence. Crow waits.

"My notes—in my robes—let them survive me—"

For the first time since setting foot into this cell, Crow hesitates. Another act. The favor is unwise. He won't risk it—

He reaches into the cross-fold of the physician's torn robes and withdraws the bloodstained book, its cover falling open to a page of anatomical notes before it's quickly slipped into his own robes. "Thank you," the physician whispers as I stare at Crow, who bows, then leaves, closing the cell door behind him.

It's just me and the physician.

As she wheezes, I refocus. She really is like Ren's mother, so devoted to helping others. She praised Cloud for her mettle and Crow for his heart.

Maybe, just now, that heart wasn't so false.

But goodness won't save any of them. *I'm sorry*, I think to her. For soon, interrogators return to the cell, and to work, until the inevitable occurs. The pain grows too much for the physician to bear. Her head lolls forward. She's not dead—yet.

Her spirit has simply left.

I've been waiting for this moment. Bracing for it.

After this—

There shall be no redemption.

I enter her body just as the guards dunk her face—*my face*—into a pail of water.

"Stop," I splutter. "S-stop. I'll confess."

三十四

FOR A LIFE

I'll confess.

The last word drips off my teeth. My flesh is lacerated, my bones crushed. It's pain like I've never known before, even as Lotus.

If all goes according to plan, I'll suffer worse.

The interrogators exchange a glance. One grabs my bleeding chin, wringing out a whimper. "Lie to us, and you'll wish even harder for death."

"Everything—I said—is true."

It would have been Plum. It should have been Plum.

But then Crow came in and spoke to the physician.

The nerve of him, risking death to use *my* chess piece.

I'll give him a taste of his own poison.

"I work—for the South," I repeat. "Crow—sent me. Just now, he tried—to silence me. He took my notebooks, afraid—there'd be evidence . . ."

The interrogators don't speak. The only sounds come from the neighboring cell; my wounds throb at Plum's wails. Her injuries won't be light. Without treatment, she will still die. *I may kill two birds after all*, I think, as one of my interrogators at last exits our cell, footfalls echoing, then fading. He's going to Miasma with my confession.

Step by step, death walks to Crow.

I wait. Time is hazy, elongated by the agony.

Then—I'm unbound. Dragged out. The smell of brewing rain. The reek of blood. It soaks the chopping block, wets my cheek when I'm pressed down.

Again, the blade falls.

I float through the palace and find Miasma in the throne hall, face pensive.

"Bring him and the wine," she finally says.

A servant delivers a goblet on a tray, and my gaze sharpens. A single-sided toast almost always means death by poison—one of the kinder capital punishments—and I must admit, I was not expecting Miasma to be so lenient. What will I do, if Crow takes the wine and stymies my scheme?

Then the sight of him, entering the room next, quiets my worry. He's killed me not once, but twice. *He* enabled Cicada to pull off the ambush at Pumice Pass. *He* caused Cloud to lose Bikong. Hate is too simple a word for what I feel for him. I despise him. I respect him. He's never disappointed me as an opponent.

He won't disappoint me now.

Ten strides from Miasma, Crow stops. He bows, and Miasma stares at his lowered head. Is she remembering Ren? Is she remembering how everyone always forsakes her in the end?

"Well, Crow?" she says as it begins to rain in earnest. "Any last words?"

Crow straightens. Without Miasma's invitation. It's an offense—minuscule, compared to whichever he's about to die for. And he knows—would have known the second the guards came for him, like they came for so many of his predecessors—that his death is sealed. So as his mind works—and it's working, I can almost hear its rhythm—it's not trying to figure out what's to come, but what led to this. Who condemned him? The physician—but why? How? He's a good judge of character. Could he have been wrong about her?

No, Crow. You were right about her. And you were right about me. You were right to never trust me. But I'm a god, and you're only mortal. Unfair, isn't it?

Such is war.

"Nothing?" Miasma says when the silence stretches.

And Crow—he takes a measured breath, one of the few he has left. "What can I say, after the thousands of words we've exchanged, if you trust the words of a stranger?"

"You admit to sending the physician."

"I admit to seeing her."

"Ah." Miasma holds out a hand, fingers spread. "I didn't realize there was such a distinction." Her hand closes into a fist; she slams it down on the arm of her throne. "I should have asked her for clarification before I killed her!"

We. We killed her, murmurs my conscience as Miasma's words hang in the air, insincere, their meaning clear. She doesn't need more evidence.

The suspicion I planted has finally flowered into a death sentence.

"Bequeath the wine," she says, and the servant proceeds, the dark liquid shivering within the goblet. My mind shivers with it. *Prove me right.* The servant stops before Crow, bows at him.

Prove yourself worthy of my scheme.

Crow bows too—to Miasma. "I decline."

The prime ministress rises from her seat.

"You can execute me."

She strides in.

"But I won't kill myself for no reason," says Crow as he's seized by the clasp of his cloak.

"You think I'm making a mistake," Miasma whispers, knuckles white around the black fabric.

Rain patters, loud in the quiet.

Miasma releases Crow.

Her hand darts forward, shoving into his torso as if she means to disembowel him. But when her hand comes out, it's with the physician's book. The bloodstained, cursed book. It holds no evidence, just notes, but it's something to hold, crush, and throw.

It smacks like a hunk of flesh upon the floor.

"A mistake," Miasma breathes. "What did I say by the river, Crow? I won't stand to be betrayed. A mistake." She chuckles. "You, Crow, are the one who's making the mistake. This?" She lifts the goblet. "This was mercy."

The goblet hits the ground too, poisoned wine joining the blood splatters on the book.

"Take him away," Miasma says, and I wait, breath bated, for the execution order. Beheading would be too quick, poisoning too irreversible without an antidote. The one method compatible with my plans is also the one Miasma favors.

Go on. Remind me of the only death fitting for traitors.

"After the feast tonight, steam him."

‡ ‡ ‡

The smells escape the kitchens within the hour. Ducks, roasted. Wine, warmed. The rain stops, and outside on the pavilion, servants go down the long, stone tables, placing cushions for each official.

Two will be absent.

Plum has been left to rot in the dungeons. After scouting out the steamer, I pay her a visit. *It's nothing personal*, I think to her as she moans, like I thought to Crow, but truly, Plum's only crime is her fate. In any case, she won't survive much longer without treatment, and she won't be treated without a stronger restoration of Miasma's trust. I was right to choose Crow, whose presence I sense in the cell next door. I start to pass through the stone wall separating us, then still. I have no reason to visit him. No reason.

His words echo through my head, unbidden.

I won't kill myself for no reason.

A lesser rival might have taken the poison, innocent or guilty. Had Crow done so, he'd have thwarted my plans.

But because he is Crow, he refused. He kept his cover to the end. He will be steamed like the other Southern spy on the junk that night. That night we kissed. I pretended to be Miasma's. To be his. But he outperformed me. The ice in my mind spreads, spidering into the place where a human heart would rest, and without visiting Crow, I leave the prison block, floating to the soldiers' mess halls as the feast commences. Wine flows and voices brim. One table breaks into an argument over who is the better general, and I remember being crushed between Lotus and Cloud at Hewan.

I'm the god!

No, I'm the god!

Now Lotus is gone forever. Her spirit died at Pumice Pass, thanks to Crow, and her body in this palace. My field of vision shrinks, until all I can see is forward, to my next step.

The next table.

The next group of soldiers.

Three are slumped over. The first body doesn't take to me, too drunken. Same thing with the second.

Only one body left now. I'm about to try it when I notice the ghost, hovering at the table's end. Or is it the soldier's spirit?

No time to decide. The spirit moves down the table, toward the body. I sink in first—and keep sinking, sucked under by the stupor.

Close your eyes.

No. I will myself up, to my feet, and stagger past the soldier's confused spirit. He's not my first victim of the day.

Nor will he be the last.

In the barracks, I bind my face with bandages, leaving only my eyes uncovered, then steal a dagger from someone's personal bundle. I go to the steam room and wait.

At last, the soldiers assigned to Crow's execution come down the hall.

"Hey, you!" I shout, pointing at one. "Back to your station."

"Me?"

"Yes, you. Orders from above." The soldier looks to his partner and I bark, "Take it up with the prime ministress if you have a problem." A bluff. Behind my back, I clench the dagger, grip relaxing only when the soldier shrugs. *Good choice.* I remember the horrible smell, the night Miasma steamed that Southern spy on the junk.

"What happened to your face?" asks his partner as I take his place.

"Burned it." I keep it simple, and my partner grunts. He faces the great doors before us.

"Let's get this over with."

I've already seen the steamer—was *in* it earlier, as a spirit—but the second time around is just as macabre. The bamboo monstrosity is at least one person tall and two in diameter. Bolted to its side is a ladder; under it is a vat of water atop a firewood urn. The other soldier grabs a torch from the wall and sets to work. I join him, mentally reviewing the specifications I gathered, from the width of the rim, to the drop from the top, to the slats at the bottom.

Once it begins, I'll have no room for error.

The fire flashes. The room grows warm, then humid. It's sweltering by the time two soldiers enter with Crow. He's been stripped of his black robes and left in rough-hewn white. Funeral garb.

"All yours," say his escorts, leaving as soon as they've passed him on. My partner grabs hold of Crow—and is shrugged off.

"I'll walk myself."

He climbs the ladder; I lift the lid. Steam billows into both our faces. Crow coughs, and my thoughts falter.

Behind Crow's every action is reason. When he asked Miasma

to spare Lotus, it was for a chance to decipher the warrior. When he told Plum that Ren wouldn't attack the North in response to Lotus's death, it was because he suspected his and Cicada's plans had been foiled by that same warrior's last words. When he refused to take the poisoned wine, it was because he didn't want to give Miasma his guilt as closure. If he's to die, let his death haunt her.

But now? I can't imagine any reason behind his actions, which leaves his emotions.

Those, apparently, I have never known.

And I never will. As Crow pauses at the top of the ladder, something pushes into my heart—a desire to peer inside him and see his every thought. *Where is your fear?* I think as he gazes down at the death awaiting him. *Where is your defiance?* His hair falls forward, veiling his face, and I wish I could make him look at me, make him see me as his rival in his final moments.

But he is no longer mine.

In the end, we were not equals.

He steps into the steamer and my hand jerks, as if to stop him.

I stop myself instead.

Join the other soldier in putting on the lid.

The coughing starts, hair-raising and vicious.

My fists harden to rocks.

This is for Lotus.

For Cloud, whose death isn't averted, only delayed.

For Ren, who deserves a better fate than that of tragic vengeance.

In the corner of my eye, I see my partner. He's focused on the steamer—and then he's out cold from a dagger pommel to the temple. I tuck away the weapon, climb the ladder, and heave off the lid. Steam roars white past me as I dive through it, waist over the rim, eyes tearing, lungs seizing—

With my qì, I clear the torrent so that I can breathe.

Can see.

Crow. I land beside him—and choke. My hands—*my knees*, they're burning—but Crow's burned for longer. I grab his wrist. *Alive.* He's still breathing, but his spirit—it's gone.

Gone.

Gone is the strategist who saw through me—first as a defector, then as Lotus. Gone is the rival who outsmarted me—he's defeated like I wanted but—

I ended him.

I really ended him.

Don't act so shocked, says a voice from the depths of my skull. *You always had it in you to be the villain. Now rise*—like the steam is rising. Like my spirit will rise, if this body expires. Is expiring. Stay put, and we'll die together. Yes, I could do that. I could, I think, gasping for air as I lose control of my qì, the steam billowing back in. I could let this body die—but it'd be meaningless. I'll never be able to join Crow. He's mortal. I'm not.

To help Ren one last time, I've sacrificed more than my heart.

I stand, face wet. *Just condensation.* I lift the body, push it over the steamer's edge. It catches. A sob escapes me. *Just frustration.* I clamber out and turn back, tugging the body down. He falls on me. We're both on the ground.

Only I get up.

Breathless, I gaze at Crow's motionless form, condensation dripping down my cheeks, to my lips. It tastes salty.

I swipe it off.

Move. You're not yet done.

Quickly, I undress him and myself, my mind on the objective. *Avert Ren's and Cloud's deaths in the Marshlands. Repair the Southern alliance.* I'll convince Cicada, as Crow. It starts with having her think she's lost him to Miasma. She needs to really believe it—as does Miasma. I pull on Crow's clothes, dress him in mine, then take out the soldier's topknot.

Our hair spills down, long.

Facing the steamer, I walk back toward it. Short of it, I kneel, hand to the ground. Five fingers, stretched out.

Do it. Do it now.

Dagger raised; dagger down. I throw the severed finger into the fire before the pain can reach my brain and then—because Crow shouldn't be bleeding—shove in my hand after it.

"A-Aghhhh!"

Not mine, I tell myself when I'm gasping at the mess of cauterized flesh. *Not mine.*

But this scheme is, and it's not yet finished.

One-handedly, I climb back up the ladder and into the steamer. I have to eject myself from my present body. Drinking is one way.

Dying is faster.

Steam is air. Water. Elements of life that become death as I pull the lid over my head. Instinct kicks in; I crawl to the walls and pound at them. I want out.

Out.

Out.

Out—of the body. My spirit shudders through the steamer's walls, into the torchlit room. My partner is still on the ground, as is Crow—

His body surrounded by a dozen-some ghosts. One reaches out to touch him.

"*No.*" I slap at it, and visions—*the red flag whipping overhead, the executioner's dripping blade*—flash through my mind as my hand passes through its. I flinch backward, then recover. "He's *mine.*"

The ghosts continue eyeing Crow.

I don't *think* ghost possession is possible, and I didn't go through living hell to find out. "*Mine,*" I snarl, and descend into Crow's body.

My first breath sets me ablaze.

My skin feels like a bladder about to burst.

Moaning, I roll myself upright and cover my face—now really blistered—in the bandages.

Tying a topknot makes me want to cut off *all* my fingers, just to stop the pain.

Standing almost has me suffocating.

Nearly there.

I lurch to the wall and grab a torch.

The soldier and Crow might share a missing finger, but that's not enough to pass a close inspection, especially not Miasma's. So I set fire to the body I shed in the steamer, then to the steamer itself. When it's burned long enough, I press on the meridian above my partner's upper lip. He comes to—cursing when he sees the flames.

I help him put them out.

"What happened?" he groans after, cupping his temple.

"You fainted." I try to deepen my voice, but it's not necessary. I sound nothing like Crow, my vocal cords burned. "I tried to wake you, but I—I think I saw a ghost."

"You didn't."

"I did. It made the fire leap *this* tall."

More curses. "Have you checked the body?"

"Not yet."

We open the lid, coughing at the black smoke. It clears, revealing the body—or what's left of it—and my partner blasphemes the gods. "We're done for."

"No. It's not our fault. It was the ghost's."

"The ghost's."

"Yes." I nod. "Like I said, the flames suddenly started moving strange, and I saw a ghost. It looked—like Lotus's!"

"Who?"

Now he's embarrassing himself. "The famed warrior! Ren's swornsister!"

"O-okay."

"She said that she wanted to burn the strategist who defeated her."

The soldier blinks doubtfully.

"Listen to me," I say, for what other option does he have?

Later, we say the exact words to Miasma. She orders to see the body and frowns.

"Lotus's ghost, you say."

We nod.

Miasma compresses her lips. Seconds crawl by like years.

"Take it out of my sight," she finally orders. She turns from us, but not before I see her clutch her head.

May *her* fate still come to pass.

‡ ‡ ‡

We bury the body on a barren hill north of the palace. As we shovel, my pain-dizzied mind flits to the physician. The soldier. I've ended the lives of two bystanders.

But they are not who I mourn. The hands I have around the shovel are closer to Zephyr's than Lotus's. The only calluses are from playing the zither. The missing finger—Crow lost it because of me.

Did you ever think you'd lose your spirit to me too? A hollowness echoes through me, stronger than even the pain. The ice in my heart gone, melted and become steam as well. I shake my head and shovel faster. The moment I stop, the moment I rest, the moment I regret, I won't be able to get up again, and I have to keep standing. Keep going.

I've come too far to go back.

‡ ‡ ‡

That night, I sneak out of the palace and steal a horse from the stables. The stars shine, same as always. But the universe has irrevocably changed. It is now a world without Crow, and as I ride, tinier stars appear at my lashes.

They flick off in the wind as if they never existed.

三十五

RIVALS ONCE

A *world without Crow.*

But there's still Ren. How long do I have before fire and death claim our camp? I don't know, have no markers of time or events out in the wilderness between me and where the battle is fated, deep in the Marshlands. All I can do is ride, unceasing, unsleeping, two days passing before reality sets in:

I'm no longer a warrior. Crow's constitution is closer to Qilin's, with some exceptions. The addition of certain . . . human anatomy was the first inconvenience; every bump in the road set my crotch aflame. Now my inner thighs burn like molten metal, forging me to the saddle. I'd say it's muscle fatigue, but that's implying I *have* muscles. I cough—and panic at the taste of blood. *Nothing to be scared of.* It's the consumption. The ache in my chest? Consumption, and not because his voice won't vacate my head.

Some people never leave.

On the third night, I finally pry myself out of the saddle and settle in a bush, needled by the cold. Shivering is torture. Sleep ushers in nightmares of a burned, faceless rider following me through the forest.

I wake, half-frozen, to angry caws from a murder of crows.

I hurry back to the road, avoiding the hoofprinted paths. Best not to run into anyone riding solo in this form.

I'm seeing double by day four.

Ugh. How *did* Crow get anywhere before?

He wasn't steamed, for one.

Did I think that, or Dewdrop? The woods are lifeless when I look to them. *Then why do I feel followed?* The sensation haunts me, and after six sleepless nights and six paranoid days, I buckle: I take the fork in the road that's been trodden.

Soon the trees are thinning, giving way to vegetable plots. Geese flap in the green. Huts appear next. I dismount outside one, a brush gate encircling its attached stable. Maybe I'll rest here. Recover my soundness of mind. A rustle at my back spins me around, but it's just a farmer, walking up the dirt path. Two baskets swing from the pole laid across his shoulders. He stops in his tracks at the sight of me, and the baskets sway forward.

I spread my hands. "Good sir. Forgive the imposition, but may I spend the night in your stables?"

The farmer doesn't speak, his eyes wide at my armor.

Rat-livers. I should have taken it off. He can't see that I'm on the verge of collapse. He just sees a soldier.

"I'm a courier, bound for Taohui." Motion tugs my gaze to the hut. A child stands in the now-opened doorway, holding a broom—no, a spear, its blade curved like a crescent. My throat tightens.

It's a miniature model of Cloud's glaive, Blue Serpent.

"Bà!" cries the child, and the farmer's face convulses. He shoos her, and my throat closes completely. *I won't hurt you.* But words are flimsy. Allegiances are stronger. What are the farmer's? If I guess wrong, he'll snatch up his child and run.

I'll just have to be right, then. "I serve Ren."

"Xin Ren?"

"Yes."

The man's expression changes like night to day; he kneels before I can stop him.

"Susu, come here! Kneel," the farmer instructs the child after she runs over, ignoring my protests. "Thank the servant of our great Xin's heavens-sent protector."

Father and daughter pay their reverences as if I were Lotus, or Cloud, or Ren herself. They have no idea who I really am, or what I've done.

I redouble my efforts to help them up.

"Our home is shabby and humble," the farmer says, finally getting to his feet. "But it'd be our greatest honor to shelter one of Xin Ren's people."

"The stables are a perfectly fine shelter."

I insist until the farmer relents. "Wait here," he says, then goes into his hut.

He returns with wine, rice cakes, and dried sausages.

Stomach gurgling, I glance to the child. Food is the first

casualty in any war, and though Ren wouldn't requisition civilian grain lightly, our troops must eat. *Feed them first*, I'd have advised as Zephyr.

"I have food," I lie to the farmer, and then, knowing he won't rest until I've accepted *something*, I take the wine and ask for a blanket.

In the stables, I pack the wine jugs up with my armor and rub down my horse. Night falls. I huddle in the hay, clinging to my blanket. I'm cold, so cold. This body can't seem to shake the chill. My teeth chatter—and clamp down at the creak of the stable doors.

In the moonlit gap stands a ghostly form.

However Crow's eyesight was before, the steaming certainly hasn't helped it, and it's not until the child has walked closer, spear in her grip, that my racing heart slows. I've become as untrusting as Miasma.

The child stops three strides away from me, neither of us speaking for a silent second.

"Are you really Ren's?"

"I am."

"You know General Cloud?"

I know her, all right. Fought with her. Died for her. "Yes, we're . . ." *friends*. But I'm not sure Cloud would agree. "We've trained together."

"I want to be Cloud," says the child, jabbing her spear. "*Yah!*" She leaps onto a haybale. "I want to kill enemies." Her eyes flash, and for a heartbeat, I recall Ku at that same age, crouched by the clay soldiers on the straw mat of a street vendor.

I want to know war, says my recall-Ku, and the words feel new. Am I misremembering? Or did I disregard them?

It's not important. I banish the memory and gesture the child closer.

"You need one more thing if you're to be Cloud." I tie my blanket around her shoulders; it puffs behind her as she jumps down and stabs a haybale. "Go now, before your father finds you gone."

Alone again, I burrow into the hay at my back. Who *am* I? I came here to *sleep*, not to encourage foolish dreams of becoming a warrior. In fact, after I succeed in helping Ren to the North, uniting the three kingdoms in the process, the child should know *more* than war. She can be anything she desires. That's the future. I just won't get to see it, a choice I don't regret.

No regrets . . .

My eyes fall shut, darkness like night behind my lids. Shine of stars. Rush of water.

Wind streams by as I face the river, standing at the stern.

Black-robed arms fall on either side of me like the chains of a drawbridge, lowered.

"Is this how you plan on soothing your conscience?" His breath brushes my ear—my chest against his as I spin. "By playing nice with children?"

I shove him backward. "Go find someone else to bother."

"There's no one else I want." He glances at the stars, perfunctory, then back to me. "What do you see in the cosmos?" he asks, and his gaze is an all-consuming inferno. His voice is the opposite: light and graceful.

I silenced it forever.

I did, didn't I? I pinch my wrist. Painless. *A dream.* In the waking world, there is no Crow. I effectively killed him, and now I miss him. Does that make me a despicable person? Let me be despicable, then. Because none of this is real, I can be weak. I can toe the lake of regret without stepping in.

Yes, let me be despicable for a moment.

"I see many things in the cosmos," I answer Crow. "An arrow that you will take for me." My voice falls, barely louder than the river. "Your end."

"At your hands," Crow says, and my heart skips a beat. A guess, or does he know? Would he forgive me, if I told him my reasons are his? To ensure our lordess wins? I doubt it.

I'm just a monster for hoping so. "I'm sorry."

My breath catches as Crow closes in.

His fingers go under my chin.

"Don't be." His eyes are darker than the night, but I feel safe, falling through them. "I would have done the same."

I can't tell if my chin tilts up because of him, or by my own volition. His lips grace mine and—

I gasp against them.

I pull away, hand clapped over my neck. Blood spurts through my fingers nonetheless. Across from me, Crow holds a dagger, blade red like the slit on *his* neck.

His wound is a mirror image of mine.

I jerk awake. The dagger stays at my throat, its blade biting skin as I shrink back, into the haybales. Before me is a face at eye level. The dagger wielder's. A torch flames in her left hand. Two people stand behind her. *Lotus and Cloud*, I think for a groggy blink.

The reality couldn't be more different.

"What do we have here?" says the crouched bandit. "Another Marshlands refugee?"

Another. How many have they seen? Has Ren marched on Cicada already? Resting was a mistake. I should be on the road.

"Out of my way," I bark. "Or I'll peel your hide."

The bandits stare at me.

And snigger.

"I'd like to see you try," says their leader. "What are you, even?" Her gaze slides to my hands, inching to my broadbelt. My weapons—are gone. The bandit smiles. "Pretty bold for a refugee. An army deserter, then?" Her dagger presses closer. "Scared of death, Pretty One?"

No, but eager for yours—words that I bite off. I'm Crow, now. A strategist with consumption, facing not one but three bandits—if there aren't more outside. My attention expands. The stables are quiet. Horseless. The weapons of the two standing bandits are coated in blood. The farmer—his child—no, *focus*. How do I get out of this?

As I think, a draft wends through the stable doors. *My answer.* If I could just use it to bend the flame of the bandit's torch—if I could just burn her hand—

My connection snaps like a thread. I breathe harder, exhausted by even the failed effort, and the bandits laugh, mistaking it for fear. Maybe some of it is. I haven't felt this weak since I was an orphan, and I glare at the draft as it moves on without me, teasing at the bandit's hair. Her torch flame wisps—

Toward the hay behind my shoulder.

The bales ignite and I vault forward, past the bandit and the two others, rolling through the hay to smother my back, on fire. Then, to my feet. To the outside. The horses are tethered to the brush gate—the bandits' and mine. My relief swells, then drains.

The farmer lies face down past the gate.

The child is a few steps farther, spear broken.

No. I back away—in the wrong direction. Shouts, closing in. *Forward. To the horses.* I haul into the saddle just as a bandit reaches me, sword flashing up. Pain, at my hip—

I kick us into a gallop.

Hooves thunder in our wake. An arrow strikes an upcoming tree. I duck and urge the horse faster, to both our limits, until the trail behind me falls quiet.

The sky lightens.

My back burns as if it's still on fire. The rest of me is numb. Too numb. I can't feel my hip, soaked in blood. I pitch in the saddle—and off, crunching into the ground.

The horse trots on.

The heavens above me swirl, clouds hiding the sun.

Dead. They're all dead. Was it because of me? Did I lead the bandits to them?

So what if you did? says the voice in my head, the same reptilian voice that spoke in the steamer. *Stop pretending to care about the peasants.*

I'm not pretending, I think back at it.

Then care about the thousands who will die in Ren's war with Cicada.

She's right. I'm right, for the voice is mine. *Keep riding*, orders the strategist. I should listen to her. But I have no strength. Haven't for days. Breath by breath, I grow more numb and cold. Coherent thought becomes harder, and it takes me a while to form a blatantly obvious one:

I'm dying. Or rather, this body is dying. It's always been sickly, but now? Steamed? Burned? Cut by bandits?

It won't make it to Taohui.

So let go of it. Find another.

No. After all my troubles? Besides, I need Crow's identity to execute my stratagem. I can't let him go.

I won't.

Shivering, I reach within myself, going deeper than before— than ever—until I come upon something shrunken like a walnut. Past the shell, I sense my powers.

I manifest the walnut outside of myself and pry at it; the shell thickens, as if my powers don't want to be touched. But they're *my* powers; they *will* do my bidding. I slam the walnut back into my chest, where it bobs, and bring the brunt of my qì down on it.

A heartbeat.

My power blasts through me, obliterating my senses. Waves roar and dunes shift, west of the Westlands. A thousand voices sing. A sea of grass dances.

And then I can see through my own eyes again. Still on the ground, still cold, but my limbs feel stronger. I lift a hand, make a fist, then glance to the grass by the roadside and focus on a single blade. I try to bend it with the wind.

Nothing happens.

Above me, the heavens are silent. Within me, the walnut is gone—and my powers with it. Bringing this body back from the brink must have depleted me. A huff escapes me, disbelieving, then another huff verging on a laugh. "You'd like that, wouldn't you, Crow?"

"I'd like what?"

Ah. I must be dreaming again.

"To punish me even from the afterlife," I say, and shiver as a draft chills me.

"The afterlife, you say." The chill intensifies. "How odd. If this is the afterlife, I did not expect to see you here too."

He comes to lean over me, his face upside down.

I bite my cheek. The pain feels real. If this is real, then this Crow looking down at me can't be.

Real.

And he's not. As my vision clarifies, I see that he's not completely solid. More like half-transparent.

A ghost. Not quite. His body lives. An ejected spirit, then.

Whatever he is, he remains in this world.

He's not gone.

An emotion rushes through me, suspiciously close to joy, joy that I have no right to feeling. He was only gone because of me. And now my powers are gone because of him. Irritation staunches the joy even before Crow says, "No need to thank me, for saving you back there."

"Saving me?" What is he talking about?

"The bandits. The torch."

That was me. *I* bent the flame. Unless . . . well, my powers were weak. If it really was him . . .

"You set me on *fire*."

"You steamed me," Crow deadpans.

I try to sit up, struggling and failing.

Crow watches, impassive.

"I interrogated myself, up to my final moments. What, exactly, tipped off Miasma? Did I slip? How could Lotus figure out my ties to the South? Unless it wasn't her, but someone else. A strategist." He leans in, bringing the cold with him. "Or the heart of one in her."

Slowly, his eyes comb my face. "That last scene of our duet. You perceived my retreat. How would that be possible, if you weren't present at the original scene? No matter how I analyzed it, it didn't make sense. I thought I'd die without knowing.

"Then, after I thought I'd died, I saw you. One among the ghosts. You slipped right into my body and reanimated me." I finally manage to sit up and Crow says, "Tell me, Zephyr: Who else did you commandeer? The physician?"

I've always had to watch myself around Crow. Concealing my true abilities—and later, my identity—gave me an advantage. But now he's a spirit.

He can't hurt me.

"I did," I say before I can think better of it.

"You killed her."

"She would have died anyway. You said so yourself."

"So I did, as a strategist. We like to pretend we're certain of everything, don't we?"

"I don't pretend. I'm a god, Crow," I say, just to remind myself. "I know how this ends. All of this. Your Cicada wouldn't have united the three kingdoms."

Crow's smile is emotionless. "A god," he repeats, choosing to react to that and ignore the bit about Cicada. "I see your opinion of yourself hasn't changed, in the time we've been apart."

"I'm being serious."

"Prove it." Crow blinks, waiting. "You can't."

Bastard. Powers can be recovered—

After hundreds of years of recultivation.

So I'm temporarily powerless. That doesn't mean I'm not still a god. I'm in this body, after all.

"I know things about the spirit you can only guess at," I say to Crow. "Want to hear one? You're entirely dependent on me. Drift too far from this body, and you'll dissipate." I eye him. No reaction. He's already inferred as much. He must have been the presence I sensed in the woods, following out of sight but close by. "I'm right, and you know it."

"Say you are." Crow crouches by me. "Then my objective is simple: I'll just have to reclaim my body." He runs his fingers over my wound, and I gasp. I can *feel* him. Not in the flesh, but in spirit, his mortal qì to my divine. He digs his fingers in and—

A flash of images. *Blood, in a handkerchief. A girl, embroidering a new, unsoiled one—*

"In your sleep, you stayed lodged in my body," Crow murmurs, the vision fleeing as he lifts his hand. "But if you were to pass out . . ." His eyes rise to mine and I swallow, trying to hide how he's affected me. "Would your spirit leave?"

"Over *your* dead body."

"Just what are you going to do, Zephyr?" Crow asks, and my mind clears of his touch, the abrupt visions it caused, even the way blood seems to be flowing faster from my cut.

I'm going to the Marshlands, where Ren's battle of vengeance against the South is fated to unfold. I'm going there, and I'm going to Cicada as Crow.

I'm going to trick her into surrendering before the tide turns.

"I'm going back to Ren." The roads and rivers to Xin City and Taohui run concurrently for a stretch before they diverge east and west. Crow won't know truth from lie until I'm more than halfway to my destination.

If he believes the lie at all. I hold Crow's gaze. I wonder what my face looks like, as his. Because my insides are confused, but I've never seen Crow confused. He's never shown an emotion as imperfect as fear or anger or impatience.

He is the consummate strategist.

But so am I, and as I stare at the face of his spirit, at his slow, cold smile, I know it's a falsehood. We might have been rivals once, on opposite sides of a war, my lordess his enemy, and his lordess mine. Now that nuance is gone. Even if I weren't going to Cicada, I've stolen his body.

Even if our lordesses weren't, we would be enemies for eternity.

三十六

A SALTED EARTH

Enemies for eternity.

Ride the horse. Stay awake. Hold on to the pain, when my mind goes slippery. Crow can follow me all he wants, but I stand by what I said: I'd sooner let this body perish than return it.

"With all due respect, you look haggard," Crow comments as I lead my mount to drink from the marsh. Since passing Bikong, tree cover has been sparse, but there are no troops to see us. They must be at the conflict between Ren and Cicada, farther south. How close is Ren to losing? I'm six days to Taohui. Will I make it? Am I feverish? The wound above my hip has finally stopped bleeding, but I'm scared to examine it. What can I do if it's infected?

The wine. The jugs, still strung to my saddle, are cracked. I hurl them, then grind my teeth. Crow's seen me arrogant, angry, flustered even, but never this temperamental, and it's not because of his body's qì. It's me.

So this is what it feels like to be desperate.

I brace for a jibe from him.

What he says is worse. "When was the last time you slept through the night?"

He has the audacity to sound concerned.

I mount the horse.

He follows. "You need rest."

"What I need is for you to be quiet."

To my surprise, Crow obliges. I ride in silence. Sunset. A night of cold sweat. A dawn of vomiting by the roadside, where I come to a grim realization: This body might fail me again, and I won't have any power to save it.

One more time, I take the road out of the wilderness.

Yichen is no hamlet, but a proper city. A line winds past its gates, hundreds of people seeking entrance. Most are refugees, their clothing tattered and browned by the earth they've walked. I've just never seen this many south—another sure sign that the Ren-Cicada conflict has erupted, displacing Marshland civilians looking to escape the fighting.

One physician stop. That's all you're allowed. I tether my horse outside the first storefront I happen upon and limp in, repelling patrons and drawing the physician.

"Heavens, young soldier!" He ushers me into the back room. "What misfortune befell you?"

"Her," Crow says as I say, "Bandits."

The physician clucks, sitting me down. "As I feared. You're my tenth this week. Let me see—ah."

He finds the sword wound first, the burns second. He peels off my robes; I see white as the fabric detaches. Partway through being treated, I start to cough. The physician ties off the last bandage and takes my wrist to read my pulse, and I can't help but think back to the last physician I met, possessed, and condemned to death. My coughs thicken.

Sighing, the physician releases my wrist. "You're awfully cold, young soldier. Dare I say cold as a corpse." Probably because I almost became one. "You also have the sequelae of many diseases." So it would seem. "And your pulse is startlingly weak. A full recovery is still possible for someone of your age, but not if you're riding day and night and hunting down bandits." As if I'd be so valiant. "You ought to be resting."

The physician leaves me to prepare my prescriptions, and *he* speaks, the bane of my existence.

"Told you so."

I pull my ruined robes back on.

"I could have warned you about the body you were getting into," Crow continues, "if you'd given me the chance before steaming me."

"Oh, I knew exactly what I was getting into," I mutter through my teeth. "We suffered two weeks on a junk together, don't you forget."

"How could I? I remember every day. The way you played the zither so angrily, unable to unlock its potential despite your skill. Who were you? I wondered. Now I know." Crow bends down, nose to mine. "A petty little murderer."

He's lucky I can't punch a spirit. "Petty?"

"Clearly you're not planning on curing me, despite your claims of being a god."

"Curing you? I—" *revived you, you ingrate.* I breathe in,

extinguishing the words. "That's not how it works." I think. Dewdrop never said anything about healing preexisting diseases, and now I can't even heal normal injuries. "Even if I could cure you, I wouldn't."

"See?" says Crow, sounding pleased. "Petty."

"You—"

The physician returns with the medicine not a second too soon, because every second I spend squabbling with Crow is one too many. *No more talking to him*, I think, reaching for my broadbelt to pay. I—

Have no money on my person.

"It's on the house," says the physician as I frown, patting myself down. "I could tell you're an empire soldier by the make of your boots." My eyes shoot to them, unable to see the difference. "Serve our prime ministress well," the physician says, and I nod, forcing a smile.

Back at my horse, I almost discard the medicine. But that *would* be petty, and sighing, I string up the parcels beside my armor and mount—

My legs give out, sending me back first into the street.

"Watch it!" a merchant cries.

"Look, Māmā, look!" A child points.

"Ouch," says Crow, crouching at my side. "That's a first, even for me. I hope you're not blaming my body."

"Oh, I am." I get up, dusting off my knees.

"Riding was never one of your strong suits."

"I improved, thank you for asking." I step into the stirrup once more. *Come on now.*

My leg trembles.

Rest, said the physician.

Rest, said Crow.

Easy for them to say, ignorant to fate. I start to pull myself up—then still. What if I tumble off again? Lose consciousness? The stakes have changed. I have a spirit following me, waiting to reassume his body. I step down from the stirrup, take the reins.

Walking never hurt me.

So long as I don't faint.

With the horse, I go down the main boulevard. A young noble dashes by, laughing as her suitor pursues her. The war has yet to touch them, but it will. So long as the kingdoms are split, they will fight. Violence will breach these walls, just like it breached Shangu, Dasan, city after city living in peace until it was ripped from them. Most people are like grass, bending with the wind, helpless to change its direction.

Crow and I are different.

Crow *was* different.

"Where are we going?" he asks, and as our eyes meet, I have to remind myself that he's not really here. Not with me. His spirit's presence doesn't negate the fact that I ended him. Not his life, but it's almost worse that I didn't.

I could have spared him the indignity of being my puppet.

"I'm here to stay," Crow says, and I blink.

"What?"

"By how intensely you're staring, I assume you're trying to memorize my face before it vanishes. But I assure you I'm here to stay. Now, where are we going?"

The insolence. I tear my gaze away. "There's no *we*."

"Duly noted. Where are *you* going?"

Ignoring him, I stop by a shop to pawn off my armor, using half the money to buy a clean set of robes. The other half . . .

"Could it be that you're heeding my advice?" Crow asks as we slow before an inn.

The physician's, not yours. But I will *not* debate with an almost-ghost.

Inside, diners pack the inn. Servers run to and fro; maids carry bowls and linens up to the mezzanine, inset with doors to rooms. A host seats me near a table of scholars.

"Did you hear?" one scholar says as my order is taken. "Miasma killed her strategist."

Reflexively, I lower my face.

"Heard," another says. "Word is she steamed him."

It's promising these rumors have spread. Now, if only I could hear rumors of Miasma succumbing to the growth in her head . . .

"That's old news," another scholar says with a dismissive wave of his chopsticks. "Miasma kills advisors all the time. Even her oldest one wasn't safe in the end." Excellent; Plum's dead. "Want to know what I heard from my cousin, the—"

"—youngest court official, smartest of her village?" The table chuckles. "We know, Kunming. Cut to the chase."

Kunming grumbles, then leans in. "The strategist was a Southern spy. A friend of our young queen's."

Our. They're loyal to Cicada.

The table grows solemn, giving Crow a moment of silence.

"A pity," one finally says, "for her to lose a trusted advisor in the face of Xin Ren's advance."

So it's started. Just as I feared. A server comes by with my bowl of congee; I stir it as the scholars continue talking. *Thousands of casualties. A salted-earth campaign. The Southern lines pushed back across the Marshlands.* Cicada trying to negotiate for peace, and Ren refusing to grant an audience. My stomach knots with every word. That's not Ren. Not Ren.

But it matches what the fate scrolls said. And Ren—she did order the messenger's execution. What if that's the Ren Cicada is now dealing with? A grieving queen?

And if it is? I shovel congee into my mouth. *You're going to Cicada precisely to reverse this fate. Now eat.* I force down spoonful after spoonful until the bowl is clean, then pay for both the meal and a room. I take to the stairs with the key.

Crow drifts beside me. "Do you still think she deserves to rule over the three kingdoms?"

Ignore him.

"Xin Ren." His voice curves up like a hook. "A lordess who reddens rivers over a personal grievance."

Don't be baited—

"I wonder *who* made it personal," I growl.

"You know best there was no emotion attached. It was all strategy. The best course of action. You'd have killed the enemy strategist too, in my shoes." Crow floats ahead, looking down at me as I climb. "Evidently, considering that you *are* in my shoes."

A door on the mezzanine opens before I can reply, releasing two girls hand in hand.

Giggling, they pass through Crow.

A timely reminder. As a god, only I can see and hear him. The girls descend the steps, and I hiss, "Ren's so-called weakness is also her strength. She feels other people's pain as if it were hers. She's a better person than *your* lordess."

"Xiaochan listens to counsel."

"Xiaochan," I repeat. That must be Cicada's diminutive—or what Crow would have me believe it is. He's too careful to slip like that. It must be a trap.

"It's good that she does," I say, pretending to fall for it. I reach for the door and suddenly Crow is in front of me.

"You're traveling to her, not Ren."

So he finally connected the dots. "Move."

"Make me."

We each hold our ground.

"Ren or Cicada, what does it matter?" I reach through Crow and unlock the door. "I told you; I'm a god. I know how this ends." Except that's no longer true; anything is possible without Plum. But Crow needn't know. "Neither of our lordesses will win the three kingdoms, according to fate. I'm trying to stop it."

"And why is that?" asks Crow, voice like silk. "Why not let Ren collect her victory in the Marshlands first? From what I overheard, it's as good as hers."

For now. "No victory is costless," I say, voice as neutral as I can make it even as the vision of the fire blazes through my mind again. "Only Miasma will emerge from Cicada and Ren's conflict unscathed." Another lie, to make my greater point: "We have a common enemy, as *you* and your lordess seem to have forgotten."

I step into the room, stilling as Crow says, "Stratagem Twenty-Four." Whispered words, just behind my ear. "Conquer Guo Through Yu."

My mouth thins.

Guo and Yu were two ancient states, living in the shadow of Jin, a bigger state that sought to control both but couldn't so long as they were united. So Jin started attacking Guo and gifting the spoils to Yu, turning allies into foes. In its final invasion of Guo, Jin obtained safe passage through Yu—and conquered Yu on the victory march back.

In this era, most would compare Cicada and Ren to Guo and Yu, the two smaller states, and Miasma to Jin. But I never believed in repeating history. With the Rising Zephyr Objective, I intended for Ren to be Jin. Defeat Cicada too early, and we expose ourselves to Miasma's undivided attention. But once Miasma falls, we will turn on the South *our* undivided attention. This has been my plan all along. Crow, deducing it, must have advised Cicada to kill me.

But he can't stop me now. Therefore, there's nothing to say—even less considering that Miasma's own body will take care of her, shifting up my plan to remove Cicada.

I'll spare Crow that knowledge as a kindness.

Silent, I take stock of the room. A bed, a table, two stools. A washbasin rests on a rack by the window. In the water, I study my new face, grimace as my fingertips meet the still-puffy skin. I look up to Crow's stare.

The water doesn't reflect him.

"Well?" he asks softly. "Is it to your liking?"

Don't be provoked. I turn from the basin and go to the bed.

Crow trails me. "I looked better before I met you." I sit and unwrap the robes I purchased. "You aged me."

Ink-black fabric spills into my lap.

Crow's color. It was the cheapest. Now I realize how it seems—that I bought it to spite him.

"Could you look away?" As soon as I ask, I wish I'd ordered him instead.

"Really, Zephyr? It's my body."

Scowling, I start undressing. My forearms are thin, my wrists vined with veins. They delve blue into the soft crooks of my elbows. There's no softness at my chest. That's all bone and skin and not so different from what little I had to work with as Qilin.

"If anything," Crow says as I inspect myself, "it's my qīngbái being compromised."

He's almost certainly being facetious; I've done so much worse than invade his privacy. But all the rationalization in the world can't stop the stone from forming in my throat. "Then don't watch," I say, but the stone grows when I find the scar behind my shoulder, where Crow took that arrow for me, and even though I *know* he saved me just so that I could burn Miasma's navy, my next words are choked. "Go haunt someone else."

"I'd never be disloyal to you."

Jaw clenched, I finish dressing.

I lie down; Crow remains sitting.

"Qilin." My gaze startles to him. "You signed the letter off as Qilin," Crow muses, my old name almost sounding pretty when he says it. I should be uneasy with all the small talk he's attempting, but I'm too tired to tell him to stop. "Why?" he asks, and he's free to waste his breath.

I just shouldn't be wasting mine with him. "It was my name as an orphan."

"I know," Crow says, and so much is embedded in those two words—my history with Ku *and* Crow's knowledge of it—that I squirm. "But you always seemed like someone who would disavow her origins. To sign your birth name on the letter . . ." He pauses, contemplative. "You must have thought I was going to die without ever knowing it. You meant it as a parting gift. How close am I?"

He stares at me, and I stare back. *Disavow her origins . . .* What gives him the sense?

Am I so transparent?

"Not close at all," I say. "I never would have expected you to die so pathetically, doomed by one lost navy. I'm surprised it cost you a finger. Must have hurt."

"Wouldn't you know, seeing that you cut off a finger yourself?" Damn Crow and his comebacks. "And you took that arrow at Bikong too. You now know, intimately, all the pains I've gone through to save you. Does it tenderize your heart?"

"No."

"Not even a little?"

"Why are you talking to me, Crow?"

"Why can't I? It seems that only you can hear me." I plug my ears, which has Crow smiling. "So you were an orphan. But you also claim to be a god. Why, may I ask, are you here and not enjoying life in the heavens?"

"None of your business."

"Perhaps you're here as punishment."

Sounds from downstairs float up to us.

"Not this time," I finally say. "I'm here by choice."

"Whatever on earth is the reason?" Crow asks, and his shock almost sounds genuine, before he says, "Aha: me."

I swipe at him and he leans back, out of my reach—mostly. Another flash—*a girl and a boy, laughing in a sunlit courtyard*— that fades as my hand passes through his spirit and Crow says, "All choices have a price. So what did you pay to return, Zephyr?" he asks, and his gentleness throws me more than the brief vision.

A front. A façade. He's trying to get me to lower my guard. And I won't lie, a part of me is tempted. I *want* to tell him, while he cares to play at niceties.

By tomorrow, he might not.

"Nothing," I say, nipping the want. "I paid nothing."

"I don't believe you. In the legends, there's always a payment. For your sake, I just hope it wasn't too great."

A front.

"Because you see, I read your letter. I found it quite moving."

A façade.

"The words you wrote almost had me believing that your heart beat faster for me."

Our gazes lock. Maybe they've been locked this entire time. It's a moment without a beginning. It could have no ending.

I look away first. "Then you were the fool."

"I was. Alas." A sigh of a word. "Why did the world have to

make a you when there was already a me?" Crow laments, and my breath catches in my throat.

"You said something similar, once."

"Did I?"

"In a dream," I admit, and wait for Crow to ask me how many times I've dreamed of him. When the silence holds, I glance back over to see his eyes closed, his face canted toward the ceiling. We're pretending, like we did in his cabin. He'd lain on the bed and I'd sat, beside him.

If I die, he'd said, *you can play my funeral dirge*.

But back then, at least, the future was a question. He hadn't killed me, and I hadn't killed him.

Blood hadn't yet salted the earth between us.

Sleep. I need sleep, not this useless reminiscing. I close my eyes, feel myself sink. But at the surface of unawareness, I can't surrender myself over. Thoughts pull at my mind—does Miasma have nightmares because of the ghosts—can ghosts touch dreams like gods—is Crow a ghost, or a spirit—will my powers come back—

Through it all, I hear laughter.

I see that unfamiliar girl, embroidering handkerchiefs. She was also in the courtyard, and the boy—

Looked like Crow.

My eyelids part. Crow is still sitting on the bed, his back near my right hand. I slide it closer.

My fingertips touch his spirit.

—"Here you go. I made it for you." The girl holds out an embroidered handkerchief to a younger Crow—

—and covers his eyes with her hands, this memory in a sunlit courtyard. "Found you, Senge!"—

—"Shuaimei," Crow greets, rising from his desk as the girl enters, in her midteens now, like Crow, but she's taller than him, and at least a chǐ taller than Cicada. She wears a handsome suit of armor, a sword sheathed at her hip.

"What are you doing here?" Crow asks, coming around the desk to meet her.

"To see you off, silly." She straightens the front of his robes. "Be careful up North. Watch your step, and watch your health."

"I will," says Crow, before a cough consumes him.

"See? Your body knows better than to lie to me." She grins as Crow blushes. Then her grin gentles. "I won't be able to write to you. So I made these for you to remember me by." She draws out a bouquet of handkerchiefs from her breastplate. "If something happens to you, I'll never forgive you."

Crow starts to reply, and I become him. We want to say nothing will happen to us, but that would be disrespectful to Shuaimei, who's been fighting pirates on the Southern rivers and seas since she turned thirteen. She knows the cost of war. Spies die all the time.

Lordesses too. "And if something happens to me . . ." She lifts her eyes to ours, and breathing becomes tricky. "I know the little cicada still has a lot of growing to do, but promise me you'll serve her as faithfully as you serve me, Senge."

-ge. A suffix that, like the -mei in Shuaimei, describes an age difference between close relationships. And here, the relationship is close, indeed: The girl presses her lips to ours, and my hand jerks away from Crow's spirit.

The scene fades.

Back to the inn. To its quiet. I try to slow my breathing as my thoughts gallop.

Shuaimei.

I've never met her, but I know exactly who she is.

A person who looms larger in the memory of the Southlands than even Cicada, its current lordess.

My pulse gradually returns to its feeble current, but my mind remains abuzz. Beyond my lids, the light changes, darkness falling.

I rise with the dawn.

Crow watches as I go to the basin. I act as if nothing is amiss, combing out my hair. It's softer than Lotus's. I catch my fingers lingering and yank the locks hard to the top of my head. The ponytail tumbles down my back.

My reflection shows a strategist. This body isn't without its flaws, but it's the role I play best. Or did. Cloud and I got captured because I failed to think four moves ahead. I was distracted, trying to be a warrior and Ren's swornsister.

I won't make the same mistake again.

I leave the inn and saddle up. Sunrise breathes over the horizon. I chew on dried ginseng for strength, riding through the day and night, not stopping until the sky is lilac and we've come to the Mica's eastern offshoot. The river flows, the water clear.

It runs red in a future where Cicada defeats Ren.

As Crow, I will see that it never happens. I trot down the

bank and knock on the doors of a fisher's shack. They open to a woman's face. "You are . . . ?"

This far South, the customs are Southern. The fisher's accent is Southern.

"I'm a courier for Cicada," I say, and no more words are needed.

Soon I'm on the water with two oars in my hands and a heart full of regret for declining the fisher's offer to row. Crow smiles at me as I struggle, and my mood darkens. His smile is falser than I could have ever guessed. Even before he became a spy for the South, his heart belonged to another.

But I shouldn't act differently. If Crow finds out I know, he'll wonder how.

"This amusing to you?" I force myself to grunt.

"Very."

I keep on. The wind casts ripples over the river. The day is overcast, clouds piled like mountains.

"Brings me back to our morning on the Siming," says Crow. "If you hadn't killed me, I'd be sitting opposite you. You wouldn't have to touch the oars—"

"Because *you'd* row?"

"As any Southern gentleman would," Crow says, and I think of that younger Crow, softer, unscarred. Able, still, to blush. "It's all in the technique. I could have taught you. A shame." He settles back in the boat, and for a breath, I mourn the boy he was. "As much as I like myself, I have to say it dampens the mood a bit to be gazing at my own face. I'd much rather it be yours."

"I shudder to think of your prior courtship experiences if you find any hint of this romantic."

The words slip out of me, but Crow grins, detecting nothing strange to them. "Prior experiences . . . I can't seem to remember any."

"Keep lying," I say lightly, even as my mouth sours. It shouldn't. I already knew the untruth of Crow's sweet nothings. He killed me, for heaven's sake. I steamed him. To be jealous now? Of someone dead? My sobriquet might as well be Pickled Peacock. We ended each other before any third person. Nothing has really changed.

Nothing.

It's just . . . Crow's words. All of them burn now, whether he intends for them to or not. "I told you before," he says, "I like ruinous things. And you were the death of me. So, you win. You're all I can think of."

I may be ruinous, but not like Shuaimei. Losing her must have destroyed Crow. She's the reason why Crow's loyalty to Cicada is unshakable, why Crow will hate me more—if that's even possible—should harm befall her or the Southlands. It's a reckoning I can't avoid.

So bring it.

An hour later, a helmet bobs by in the water. A broken war flag drifts past next, camp of origin undiscernible.

A li or so down, bodies appear, strewn in the shallows.

I stop the boat on the east bank of the river—the bank closer to the South. Crow says nothing as I step out.

I walk. And walk. The plain turns to mud, and the mud tells a story: Camps, once standing, have been routed by attacks. Repeatedly, Cicada's troops have been pushed back. There is not a Southern soldier in sight for many li, and by the time I'm finally stopped, I'm far too close to the Southlands encampment.

"Halt!" The soldiers I face are more bandaged than armored. Barely a threat. I'm more focused on what's over their heads. *Taohui.* My knees weaken as I behold the forted city nestled in the misty foothills of the Diyu Mountains.

I've made it.

I'm not too late to save Ren.

"Declare yourself!" demand the soldiers, and I sigh.

"Crow." This is where they bow and welcome back their strategist, immediately. Or not. I guess their defeats are weighing on—

They encircle me, spears pointed.

"Intruder. You're a spy from Ren."

What nonsense is this? "Why don't they know you?" I snap at Crow.

"Who are you talking to?" bark the soldiers.

Rat-livers. "No one."

"Zephyr, making an oversight?" Crow tsks. "I never thought I'd live to see the day."

You didn't, unless your definition of "live" extends to being a spirit.

"I've been planted deep in the North for over three years,"

Crow continues. "No one here has seen my face. But if you knew the code word . . ."

He trails off, his tone almost suggestive.

"Bastard."

"What did you say?" The soldiers, again.

"Nothing." In my head, I throw every profanity I know at Crow. *Code word.* He'd never tell me. His spirit might hold a helpful memory, but touching it now would be too suspicious, and admittedly, I don't want to.

Crow's past has distracted me enough.

"Take me to Cicada," I tell the soldiers. "*Now.* If you harm me, she'll chain you in the lake like her Fen pirate."

There. I know something only a Southlander would. They'll think twice before—

—binding me.

Crow laughs quietly.

"You'll regret this," I hiss as I'm hauled to the camp. "You don't know who I—"

A soldier moves in with a gag.

Ten hells. My nose is pinched when my mouth won't open, and I'm just about out of breath when I hear a voice.

"Senge?"

It's her. My lifesaver. The guards block my view of her, but I know her voice. Apparently, I also know her diminutive. *Xiaochan,* Crow let slip.

Little cicada.

But I trust the boy I saw more than the spirit staring at me now, waiting for me to speak. And speak I do. Two syllables. Not Shuaimei, for that would be wrong too. The suffix -mei—*younger girl*—can stay, but *shuai* means "general."

It also means "cricket."

I change it to *chan*, for *cicada*. "Hello, Chanmei."

三十七

EMPTY FORT

*C*hanmei.

The first time I ever visited Crow in the capital, I saw him murmur a name in his sleep. Too quick for me to decipher, but even then, I knew it wasn't *my* name. I will never haunt him like Shuaimei. Cricket. Crow's first lordess and older sister to Cicada, his lordess of the present, whose diminutive must be Chanmei by induction.

"Hands off him!" Cicada shouts, and the soldiers release me. I face her as she descends from the litter.

She reaches me in five strides. "You're alive. You're alive. You're alive—"

Smack. My head whips to the side, my right cheek on fire.

"How dare you scare me like that!" Cicada lowers her hand and I blink, stunned speechless, as Crow's gaze flames in the corner of my watering vision. Being slapped is apparently a better fortune than I deserve; he yearned for me to say *Xiaochan* and blow my cover. Well, lesson learned. Even as a spirit, he will do his utmost to defeat me.

Indeed, Crow, the two of us can't coexist in this world.

And we don't. Crow can glare at me to his heart's content, but only I can say "Gentler, please" to Cicada with a wince. "I really was steamed."

"Thanks to who, I wonder," Crow says, voice dark.

"I don't care if you were steamed or roasted," Cicada snaps at me. "For two weeks, I thought you were dead. *Two weeks.* Couldn't you have ridden faster?" Before I can reply, her hand rises again and my eyes flinch shut.

The second slap doesn't come.

"You're bleeding." I open my eyes to see Cicada frowning at my waist. I look down myself, surprised to feel a wetness in the black fabric. "And your face is ice-cold. Summon the phy—"

"Wound's dressed," I interrupt. "I saw a physician on the road here." I save the details of how I'm dying from a dozen other ailments. I'm sure Cicada knows, as the childhood friend Crow once spoke of—or was that Cricket? *Focus.* Cicada is oblivious to Crow's spirit; whatever they had was no sworn siblinghood like Cloud's, Ren's, and Lotus's. I am Cicada's strategist before I am anything else, and as a strategist I now say, "There's no time, Chanmei. I can wait, but the war won't."

Cicada's demeanor instantly shifts. "You're right. Come."

She leads me through the Southlands camp, and as we walk, I remember who she is: an actor who's had to put on many faces to survive in a court that worshipped her sister. Would it hurt her to know Crow did too? Or does she already know?

Focus.

We enter the command tent. "Advisors," Cicada says, "look who's returned."

Blank stares. I'm wondering if it's my hair, still in its high ponytail, when an old advisor blanches.

"G-ghost!"

My gaze jerks to Crow. He smiles, and a vein in my temple twitches. Of course they're not referring to him.

They're referring to me, the spy Miasma allegedly killed.

"I'm very much alive," I say to the advisors, who flinch. The ghost speaks. Then, slowly, questions start to bubble. How did Miasma find out? What ordeals did I undergo, and how do I live to tell them?

"He must have turned," the old advisor says. "He's been sent back as *their* spy, in exchange for his life."

"Say one more word and I'll take *your* life to pay for everything he's suffered," Cicada snaps. She faces the rest. "Crow is the reason Miasma hasn't exterminated us yet, or have you all forgotten that?"

"Miasma isn't the one at our doorstep," someone argues. "Ren is."

"Who we could still be allied with," another mutters, "instead of Miasma—an 'ally' who doesn't even reply to us in a time of need. It's as if she thinks we sent spies!"

"Well, we did," mutters another advisor.

"So? Did she have proof? Did she?" the advisor asks, gaze wheeling to me.

"No," I say, because it's true. Crow never confessed. Any evidence was circumstantial. The least I can do is acknowledge this feat even if it goes unappreciated. The advisors resume their bickering, and Cicada's hands fist. These same men pleaded with her to swear fealty to Miasma when I came to her court as a Northern delegate.

Spineless bunch. "We can salvage the situation," I speak over them. "I'm here to tell you how."

I stride to the hanging map; the tanned hide is poxed with Ren's encampments, denoted by red flags. The war is but a week old, and Ren has already regained all of the Marshlands, backing Cicada into Taohui. Soon, she'll have nowhere to retreat but across the Diyu Mountains, into the Southlands, and who's to say Ren won't invade that too? To the advisors in this tent, the war is all but lost.

But I've seen the fates, the fires, the loss that's converted to a win. And now I see how.

Ren's fatal weakness lies in the layout of her camps. Only I discern it.

I, and Crow.

"No." It leaves him as a whisper, laced with horror. He knows exactly what I'm about to do: Steal the victory that Cicada doesn't even realize is in her jaws.

"At this hour," I say to everyone in the tent, "we need to remember who the real enemy is."

"Don't listen to her," Crow says to Cicada. "This fight is not over. Ren's camps—"

"We need to make peace with Xin Ren," I say, not bothering to raise my voice over Crow's. "More than that, we need to rebuild trust. Restore the alliance. Even if we could win against Ren, our battered army will have to face fresh empire troops."

As I speak, Cicada paces to the throne-like chair set before the map. She sits, tapping her fingers on the arm.

"*Ren*," she seethes. "Who would have known that she'd be capable of such bloodshed?"

"It's to be expected," I say, "given her swornsister's death."

"She should blame Miasma for it!" Cicada explodes, then takes a deep breath, reining in her emotions. "We've already tried suing for peace. November crossed enemy lines this morning with our latest bid."

For a second, I can't speak. "What did you send her with?"

"A wooden replica of General Lotus's body," chimes in an advisor.

Spineless *and* good-for-nothing.

"I heard Miasma only sent Ren the head," Cicada explains, seeing my expression. "I'd want my own swornsister interred whole."

If that were your swornsister, you wouldn't want her in the ground at all.

But Crow wouldn't say those words, and Cicada sighs when I don't reply. "We'll wait to hear her report when she returns."

"If she returns," mutters an advisor. "Her sister was Ren's strategist."

"We don't speak of that in this court," Cicada snaps.

"It seems relevant. What if she defects?"

Toad. Ku and I have our history, but I won't stand for strangers slandering her. Would Crow? It's too early to know. *Don't risk it.* I hold my tongue as Cicada rises.

"I'll only say this once." Her gaze falls steely on the advisor. "I trust November with my life." She looks to the others. "She would never surrender to Ren, but the next person to insinuate as much can, because I won't have them in my camp."

Her conviction is as deep as a Northern winter, and grudgingly, I commend Cicada as her advisors shiver, their detractions frozen within their lips. A part of me will always be bitter that she's replaced me as Ku's protector, but wasn't I a replacement too? A sound comes from outside the tent, and Cicada's gaze lifts. "That must be her."

Before I can prepare myself, Ku is striding in. She stops, stares at me, and I stare at her. My sister—or so I thought for eight years. What if she can also see Crow's spirit like she saw Qilin's? "Is it safe?" Ku asks, and I don't know how to answer.

"It's safe," Cicada says.

Ku rushes for me, body rocking into mine. She hugs me tight, and my mind empties. My arms—my hands—what do I do with them?

Just follow Ku's lead. Clearly, she loves Crow. And I am Crow. My arms go around her, my mouth opens. I—

I don't know what to call her either.

I grow aware of Crow's cold stare. He won't give up Ku's pet name now, not when I just told his lordess to surrender when they should fight on. But silence won't do. My arms tighten around Ku. "Look who's gotten tall."

I hope my voice is steadier than my heart.

"She's been asking about her mentor every day," says Cicada, a smile in her voice. "Haven't you, Xiaoqiu?"

Xiaoqiu. Little autumn. Autumn for November, Ku's sobriquet. Crow was Ku's mentor.

I internalize one fact after another.

"Enough with this," an advisor breaks in. "What did Xin Ren say?"

"No truce." Ku lets go of me, facing the men. "Xin Ren said she spared me on account of her old strategist. A legion under Sikou Hai was marching toward us when I left."

The advisors moan, but I'm relieved, so relieved that Ku's refusal to say my name hardly stings. As long as a glimmer of the Ren I know still lives, I'll lead her back to herself.

"So we have our answer," says an advisor, patting at his brow with a handkerchief. "We must retreat."

The others murmur in consensus.

Cicada's eyes flash. "And cede Taohui too?"

"There's no other option!"

I won't gloat. I won't. It takes a seasoned strategist to see that all is not lost. Ku isn't there yet, and I dispatched the person who is.

"I have a plan," I say as the temperature rises in the tent, but the advisors only shake their heads.

"It's too late to do battle, strategist. Xin Ren's almost upon us and we have nothing but a city of civilians at our backs."

"I have a plan," I repeat, "to make Ren lay down her arms without spilling a drop of blood."

Silence.

Smug, Cicada looks to her council. "Don't act so shocked. No ordinary person could have fooled Miasma for so long."

Would have been longer, had I not involved myself.

"Tell us what to do, Senge," Cicada says, and all eyes are on me, but I only feel Crow's. They bore into me as I lure his lordess away from a war she would have won.

"There's nothing for you to do. I'll deal with Ren myself."

"With what?" demands an advisor. "With our wounded soldiers?"

"No. With a zither, and just a zither."

‡ ‡ ‡

As servants set up the instrument atop the fort's walls, I glance to Crow. Only he was present when Cicada pulled me aside before I could cross the short li between us and Taohui.

She showed me a letter from Miasma.

Ah! The terrors of Charity Ren! I'm sorry to hear she's giving you so much trouble. One would think she'd be easy to deal with, now that I've done you the favor of killing her swornsister. But not every army is equipped to squash a fly, no?

Unfortunately, the situation at the capital is fraught, with rebels and spies afoot. Famine persists and I have no grain to spare either. You'll have to understand, then, why I'm unable to come to your aid. I shall wish nightly instead for your swift and decisive victory over our shared foe.

Your Prime Ministress,
Miasma

"I've had to keep this from every white-head in my court," Cicada had said under her breath. "The mockery! The disrespect!

And this was before I received reports of what she'd done to you!"

I'd nodded along, focused on the date. Fate had said Miasma would fall not long after the physician. Now it'd been two weeks. Was she going to die or not? Then there was the matter of Cicada. I'd planned on removing her after saving Ren. Was this the moment? We were alone in the tent. I had no weapons, but I had my hands. But kill Cicada, and her advisors would take over. They'd be harder to control. Best to have Cicada's help in defeating Miasma, as I'd conceived in the Rising Zephyr Objective.

"She can keep her troops," I'd said to Cicada, voice calm, as if I hadn't just considered her murder. "And she can keep this letter. Does the camp have a pigeon to spare?"

While the bird was being procured, I'd drawn a diagram on the back of Miasma's letter, labeling it as *Ren's camps*. Among the empire's many advisors, there had to be one theory-literate enough to spot the golden opportunity and urge Miasma not to sit and wait, as she had in Dasan, but to attack. To drive her troops southward, into the Marshlands, and take advantage of our divided front.

By then, we'll be united as one.

Crow had watched while I'd sent the letter. He knew exactly what I was doing: Stratagem Fifteen, Luring the Tiger Out of Its Lair, all the better so that we could defeat it. We'd defeat Miasma, then we'd turn on Cicada as he'd predicted.

He doesn't need to speak now for me to know how it feels to be unseen, unheard, unheeded.

I wait for the servants to leave, wait until it's just me and Crow, alone on the ramparts.

I go to stand beside him.

So, Miasma. I should ask him about her even if he refuses to answer. Hells, I could even ask about Xin Bao, useless as she is.

It'd still be more useful than what actually comes out of my mouth: "Like I said, Cicada wasn't fated to win."

"Don't, Zephyr." Crow leans his crossed elbows on the battlements, gaze forward. "Has anyone told you that you're very bad at comforting people?"

"I'm only stating the facts."

"You must really take me for a fool if you think I can still trust a single word of yours."

I can't trust your words either. My mind flashes to Cricket, and I sound alarmingly mopey when I mutter, "It's the truth."

Control your emotions.

"How's this for a truth?" Finally, Crow looks at me, his attention bruising. "Ren would have died first. The incoming battle would have been won by us, if not for your interference."

There's nothing to refute. It's all true. I should be proud it is, but under the heat of Crow's gaze, my pride shrivels. "I'm just looking out for my lordess, same as you."

"How can I look out for Cicada, Zephyr? *How?*" demands Crow, so forcefully that I almost step back. Almost. I won't be cowed by a spirit with no body, no form, no breath behind his words. He can't touch me. Can't physically hurt me.

Then why does his anguish scorch?

"You're still here," I offer, voice small.

"Yes." His is acid. "As a spirit. The playing field is a little unfair, wouldn't you say?"

"You didn't play fair either."

Crow blinks. A grin bitters his lips. "You can't still be wounded that I called the soldiers on you."

"I came to you as a strategist."

"No, Zephyr." He says my name like a punishment. "You came to me disguised as someone else. You knew my secrets when they should have died with you at Pumice Pass. Now you're here, in my body, speaking with my mouth. Let's talk about unfair odds, shall we?"

"So you're giving up?" I shouldn't be goading him on, but I can't seem to help it. "The strategist I respected wouldn't have settled for anything less than total victory."

"Where was that respect when you shut the steamer's lid?"

When I don't reply, Crow turns away, facing the battlements again.

See? chides the voice. *That's what you get for straying from the objective. Who cares about his feelings? Ask about Miasma now—*

"You may think you're a god incarnate, Zephyr, but in reality, you're just a cheat."

Cheat. He's figured out how I arrived at the diminutive Chanmei. He's going to accuse me of looking into his spirit, then tell me all the ways I'm not like Cricket, and I'll have to pretend not to care—no, not pretend. I don't care.

I *don't.*

But then Crow says, "You might have all those advisors believing that you're about to accomplish Empty Fort, but it's a legendary stratagem for one reason: No one living has successfully turned away an army from an empty fort. But you will, because you have a cheat. In fact, here it comes. Look."

Crow's eyes remain on the horizon, and at first, mine remain on him, his words cutting me long after he's gone silent.

Good. That's what I need—a constant reminder that nothing exists between us but hurt. I look to the horizon too. Smeared with mist, then dust. A growing haze.

Legions of troops ride out from it, led by a figure in black.

Sikou Hai. I identify him by his mask, a burst of gold covering half his face.

Just as I can see him from this distance, he can also see me—a lone figure atop the battlements, bare of soldiers and banners. Down below, the gates are wide open. A trick, he'll be thinking. Soldiers are inside, lying in ambush. Or—the fort is actually empty and it's as Crow said: a last resort that only exists in legends. Cataloged as a stratagem of desperation, Empty Fort precedes only Stratagem Thirty-Six:

Retreat When All Else Fails.

But it won't come to that. I'm here with my favorite weapon.

I touch the zither strings, aware of Crow's missing finger, but not worried. I've made music with more unfamiliar hands.

The first notes emerge, supple and resonant.

I play the song Sikou and I composed by the lake, when I was Lotus. We had no audience. Now twenty thousand troops listen, but only one person will understand the significance.

Sikou Hai. Your mind must be racing. The setup was enough to make him pause, but this song—it means something to him.

It'll compel him to approach, and him alone.

Sure enough, he pulls away from the ranks. I can only imagine the soldiers' reactions. A literati like him, riding out undefended? He's asking to be killed.

Little do they know that a strategist can stomach risk as well as any warrior.

Sikou Hai stops his horse in Taohui's shadow.

"Greetings!" he calls up to me, his voice carrying over the music. "We have not met, but I assume you're one of Cicada's strategists?"

"I will haunt you in this life and the next," Crow vows to me.

"Be my guest," I say under my breath, then call down to Sikou Hai, "I am. Won't you come up to talk?"

I can imagine my disciple's thought process. At this range, I could have already shot him. Whatever my intentions, it's not to kill him.

He dismounts and takes to the steps. I continue playing, the notes trilling as his head appears at the landing, then more of him. My fingers stop.

Don't stare.

"I do believe that's my cloak," Crow says.

I wish I could deny it, but he's right. The black cloak I saw from afar is made of feathers, closer up.

Why is Sikou Hai wearing it?

"You steal everything, don't you?" Crow goes on.

"You—"*left that behind for me, I'll remind you.* But I can't reply, because Sikou Hai is here. He clears the last of the steps, and what he's wearing becomes the least of my concerns.

"Where did you learn that song?" he asks me, and I'd planned on saying *From you. Don't you recognize your mentor?* But as the wind rises, I chill. The last time, I told them who I was. Sikou Hai. Tourmaline. Cloud. I told them everything, and look at the result. Sikou Hai should have dissuaded Ren from this campaign. Did he try and fail? Or did he learn nothing from my mentorship, short as it was, and let his queen do as she pleases?

"I don't believe the song is important," I finally say. To know my identity, he must earn it.

Sikou Hai frowns. "Actually—"

"You've brought twenty thousand troops before the city walls. Do you aim to defeat us?"

"If there's an army to defeat."

I hold Sikou Hai's gaze; his is steady.

"He's not bad," says Crow.

As if I'd mentor just anyone.

"You're right," I say to Sikou Hai. "We have no forces behind us. The city is for your taking. But do you want it?"

"Your meaning?"

"Tell me what you truly think of Xin Ren's campaign against our queen, and I'll tell you how I know the song."

I've put Sikou Hai in a bind. To speak ill of his lordess in front of me, the enemy, is to betray Ren. He won't do that. But a wise strategist knows when to walk the line.

"We should still be allies," he finally answers.

Five words. Not outright treason, but as close as I need it to be.

"I picked my disciple well," I say, rising from my zither. "Miasma tried to kill me. So did Crow, this body's previous owner. Pity for him, I killed him first."

"Crow. Cicada's spy." I nod, and Sikou Hai steps toward me. "You tortured the song out of Zephyr."

"What? No!" I say while Crow sniffs, as if torture is beneath him. The hypocrite. He'd have used any means to crack the mystery of Lotus, had Miasma spared me. "*I'm* Zeph—put away that knife, you fool!"

Sikou Hai advances another step, blade in his hand.

"Listen—" I back up. "*Listen*: This is a lost battle. Ren's camp formations are atrocious—covering an area too large to be properly defensible, and packed too close together. You're lucky no one from the South has realized it yet, but once they do, they'll attack the way that I once attacked Miasma—with fire. They'll be aided by the westward wind, set to move in tomorrow." And I'll be powerless to avert it. "Ren's loss of the Marshlands will be final."

As will the loss of her life.

A shadow of a bird wings over us. My eyes stay on Sikou Hai, his person unmoving—

His eyes suddenly glassy.

Heavens spare me.

"Rising Zephyr—" He steps toward me and I back up more.

"*Don't.*" Being cried on is one indignity I refuse to suffer. "I'm alive, so treat me that way."

"I—I'm sorry." Sikou Hai swipes at his eyes. "It's just—we

saw the head and Ren—she's fine!—but she wouldn't eat. And Tourmaline—"

"What happened to Tourmaline?"

"She's fine too," Sikou Hai says, quick as my tone is sharp. I stare him down. "When you didn't return or, well, reappear as someone else, I suspect she thought she could recall your soul with another body as a host."

Another body as a host.

"Her own," I hear myself say.

"Cloud stopped her."

Tourmaline. The steadiest of us, driven to such ends because she knew I was Zephyr. And Ren—on this rampage because she *didn't* know. To the very end, I was Lotus to her. Should I have chosen differently? Would that have led to less suffering?

Stop. They're all alive. That's what matters. Sikou Hai is relying on me, and Crow is watching me.

I can't show weakness in front of them.

"Name my sobriquets," I order my disciple.

"P-pardon?"

"Name them."

"R-rising Zephyr." Sikou Hai's voice stabilizes. "Fate Changer. The Dragon's Shadow. Tactician of Thistlegate."

"One more: God Among Strategists." Sikou Hai rapidly nods. "And as a god, I've returned. I'm back here, today, to end this war." I take my disciple by the elbow. "Together, you and I will bring Ren into Taohui to meet with Cicada."

"She won't come. Not for a peace talk."

I can feel Crow's eyes on me, judging me for my choice of lordess. But Ren spared Ku.

Ren will listen.

"I brought you up here, didn't I?" I walk Sikou Hai down the battlement stairs. "Trust me that I can bring Ren in."

"And then?" asks Sikou Hai. "How will we convince her?"

"Leave it to me."

三十八

BEYOND THE GRAVE

*L*eave it to me.

An hour passes. Two. At three, Ren enters the city as I knew she would when Sikou Hai did not return to her. Gongs herald her arrival as she sweeps into the magistrate's hall, where we wait.

From my current position, I can't see my one true lordess.

I lie in darkness, able only to see Crow as he hovers by my head, shaking his.

"It's not nice to tease, Zephyr. Besides, Deck the Bare Tree with Silk Leaves means to disguise the dead as living, not this reversal of yours."

Is it really a reversal if you're already half corpse? Maybe more than half, given the ice-cold skin and barely there pulse. I'd utilize both even if it didn't pique Crow, but I'm beside myself that it does. If only I could rub it in—but I keep my silence. I may be in a coffin, but I'm not in the dark about what's to happen. Everyone is where I want them to be. Play my pieces right, and I'll turn Ren's loss at Taohui into a win.

Fate stops here with my artifice.

I hear Cicada greet Ren. Her voice is fuzzy compared to the honed blade of my lordess's.

"Where is Sikou Hai?"

"Here, unharmed," Cicada says.

Footsteps, followed by Ren's quiet words: "Let me see you." To Cicada, louder: "You've really made a habit of targeting my strategists." Scuff of a bootheel, as it turns. "We take our leave."

Voices—first, Cicada's: "Slow your step. I have a proposition." Sikou Hai's: "Listen to her."

A breath, drawn in. Ren's. "Your strategist already has my answer."

"I know," says Cicada. "Our terms were insufficient."

"Whatever you offer—"

"What is this campaign, but one of revenge?" Cicada interjects. "You fight to avenge your swornsister. I know the desire; I'll fulfill yours right now." The coffin lid is slid back; light hits my made-up face, tinting my closed eyelids red. "Here is the person responsible: A spy of ours, planted in the North."

"Ah yes," Crow murmurs to me. "Scapegoat the corpse."

"He orchestrated the execution of your swornsister without my approval," says Cicada. "But it doesn't matter, because now he is dead, poisoned by Miasma herself."

"Merciful," says Crow, "compared to your royal treatment."

"Our quarrel"—Cicada again—"should rest with—"

I'm suddenly jerked up and out of the coffin.

Don't tense. Don't breathe. Easier said than done when I've been seized by the throat. *Don't. Cough.* Around me, words fly like darts.

"Release him, Cloud," orders Ren.

"He killed Zephyr and Lotus!"

"He's dead!" snaps Sikou Hai, my ever-faithful disciple.

Not dead enough, apparently, for Cloud. My body swings as she moves, presumably out of Sikou Hai's reach. "Touch me again, and I'll break your arm."

"Gao Yun."

"Cloud!"

Hands fight over me like wolves over a kill.

Stay. Limp.

Just when I think my act will crack, I'm flung back into the coffin. I dare not open my eyes, but I can envision the scene. Cloud, enraged. Ren rooted in place. Tourmaline is here too. That was her "Cloud!"—perhaps the only voice that reached Cloud's heart. I know it reached mine. It's the first time in months that we've all been gathered in one room. The first time, since I died as Lotus, that I'm with them.

A throat clears. Cicada's. I can envision her too, in her ceremonial robes, not mourning. *Too insincere*, I'd told her. Only two soldiers flank her—*any more reeks of an ambush.* Ku is waiting in the wings—*let's not remind Ren of the last bid for truce*—and to Cicada's right stands a masked advisor. I'd picked him out myself, told him not to speak, then passed him the full-faced clay mask.

Why? Cicada had asked.

Just trust me.

And so far, Cicada has. She's been doing everything as instructed. *It'll be an uphill battle*, I told her while Crow stared at me. If looks could kill, I'd really be a corpse. *We can't bring the swornsister back, but we can provide closure.*

A life for a life. A head for a head. Last time, I was caught off guard by Ren's emotions.

This time I would speak to her through them.

"The culprit is dead," Cicada says, picking up where we'd left off. "What's more, we're willing to cede the Marshlands to you." Her voice is smooth, so unlike how she'd sounded when I'd encouraged her to make this trade. *We'll get it back*, I'd assured her, placing my faith in Ren.

"To renew our alliance," Ren now says to Cicada.

"Yes."

"You want that."

"Yes, we—"

"Were you thinking of our alliance, when you collaborated with Miasma?" The hall goes quiet. "Will you pin that on this dead spy too?"

"Thank you," says Crow, sounding vindicated.

For a long moment, he has the last word.

"Do you know why I sided with Miasma?" My heart skids when Cicada starts improvising. "When my sister died at the hands of the Fen, Miasma seized upon our weakness. She stole the Marshlands and made a gift of them to that uncle of yours, Xin Gong.

"All my life, I'd been told that you were different. But you refused to return the Marshlands, just like Miasma. So why not side with her?

"Then she killed my strategist." Cicada's voice thickens with emotion, naked, and I feel naked too, remembering how it felt to hold Crow's limp wrist in the steamer. "She reminded me of who the real enemy is.

"Haven't you heard the reports coming out of the imperial city?" When Cicada speaks next, she sounds farther from the coffin. "Unrest is mounting. Rebels rose up against Miasma, and she killed them, down to the ninth relative. She killed dozens of officials too, and a renowned physician." Voice, a little more distant. "Shouldn't you be saving Xin Bao from that blood-soaked palace?" And more distant. "Shouldn't the welfare of the people trump your vendetta?"

Swords unsheathe—from Ren's side. My breath lodges in my throat. Cicada must have stepped in too close.

At last, after what feels like an eon, swords return to sheaths and Cicada says, "If you won't listen to me, listen to your strategist. She always spoke on the importance of our alliance."

A servant will now be delivering a brocade pouch to Cicada, who will personally offer it to Ren.

If only I could watch as Ren lifts out the silk scroll.

If only I could see her expression as it unfurls.

‡ ‡ ‡

"You have some explaining to do," I'd muttered to Sikou Hai after entering Taohui. I'd already told him what was set to happen, then handed him a sheet of paper—"for coding our future correspondences." With the magistrate hall coming up, it was now or never.

Ask him. "Since when did you start carrying a knife?"

"Ren insisted."

I should have guessed. She'd also added a switchblade to my fan.

Ask him!

"And what about that cloak?" I'd muttered, tacking on the question like an afterthought. "Why are you wearing it?"

Why do you care? I feared Sikou Hai would ask as Crow's gaze smoldered over me.

But Sikou Hai simply answered like a disciple would his master. "I found Cloud in your shrine, burning it. She said it was the enemy's when I tried to stop her."

"She's right. It is the enemy's."

"So? You'd kept it, surely for a good reason."

It pained me not to correct him.

"I rescued it," Sikou Hai had said with pride. "I rescued these too." He'd removed sheaves of paper from the cross-folds of his robes, and I'd stared at them.

"You've been carrying these with you on the march?"

"They're safest with me. I will preserve them with my life."

At first, I didn't know what to say. "Fool!" I'd snapped, but my voice wavered. "What if you'd gotten blood on them?" Then I'd snatched the papers—"Careful!" cried Sikou Hai—and gazed down at my own calligraphy. I'd had my doubts about the corpse-in-a-coffin tactic—*too tawdry, too volatile*—but those doubts receded as I traced the words.

Why not harness Ren's response to another vestige of myself? "Since we have them," I finally said to Sikou Hai, "we might as well use them."

Now, in the hall, I imagine Ren holding the scroll. On it are the words I wrote, after months of practicing as Lotus, months during which I was preoccupied with the Southern alliance. I had to repair it. I had to. Over and over, I'd written out the goal. There's a saying that ink is like a scholar's blood.

I'd bled my wishes out onto paper:

Ally with the South again.
Ally with the South again.
Ally with the South again.
Ally with the South again.
Ally with the South again.

The words consume the entire sheet. And the sheet—it starts trembling. A sound so small, but it fills my lightless world. In my mind, I'm beside Ren, watching her as she reads. *See?* I tell her. *I'm here. I never left.*

Let me serve you a little longer.

"You killed her." The moment ends, shredded by Cloud. "You killed her at Pumice Pass," she snarls, "and you dare to present this?"

Paper tears.

"Cloud!"

Ren's voice is pained, but pain is good—this will work—

"She's wrong, you know." I almost jump, which would be

Crow's goal. Show Ren that the corpse lives, and this alliance will crumble.

"Chanmei didn't kill you," Crow continues. "I did."

Semantics. I already know they both planned the ambush—

"In the beginning, I asked her to spare you. 'Have her join us,' I said. But you refused, so what could I do but end you?" It takes everything in me to keep my eyes closed as his voice drifts near. "Remember? How you took my face in your hands? You thought you had me in your ruse. But all the while, I had you in mine. I knew you'd found the antidote in my pocket. I replaced it with poison. It'd have killed you, had you not been caught in the ambush we set for Ren's warriors."

He's lying, like he lied about Cicada's diminutive.

But I recall my nausea at the Battle of the Scarp, how sluggish my mind and body felt.

"Only at your shrine did I come to terms with what had really happened: The arrow killed you before my poison could. I held it by the shaft, and waited. Guilt had plagued me; I waited for the truth to absolve it. But the guilt stayed. I killed you. The moment I chose between you and my kingdom, I killed you.

"And even as I am, I will choose again. I will kill you again. I will take back this body and you can haunt me for a turn." He has no physicality to him, but I swear I can feel his breath on my cheek as he murmurs, "Well, how was that for a try? Did I rattle you?"

No, I think, even as my heart pounds faster than it has in days. If anyone could challenge me from beyond the grave, it *would* be Crow, but not for the reason he thinks. Instead of remembering the night Crow described—the night I kissed him, then stole the poison—I remember her. *Shuaimei.* The true object of Crow's affections. For me, he has nothing but hate. And I—I hated him too, right after realizing he was Cicada's spy. But now I feel only empty. That he meant to kill me is ground we've covered. I mind the lies more. *Stop, Crow.*

I know you never really grieved me, so stop acting.

"You're right," says Cicada, and I return my mind to the hall. My goal is in reach. No one can shake me, not Cloud, not Crow.

"You're right," Cicada repeats to Cloud. "We did kill Zephyr. We saw her as a threat, one that would be later used against us. But should the heavens see our alliance as genuine, then your strength can only be mine and mine yours. Such a transgression will never repeat itself."

"Oxshit. You grovel because you're losing—"

"That's enough, Cloud."

Silence falls for Ren.

What will she say next? Will she be the lordess I followed out of Thistlegate, drawn to her values, or will she be the person I need, but also fear her becoming? My heart and mind are at war when Ren says, "The Westlands accept your terms. Our fight ends in the Marshlands."

And it's what I wanted, but my heart twists at the tiredness in her voice. "I'll ride to the front lines myself to send the word."

"You must come south first and formalize the alliance," Cicada says.

Wait. No. Miasma will soon be receiving my drawings of Ren's camps. We need to unite our troops—

"The soldiers' lives take precedence," Ren asserts. "Formalization can wait—"

"We'll write to the front lines." Ku's voice, emerging from the wings. "Have them lay down their arms."

Insufficient for Ren. I know that even before she says, "Sikou Hai, you send the word."

"Queen Xin . . ." Sikou Hai pauses. *You can't actually go south*, I will him to tell her. He must convince her—

"Sikou Hai will pass on the word personally to Aster, Bracken, and our generals," Ren announces before he can.

"Then my strategist November will join him and communicate the same to our generals," Cicada says, and before I can even think about climbing out of my coffin to stop this madness, Cloud is speaking.

"Go south, then." Her voice moves closer. "Go alone." Even closer.

Swords unsheathe—and clang, blades intercepted.

"I could kill you now," Cloud says, and I just *know* her glaive is pointed at Cicada. "You'd be easier to cut than wheat."

"Gao Yun!"

"But it's on account of the sister I thought I knew—"

"Cloud, no—"

A gasp. Something patters. A metallic smell curls up my sinuses. My eyelids loosen; through my lashes, I see a hazy Tourmaline, one hand on Cloud's arm. But she couldn't stop her; Blue Serpent's blade is red with blood.

More blood pours from Cloud's other palm.

"—I'm giving back the oath we swore. I can't share this heaven and earth with someone who killed our swornsister. I can't share it with someone who sides with them either."

With a snap of her cloak, Cloud strides from the hall.

No.

"Lordess—Queen—" Tourmaline starts.

"Let her go."

No, Tourmaline. Go after her. But she listens to Ren's order, and I let my eyes fall back shut, fighting the urge to screw them. Cloud lives; Ren lives; I ended the battle that would have killed them.

But did I also end their sisterhood?

In the dark, Crow's voice returns.

"Everyone says Miasma is cruel." Someone slides the lid back over the coffin, sealing me in with the spirit who haunts me. "If only they knew you."

三十九

SOUTHBOUND

If only they knew you.

If only Ren and Cloud really did. Then I'd tell Ren not to go south.

Tell her to chase down Cloud.

Instead, I have to play dead as Ren says, "Let me have a word with Cicada." I'd like to as well. What is she thinking, suggesting a detour? Crow would know, but my mind is Zephyr's. So is my heart, lurching when I hear Ren's voice again, over the din of the departing soldiers.

"His name was Crow, wasn't it?"

Cicada waits, for the last boot thuds to fade, for the hall to empty of everyone but Ren and Tourmaline, who I heard insisting on staying. "Yes," she then says.

The answer echoes through the quiet.

He must have meant a lot to you. I sense the words on the tip of Ren's tongue. It's a strength and a flaw, her ability to empathize with anyone.

"I know we both still have our doubts," she settles on. "Our losses too, from the last time we joined forces. You'd like to formalize the alliance. I understand why. But we can formalize it here in this hall." *Yes.* Thank heavens Ren has the sense. "As for the Marshlands, there's no need to cede them. They were once the South's, and so to the South they should return." Ren says it as eloquently as I always knew she would, had I reminded her of Cicada's outstanding request. "After our war against Miasma is won, I will oversee their transfer to you. You have my word."

And before the war is won, I will ensure that Ren's troops still have access to it, now that I'm Crow. It's perfect, I think, as Cicada's voice sounds.

"Unfortunately, I need more than your word."

Thump-thump. The heavy crash of armor.

What—

The coffin lid slides away to Cicada's face. "Are you okay?" she asks, helping me up.

I don't answer. Can't. Mind blank, I stare at Ren's and Tourmaline's bodies, heaped on the ground.

"I know, I know. I shouldn't have been so hasty. But we'll never get a chance like this again!" Cicada waves a hand excitedly, and I spy the tiny reed tube between her fingers. *A dart shooter.* Filled with needles, tipped in poison.

I suddenly feel poisoned as well.

Don't panic. Stay Cicada's strategist. "The Marshlands—"

"Are most definitely ours now." Cicada's eyes gleam. "With Xin Ren as our hostage."

Hostage. Not dead. No relief fills me at the fact. "K—" *Wrong.* I cough. "November—she's with Xin Ren's people—"

"Precisely, so they won't think I have the nerve to capture their lordess. But they also won't hurt her, as they've already proved once." Cicada helps me out of the coffin. "Isn't it perfect? As far as her troops know, Ren agreed to come. And with a warrior like that for protection? What could possibly happen to her?"

With a slippered foot, she nudges Tourmaline, whose eyes are open. So are Ren's. They're immobile but conscious to witness the betrayal. "How long do you think it'll take for their troops to realize they didn't come with us willingly?" Cicada asks, and I taste bile.

Even if they realize it, Sikou Hai will assume everything is under control with me here as Crow.

"A while," I say, seeing no point to lying.

"Then let's go. Let's make it home before their armies come to their senses."

She clucks, and the two soldiers step forward to haul Tourmaline up. Cicada crouches by Ren and takes one of her arms. "Help, Senge!"

I should have killed her when I had the chance.

I should have wrung her neck.

But what can I do now?

I go to her as ordered and help her drag my lordess.

‡ ‡ ‡

Shame on me, and shame on Crow for his choice in liege. *Xiao-chan listens to counsel?* And I thought *my* lies were bold.

But try as I might, I can't sustain my anger at Crow. He promised Cricket he'd serve Cicada. What would I have done, if I'd reached Ren too late at Taohui and her dying wish was that I serve someone else? I don't know. I didn't reach Ren too late.

I succeeded—in making her Cicada's captive on this southbound boat.

Belowdecks, I relegate myself to the shadows while Cicada, lantern in hand, approaches the crate. Light falls over Ren in one hay-scattered corner. Tourmaline is in the other. Both are still slumped from the poison—refreshed as we'd crossed the Diyu Mountains—but it's wearing off. Tourmaline stirs, and Ren's eyes crack apart. She grasps at the bare hollow of her throat and Cicada says, "I believe you're looking for this."

She opens her hand; the pendant drops down, hung around her fingers.

Mine are crushed in my fists. I couldn't stop Cicada from taking the pendant or opening it, extracting from it a pearl of paper that she now unfolds.

"You really are a caricature of yourself, wearing this by your heart . . ." She holds up the sheet, fully spread. *Free me from Miasma*, it says, the words finished off with Xin Bao's seal.

"Is this why you're so committed?" Cicada asks Ren. "Because you're following an imperial edict?"

Silence.

Cicada refolds the decree and places it back into the pendant. "I'm told you only met your empress once." She clicks the two halves shut. "I'm sorry you couldn't see her before she died."

Everything stills.

It can't be true. Not according to fate—unless I've triggered a change. But *why* would Miasma kill her puppet? I look to Crow and he stares back at me, as if daring me to ask him. *Damn you, Crow!* I can't ask Cicada either. Xin Bao's status is either a fact I should know, or—

"A lie." Cicada smiles. "Xin Bao is alive, at least as of a week ago according to my spies." A servant sets a cushion before the crate, and Cicada sits. "I just wanted to see your reaction."

Ren's eyes close, a lifetime of relief to a single blink.

Another servant delivers a pot of tea and two cups. Cicada pours.

She pushes a cup through the bars.

"I last had this tea with Zephyr. I liked her. She was the one who told me I should speak and act my mind. She made it look so easy, even as she proceeded to be wrong on every count, including our alliance. She led you astray."

It's true. If not for me, Ren and Tourmaline wouldn't be on this boat, traveling away from the Marshlands just when my diagram to Miasma is spurring her to bear down.

"Maybe she meant to trick you like she tricked Miasma," Cicada muses, and fury pains my lungs.

"I am not Miasma." A dry rasp from Ren. Just those words, her first, and none in defense of Zephyr. *Good*, I think as the pain in my lungs mounts, forcing out a cough.

I don't deserve defending.

"No, you're not." Cicada drinks, and sets down the emptied cup. "You're worse. You hemmed and you hawed about taking your uncle's lands, and still they landed into your lap, through no effort of your own. Face the truth, Ren. Among the three of us, you're the dimmest, the least deserving. Need a reminder? Come here, Crow."

I've changed my mind; for Cicada, death would be too kind a punishment.

I emerge from the shadows, face bare. I'd planned on donning the advisor's mask, had Cicada not wrecked the re-alliance. In the light, I see her pleased expression. I absorb Ren's and Tourmaline's next, their reactions to me no longer muted by the poison.

"Soulless." The word cuts deeper than Cloud's worst, coming from Tourmaline. "You won't be reincarnated in the next life," she says to me, and if only she knew the price I've paid to return and win, though at this rate, a loss might be more likely. My nails dig into my palms.

Who cares about the next life if I can't have what I want in this one?

"Sit with that a bit," Cicada says to the two of them, rising to her feet. "The knowledge you were deceived by a corpse. Let's go, Crow."

"In a moment. Let my presence taunt them more."

Cicada nods, then departs first, leaving me with the lantern and the captives. She trusts Crow this much, at least.

Too bad she didn't trust him enough to listen.

But she was right on one thing: I was wrong. Not just about Cicada, but about the Rising Zephyr Objective. I squeeze my fists harder, warmth welling under my nails. I should tell Ren and Tourmaline who I am and save them—

"So the act is up." Ren's voice. "I was willing to let it pass the first time I noticed, but then, of course, your lordess had to make a point of it again and again."

The first time? My brow furrows. "Elaborate."

"I saw you flinch in the coffin."

First Cicada rendering me speechless, now Ren. "Why not leave when you realized the deception?"

I try to sound collected, but my breath hitches when Ren says, "Because Qilin was right. No matter how much I wish to make you and your lordess pay for Lotus's death, Qilin was right. We cannot march north without you on our side. And if the alliance is not to be and your lordess kills me now, then at least no one else will have to die for a dream doomed to fail."

The boat murmurs and creaks. The lantern at my feet sputters, light wavering. But not Ren. I thought I was leading her out of the shadows, but once again, she's leading me, just like she did at Thistlegate.

If she still believes in the Zephyr who came up with the Objective, then I must too.

It's not time to give up on this disguise yet.

I'll just have to think of a solution. I turn away, stiffening when Ren asks, "Did you ever care for her?

"When you came to her shrine," she says as I turn back, "you said it was to pay your respects. I thought then that you might have been a friend. Were you, or was it another act?"

"Of what difference is it to you?"

"I'd like to know Qilin had a friend while she was here in this world."

I did. I do. She's right next to you. But I keep my eyes on Ren as Crow, blithe smile and all. "I did care for her," I say, and on a whim, "I loved her. She was my sun. My air." Anything to make Crow cringe after the litany of lies he spewed in the coffin.

"She was my only equal in this realm," I wax on. "But it was not enough to save her." I crouch, meeting Ren's gaze through the bars. "I respected her because we were the same: We chose our kingdoms over each other."

Wait for me, Ren, to turn this around.

I won't let you down.

‡ ‡ ‡

I lock myself into my cabin for the rest of the night, stewing in my thoughts. Cicada told me she'd take them as hostages, but can I trust her? Would she lie even to Crow? I can't know, can't check. I curse, and thunder rumbles. Is it my powers? No, still depleted. I seethe as the storm brews without my permission, the river growing as restless as my mind.

Cicada, restless too, returns to Ren like a cat who can't resist toying with a mouse.

"I'll give you a choice," she says to Ren as I assume my place beside my false lordess, my real one so excruciatingly close. "A finger to free your warrior."

"Done."

"Ren—" Tourmaline starts.

"*I* am not Miasma," Cicada speaks over her. "The South is above such barbaric tactics." I beg to differ; her treatment of the Fen pirate was hardly civilized.

Still, it's clear that Cicada prefers mind games. The rest of her remains opaque. How can she taunt Ren, then sound genuinely curious when she asks, "What's that?"

Ren holds up a mass of hay, woven. "Soles for shoes, I hope."

"Even your talents are disappointing."

Ren smiles, amused rather than affronted. "When my mother fell ill, we had no money. Only hay in the stables." She picks up a piece from the bottom of the crate and weaves it through. "I'd make shoes and try to trade them in for medicine."

"These pity stories might work on your followers, but not me." A second passes. "What was your mother ill with?"

"Typhoid."

"The epidemics never reached the Westlands."

"We'd left by then." I'm thinking Ren will leave it at that when she says, "My uncle had banished us." She even answers Cicada's nascent question. "It was over a prophecy, given to him by a wandering sage." She pulls on the hay strand, blending it down into the mass. "Someday, the sage said, I would betray the clan."

Cicada sniffs, but I focus. I already knew Ren was genuine about the alliance, enough to abandon the war of reprisal, to look past the betrayal, but will Cicada meet her halfway? "Is that why you fight for Xin Bao?" asks the Southlands queen. "To prove a prophecy wrong?"

"She's family."

"I didn't see Xin Gong lining up to save her."

"She's family," Ren repeats, a reason unconditional in its simplicity.

"So was your swornsister, Lotus," Cicada counters. "You

surprised me, when you went on your rampage. Frustrating as it was, you almost had my admiration." She sighs. "And then you returned to being the Ren we all know."

"And who would that person be?"

"Oh, stop playing the fool."

"No, really: Who is this person everyone in the realm seems to know better than myself?" Through the shoe, Ren weaves more hay. "I'm sure you know this feeling too, of being tugged in a hundred different directions, by a hundred different voices. They all live in your heart, and they are all at odds. In avenging Lotus, I thought I was listening to myself. And I was—but I wasn't listening to the people or to my late strategist, who make me a leader. But is a leader all that I am?" Ren's voice goes quiet. "I don't know. Can a person be more than one thing at once?"

Yes, I want to say. I was a strategist and a warrior—

And I failed as both.

"That's exactly your problem," Cicada says. "You think too much about other people."

"If a kingdom is made up of people, so is a person."

"So if you were doing something you believed to be right, but the world thought it evil, would you see it as evil?"

"Yes," says Ren without any hesitation. "You must too."

Cicada makes a face. "What makes you say so?"

"Because you said you're not Miasma, and Miasma doesn't care what the world thinks."

"It sounds like a freeing way to live."

"Maybe," concedes Ren. "I thought so, some days. Other days, she seemed like the least free person on earth."

"You know her well."

"Well enough. Did you know"—Ren lowers her voice, and Cicada leans in—"our parting words were that I'm only allowed to die to her sword? It's a glory she won't let anyone else claim, unless they want war." A beat. Cicada frowns, and Ren laughs. "A joke!"

To Ren, it might be a joke, but not to Cicada. Clearly this wasn't something she considered before she darted Ren, and I see an opportunity when Cicada says, "Are you sure it's just a joke? My strategist here did once caution me against stepping over Miasma to get to you."

Finally, a gift from Crow.

"What did he say would happen if you did?" asks Ren.

Cicada looks to me, and this is my chance. I take the leap and say, "She'll retaliate. She might even come south." May Cicada think twice—

"That's a worry you needn't have," Ren laughs again, and now *I* frown. *Just lie, Ren!* Cicada still appears unsure, and Ren goes on, "If you want to bet on it, you can write to her. Tell her you've taken me hostage. If Miasma doesn't come, I ask that you wear my straw shoes for a month."

Before my eyes, the tension in Cicada is defused. Ren's joking indeed. "And if Miasma does come knocking on my doors," says the Southlands queen, "I'll hand you over alive for her to steam."

"Or fry. Sometimes she likes frying."

Disdain crimps Cicada's lips—or is she suppressing a smile? When she leaves, I almost sense an air of reluctance. But Cicada and I also had interesting conversations, and it made no difference.

Ren is the difference. Only Ren could show her captor such sincerity. She is the sun in this dark, war-torn world, and I'll force Cicada to behold her.

I just need another plan, preferably one that works with Ren's strengths and not against.

‡ ‡ ‡

By morning, the rains abate. We're due to dock at dawn on the banks of the Gypsum, west of the Southern Court, and on Cicada's orders, I send word for a carriage to be readied onshore to cover the remaining distance.

When I return belowdecks, Cicada is before the crate and Ren is holding up a pair of finished shoes. "For you."

"To gather dust in my bureau." But Cicada takes them, and for a change, Ren asks her a question.

"Why do you hold so much anger toward our empress?"

"Yours," Cicada says. "Not mine."

Ren waits.

"She's complicit in Miasma's crimes."

"She's only a child."

"She *was* a child." Cicada stands taller, head erect. "She didn't grow up. I did the day the Fen killed my sister."

While the Fen's incursions into the Southlands are no secret, Ren knows more than the average peasant. *Behind every tree that dares to grow tall is a taller mountain*, I'd once told her. *Miasma was the Fen's.* Now Ren's eyes soften, but Cicada has already swept away. "How dare she compare us," she mutters, and my thoughts churn as I follow. The Fen pirate attack is still an unhealed wound for Cicada. If I were to press on it . . . if she bled for a single, vulnerable moment . . .

It's a plan. Risky, but it just might work.

Crow will despise me for it.

"You've been quiet," he remarks after Cicada and I part to our respective cabins.

"As have you. Isn't this what you and your lordess have always dreamed of? Ren brought low? Used for ransom?"

"Is it? Ah, right," says Crow. "You only have my body, not my thoughts."

He still thinks I got lucky with Chanmei. How easily I could shatter that assumption by telling him about Cricket.

But some of us have self-restraint. "A good thing I don't have your thoughts. It must be depressing, serving a lordess who doesn't respect you enough to listen."

"Is it a revelation to you that people can be surprising?"

"'Surprising' is *quite* the euphemism."

"Not everyone is a chess piece, Zephyr, least of all the people we serve. I grew up with Cicada. I know her."

"*Knew*," I correct. "You knew Cicada. She grew up more, without you."

Crow's expression changes, a shift so minute, only a person fluent in his face would notice. I try not to, but it stays with me—the way I hit at a truth atop a deeper, more painful truth. Cicada grew up without Crow at her side.

Cricket also died without Crow at her side.

I didn't mean to remind him. Crow's to blame for starting the conversation, I tell myself as I enter my cabin and sit, reaching for the cup of tea on the table.

"The steam," Crow says.

"What of—"

I break off.

The rising vapor is tinged green.

My hand jerks away, knocking over the cup. Liquid pools, green as the glass bottle once offered to me on a palm.

The Elixir of Forgetting.

Remember yourself, Nadir had urged when I'd returned to the heavens after dying as Qilin.

Remember myself, and forget the mortals.

My gaze flashes up. "Come out!"

No one does.

"Come out! I know you're here!"

No response.

The boat sways around us.

I stand and look under the table. Under the bed. Between the blankets. I sit back down, chest heaving, and stare at the cup.

The spill is gone.

But it was there. I saw it. The trembling starts in my fingertips and crawls up my arms. The Masked Mother had promised me that my sisters wouldn't be able to stop me, but couldn't they have, just now? I'd have drunk the tea, if not for Crow—

Crow, who had no obligation to alert me. Maybe he didn't understand what he saw, but he saw enough. He knew the tea had been tampered with. Did he speak up to save his own skin from some supposed poison?

202 ‡ JOAN HE

I should let him keep thinking that.

"Did you know what that was?" I hear myself ask instead. Crow waits, silent. I look to him. "A tea for forgetting."

"What would you have forgotten?"

If Nadir and Dewdrop are trying to stop me from changing fate and paying the Masked Mother's ultimate price for it? "Everything I'm trying to accomplish."

"I see." Crow glances to the overturned cup. "If only it hadn't spilled then."

His tone is light. His expression. It's so at odds with the moment that a laugh escapes me. Crow smiles, rueful, and I grow rueful too. Letting me drink the tea was Crow's *only* play in a game where I hold the pieces. He threw his one chance away. Would he do it again, knowing the tea's effects?

No, I think; then, as I stare into Crow's eyes, I grow uncertain.

Surely not.

Surely he'd let me drink the tea.

Right?

It doesn't matter. Not the choices Crow would or would not have made, with all the information, or what my sisters think. I hold my arms around myself until the trembling stops. *Dewdrop. Nadir. If you can hear this, then for the last time—*

I want this.

I don't regret my choice.

And if you really just tried to drug me to stop me—

Then I'd rather not have you for sisters.

‡ ‡ ‡

We dock and travel by carriage, as planned. Cicada again darts Ren—"I've had enough of her righteousness"—and like before, I can't do anything to stop her.

That all changes tonight.

At the Southlands capital, Cicada has Ren and Tourmaline put into cangues. The wooden boards are yoked over their heads, their wrists slotted through the holes under their chins. I watch the mechanisms carefully, tempering my rage as rope is wrapped around their waists and Cicada leads them through the streets like animals, all the way to Nightingale Pavilion.

She's outdone herself, judging by the court's stricken faces when we step in.

"Tomorrow, we'll send word to Ren's troops that I've captured their lordess," Cicada declares from her dais. "We'll demand the immediate return of the Marshlands if they want her back alive. Any questions?

"Good," Cicada says when none are forthcoming. Her advisors clearly don't know what they're dealing with. I do, though, and tonight, after the feast "to commemorate the occasion," I will rip away Cicada's shell and remind her that at her core, she is still the girl I first met, desperately trying to prove her worth.

My mistake was not in underestimating her this time, but in overestimating her capabilities as a staid leader.

‡ ‡ ‡

The feast begins at dusk. Partway through, I slip away, the revelry ambient as I delve into the courtyards. It's been half a year, but I remember where to turn, which galleries to take.

The path to my destination.

When I return, my robes are wet. I change into a dry set. The sky has darkened, as has Crow's silence.

I knew he'd wish, in retrospect, that I'd drunk the tea and forgotten.

The feast winds down, and Cicada rises. At her waist, she wears Ren's double swords like ornaments. Ren and Tourmaline, meanwhile, remain in their cangues.

Cicada walks to them. "I'll offer you one chance at freedom. Submit to me."

"I cannot," Ren says, "as your ally."

"Very well, then." Cicada takes the rope; I join her. "Perhaps you'll change your mind after seeing how we deal with enemies of the South. Guards, bring up the Xin warrior."

We leave the feast courtyard, Cicada leading Ren at the front, Tourmaline escorted at the rear, and I between them. I know where we're going—Cicada couldn't resist showcasing her prize captive to Zephyr either—and as we walk, I sidle up behind Ren. I make sure Cicada is focused on the path ahead, a path that eventually bends around a courtyard's wall. Before Tourmaline and the guards can clear the corner, I reach under the back of Ren's cangue.

Two pins fasten the wooden halves. I find the first and slide it out. The cangue loosens, and Ren breathes in. "What are you doing?"

"Quiet."

"Your lordess has not ordered me freed." She pulls away just as I reach for the second pin. Tourmaline and her guards round the corner behind us, and I shorten my strides, growing the gap between myself and Ren.

So close. The pin stabs into my fist. *So close!*

But not close enough. All too soon, we're at the final moon gate. The guards hold Tourmaline back, condemning the warrior to watch as Ren is tugged forward. A draft hugs us as Crow furiously circles Cicada. Undeterred, she unlocks the doors and pulls. The halves of stone open. Light from the lake beyond ripples over the Southlands lordess, who doesn't step through immediately.

Instead, she waits.

Has Crow succeeded? Dare I hope he has? Not everything has gone to plan. *Will Ren be ready for what's to come?*

Will one pin loosened be enough?

It will have to be, because Cicada was only waiting for Ren. "After you," she says, and follows in Ren's wake. I follow in Cicada's, my gaze on the back of her head as she descends the steps. Her emotions are hidden to me. Her thoughts. But I can sense the moment that both shift, as she notices the trail of wet footsteps leading out from the lake.

The lake that holds no pirate.

四十

SPLIT STONE

No pirate.

Ren wouldn't know there should be one, chained to the slab center-lake, but Cicada does.

The night goes hush.

"Guards." She begins to turn, her coronet glinting—

—then *pinging* off the steps as she's knocked flat. The pirate leans over her, hands at her neck—then he's flying back, bowled over by Ren. The two land halfway to the lake with a bone-splitting *crack*, and something between my brain and body snaps. *Ren!* I should go to Cicada—I'm Crow—but *Ren. Let go!* I want to shout as she locks her legs around the pirate. He's malnourished but unchained, whereas Ren's wrists are still cangued.

You've done enough! Let go!

But Ren is Ren, and when the pirate twists free and launches up the steps, she hurls herself after him, yelling *"Cloud, now!"*

Consciously or not, the pirate slows, searching for the new threat. Ren closes the gap, and I move too, to Cicada. I help her sit up just as the pirate seizes one of Ren's swords hanging from

Cicada's sash. Fabric tears—the weapon now his—and I brace, prepared to block the attack.

Not prepared when the pirate rounds on Ren.

He swings, and I can't breathe. Even as metal strikes wood and the pirate stumbles, sword lodged in the cangue, I can't. Breathe. Someone darts past us. *Tourmaline?* Nearing the duo. *How—?* The pirate frees the blade, and my confusion melts. *Faster, Tourmaline.* He lifts the sword over Ren.

Faster!

The sword falls.

Out of the pirate's hands.

He stumbles. Lurches.

Collapses backward on the steps.

Under my palms, Cicada's shoulders jerk, her breathing ragged. She lowers the dart shooter—and raises it again as Tourmaline storms toward us, her cangue in splintered halves around each wrist. I struggle to my feet, putting myself in her path as Ren calls out, "Tourmaline. Stand down."

"She has Virtue."

"I know." Ren climbs the steps, and I breathe. *She's okay.* Only her cangue is damaged. Tourmaline snaps it off entirely, and Ren faces us. "Did he hurt you?"

"No," says Cicada. I help her up. "He barely touched me."

Because of Ren. She acted as I predicted, rescuing her captor—not that I expect Cicada to thank her.

Together, she and Ren stare at the pirate sprawled on the steps. His eyes are closed, blood trickling out the corner of his mouth, the dart in the left side of his neck.

Ren squats and checks for a pulse.

"Well?" Cicada has the gall to prompt.

"He lives." Ren withdraws her hand. "He must have hit his head."

Here is where Cicada offers an explanation, and at last, she does. "He was a prisoner of mine." She looks to the side. "A Fen pirate. I don't know how he got free. But I'll take care of him."

She calls for the guards.

None come.

"They're incapacitated." Tourmaline bows to Ren before Cicada can speak. "Forgive me for breaking orders."

In the silence, a picture emerges, one where Tourmaline could have defeated the guards whenever she wished. That she didn't is because of Ren's orders—given, I realize, to preserve Cicada's illusion of superiority. Only then, Ren surmised, would the girl speak her mind and heart.

She's been putting on a show again, without my help.

Something twangs in me, even though this is good. This is good, that Ren can fend for herself. My gaze falls to the stone step under her feet. It's cracked, like Ren's cangue. Was that the sound from earlier? Wood breaking stone? It should be impossible. But nothing is.

It just takes the right person.

Ren reaches for the fallen sword. "Even stone can split." She rises, careful and slow, with the weapon. "I may have lost my strategist at the Scarp, but together, we defeated Miasma's navy there." She faces Cicada. "United, we can defeat her again."

"And after Miasma?"

A simple question, but Cicada places it like a chess piece. After Miasma is Xin Bao.

How will Ren respond, knowing her and Cicada's differences?

"After is after," Ren says. "Until then, let's protect each other, eh?"

Cicada raises a brow.

"I don't want to pretend we have the same goals, but we can be equals. You have my word, and if that's not enough, you have my sword." Ren nods at Virtue, strung to Cicada's sash. "Keep it."

The cicadas start to sing. Or maybe I finally have the mind to notice them. At last.

Everything is happening as I orchestrated.

"Your Highness!"

A soldier, at the top of the steps. "It was her!" he cries as we look to him, pointing his sword at Tourmaline. "That warrior! She attacked us—"

"Yes, I've heard," Cicada says, voice dry. "I take it that the others have not yet regained their senses." The soldier hesitates, then nods. "Casualties?"

"None, Your Highness."

Cicada's silence is singed. Honorable Ren and her warrior, I can hear her thinking, being oh-so-careful not to hurt the enemy. What a joke she must seem to them! "Take them back to the feast courtyard," she commands.

"By myself?" asks the soldier, and I can hardly fault the quaver in his voice.

"I see no one else."

"Should I take them as prisoners?"

"Just take them!" Cicada snaps. "Keep them in the courtyard and await my arrival."

"Lead the way," Ren says to the soldier, which only seems to fluster him more. He reaches for Tourmaline—rethinks it—then leads the way, as suggested, with Ren and Tourmaline following freely.

Cicada lets them go. She unstrings Virtue from her sash. The cicadas continue to sing.

An ungodly peal interrupts them as Virtue hits the steps, chucked down.

"They're exactly the same," Cicada growls while I blink at the new crack in the stone, crossing the one made by Ren's cangue in an X. "Exactly the same!" Cicada kicks the sword, and my eyes narrow. Gifted or not, it's still Ren's. I bend for it, then notice a glint several steps lower.

Cicada's coronet.

Retrieve that first. I do, returning to Cicada as she says, "When she called out for her swornsister—it felt genuine. She really wanted to help me. And in that moment . . ."

"You saw Cricket."

Cicada's gaze swings to me. I hold it, confidence rewarded when she nods.

"I felt Cricket's judgment, as if she were standing right here, if I were to let the pirate kill Ren." She stomps on the sword. "They're exactly the same in all the worst ways!"

The tinny reverberation of metal against stone fades, the cicadas reasserting their dominance. But *are* they cicadas? A cicada's cry is harsher, closer to a screech. This song is sweet.

Cricket song.

I glance at the coronet in my hand, circumference smooth save for a seam. The metal's been cut, resized instead of reforged. Another head was meant to wear it.

Cricket's.

"She can't stop me," Cicada whispers, sinking to a crouch, arms around her legs, as my grip hardens around the coronet. If Cicada speaks as though Cricket still lives, that's because she does in the minds of many, including Crow's. He loved her. Cicada may have loved her sister too, but step by step, she's also trying to prove to the court that she is not Cricket. Her grudges run deeper. Her dreams are grander.

She hungers after the empire.

Enemy though she may be, I can relate to her ambition. Then Cicada whispers, "Just watch me: I *will* kill Xin Bao," and my empathy dies. I settle the coronet on her head; her eyes flick up. "You support my aspirations?"

"Of course," I say—hissing as Cicada kicks me in the shin, standing faster than I can blink.

"Don't lie. You've been quiet ever since we took Ren hostage. I know, Crow, I know," she says, and I can almost hear her thoughts in the silence.

I know you loved my sister.

I know you too think I'm not as good as her.

And if she says so? How do I answer? Do I tell what I think is the truth? Or do I lie?

"You don't think I should covet the throne," is what she says out loud, to my relief—and interest. Crow approved betraying the Ren-Cicada alliance. But I suppose neutralizing Ren, Xin Bao's protector, isn't quite interchangeable with killing the empress. If I were really Crow, I'd protect Cicada *and* her legacy. Even Miasma dares not wear the crown of empress-slayer.

But I'm not Crow. I don't have to want what's best for his lordess. "I've been gone a long time, Chanmei," I say. "And now Shuaimei's gone too. For over a year, you've run this kingdom alone. I trust you to know what you want."

"So you don't disapprove?"

I shake my head.

"You don't mind that I've changed?"

"I've changed too," I say, hoping Cicada might agree and tell me how, so that I can be a better Crow.

But even on this she doesn't cooperate. "That's questionable. Though, I suppose your standards have lowered." She gives me a sidelong look. "I really did ask that she join us, after I received your letter."

She? Who is she?

Crow's voice comes back to me.

I asked her to spare you. Another lie, I'd assumed. But *Cicada* would have no reason to lie. Then *why*—

A moan rises. *The pirate.* Still down—

A finger twitches.

Before I can say a thing, Cicada picks up Ren's sword, marches over, and smacks his head. He stills once more, and Cicada sighs.

"He'll need to be moved back to the lake." She glances to the moon gate. "I can't believe our guards are so useless."

Not useless, just unlucky to have faced Tourmaline for an opponent. "I'll rechain him."

"You? Can you even move him by yourself?"

I'll show you. I grab the pirate by the armpits and tug.

He doesn't budge.

Cicada sighs again. "Clearly not. Slow down, before you get another ulcer."

"Another?"

"Am I misremembering?" Together, we haul the pirate, Cicada grunting with every step. "Was it—someone else—who almost broke—their spine—" We splash into the water. "—giving November a piggyback ride?" Cicada gasps out, then curses. "This is much harder than moving Ren," she says, and I snort, to my chagrin, then blame it on the absurdity of the situation.

"I trust that you can secure the chains?" Cicada pants when we reach the slab at the center of the lake.

"Yes," I pant back.

"Good. I'll have your head if he escapes again."

"Why mine?" She splashes me and I raise my hands. "Okay, okay! My head, then. What are you going to do?"

"Return the sword to Ren. I don't want it." Cicada picks up her skirts to go, then looks back. "Make sure you change into dry clothes. An ulcer might not kill you, but pneumonia will."

Is this what it's like to have a childhood friend? Hauling bodies together? Getting kicked, splashed, insulted? If so, I wasn't missing anything.

Still, as I watch Cicada walk up the steps, I find myself

wondering if she would want what she wants if she were born into a different role. Not the heir to a kingdom, or the younger sibling in the shadow of an older, but just a girl.

Just a girl.

But of course, she's not just a girl, no matter how much she acts like one around Crow. And I'm not just Crow. My gaze falls to her wet tracks, overlapping with the pirate's.

I made sure not to leave any when I was here, earlier.

Yes, I was here. Masked, I'd shucked off my boots before wading into the lake, where the pirate was chained.

I'd put my lips to his ear.

Listen closely, if you want vengeance.

Within the hour, I'll lead the Southlands lordess through those gates. You'll have but one chance.

Avenge your brethren then.

I'd loosened his chains partially, enough to grant me a head start. Otherwise, he'd surely have caught me and asked why I was helping. I wasn't. I was only setting the stage for Ren to save Cicada, thereby marking the Southlands lordess's heart in a variation of Injure Yourself to Wound the Enemy. The pirate was but a pawn. He's served his purpose.

Now to end him, lest he talk upon waking. As soon as Cicada is gone, I crouch and plunge my hand into the water, searching the lake bed for a suitable rock. I'll make it quick and merciful, compared to Cicada's treatment; I still remember watching the monks torture the pirate. Granted, I hadn't believed in things such as qì and spirits then. I also hadn't murdered someone. Or worse.

Oh, I've done so much worse.

Isn't that right, Crow? He was my lone witness as I'd freed the pirate, and how his disapproval chilled me to the bone. He's been quiet since, and while I'm used to feeling alone . . .

Now I'm too alone.

I look up.

Crow?

Slowly, I rise, knee-deep in the lake.

He's nowhere in sight. Not beside me or before me.

Which leaves . . .

Turn—but denial roots me. Mortals *can't* take empty vessels like gods, and Crow is mortal. I've touched his spirit. I know this for certain. But then I hear it.

A clink of chains.

I turn, water sloshing around me—

Splashing as I'm pushed in.

四十一

A SMALL PRICE

*W*ater.

Becomes fire, down my nose. *Stop breathing. Go limp*—but my assailant isn't tricked. He yanks me up and I gasp—then choke. My hands scrabble at the chains, pulled taut across my throat. Air—I need—air—

My limbs start to lose feeling.

My spirit, loosening . . .

No. If only I were stronger—or had a weapon—

There is one. I release the chains. *Left side.* I reach up.

I slam my palm to his neck, driving in Cicada's dart.

The chains slacken, enough for me to grab them. I splash for the slab and lash the pirate back to it.

For several seconds neither of us speaks. We're both panting too hard. My lungs ache as if they'll never fill again. But even if I were on my last breath, I'd save a word just for him.

"That desperate, Crow?"

The pirate raises his head.

He stares at me through his bangs, running like ink over his eyes. Not Crow's eyes. But for a flicker, I see his dark lashes. His delicate jaw. His lips, dewed with water.

Lips that part. "She could have died."

His voice cracks the illusion. Even if it's his soul, somehow vested in the pirate's body, this voice is most definitely not Crow's. It's rougher. Rawer. Or maybe I'm finally hearing Crow's true emotions.

"She *could* have died," I repeat after him, allowing him this concession. "But she didn't."

"You put her in danger."

"So what if I did? She's not my lordess."

"And November? *Ku?*" The name spills out of him like poison. "Not your sister, is she?"

"What does that have to do with anything?" Crow stares at me, cold and silent, and I harden. "Ren moved to save Cicada without batting an eye. How's that for benevolent?"

A scoffing breath leaves him. "How benevolent can yours really be when her strategist is a thief? Coward? Monster?"

The water trembles between us with every hurled word.

"Go on," I say when it finally stills. "I will always welcome more sobriquets."

Crow holds my gaze, his chest rising and falling. He bows his head. His voice, when he speaks again, is low.

"You're not human."

My heart stings as if struck.

The sting dulls to a throb.

No, I'm not. Nor will I ever be.

I gave that up by coming back to Ren.

"How many times do I need to tell you, Crow?" I crouch before him in the water and crook a finger under his chin.

"I'm a god." A reminder to him, and to myself. I've seen more sights than Crow will in his lifetime. With a single gust, I've killed thousands. The words of a mortal are nothing to me. My existence does not begin and end at the place where my finger meets his chin, my skin on his . . .

My skin. On his.

Something in me keens. *He's real. I can feel him.* His breath, on my face. The pirate's body is but a bridge; Crow stands at the end of it. My thoughts stutter off. What was I going to say? What was the point I was trying to make?

I release him.

"I'm a god." Weak. "I'm a god," I repeat more fiercely, "so take it from me: Entering a body is easier than leaving."

"Maybe I won't leave," Crow says, flint-tongued.

"Suit yourself." I rise. "Stay for as long as you like."

Turning from him, I stride through the lake, ignoring the part of me that yearns to be in his physical presence for one more second, even if all he has for me is hatred.

Walk faster.

Don't look back.

It'll all be worth it, in the end.

I reach the steps and climb them, almost at the top when a familiar draft kisses my skin. I glance to my right and there he floats, moonlight limning his spirit.

"That was fast." I look back to the lake. The pirate is still chained to the slab. Is that blood I see on the stone behind his skull, or just a shadow? "What did you do to him?"

"What he deserved for killing my lordess's sister."

His voice is matter-of-fact, neither cold nor impassioned, but because I know what Cricket meant to him, I can hear the underlying emotion, a bottomless ocean that makes his fury at me seem shallow in comparison.

"Cicada shouldn't have kept him alive to torture," I finally say. "It's only because she did that I had a weapon for my strategy."

Crow doesn't speak. I wonder if he agrees. Perhaps our visions for the empire weren't so different. If the two of us still lived—him as Cicada's Crow and I as Ren's Qilin—perhaps we could have worked together. Perhaps—

I didn't need to kill him.

As an emotion, remorse is both useless and craven, and when Crow says, "I kindly ask that you refrain from voicing whatever it is that you're thinking," I'm grateful that he's not like Dewdrop. I'd never be able to meet his eye again if he could read my precise thoughts.

"Don't presume to know me." I reach out to push the stone door.

"I don't." Two soft words. "Or should I say, I won't anymore." One softer sigh. "Indeed, I respected you once."

My palm stops before the door.

Resist—

"Once?"

"What you showed today wasn't strategy." I nail my gaze to

the door as Crow says, "It was a gamble. Your 'weapon' could have very likely killed your own lordess. That he didn't, you owe to nothing but luck. Your fate seems to be blessed with a lot of it for your risks to pay off."

Fate? A mirthless smile contorts my mouth. Crow doesn't know the first thing about it. As for risk? "Didn't your mentors teach you, Crow? All strategy is risk." I push open the door and walk through the moon gate without a backward look. "You're just upset that I was willing to risk your precious Chanmei."

Courtyard after courtyard I pass through, all the way to the one that servants showed me to upon my arrival as Crow.

I stop outside his rooms, waiting for his draft to join me.

"If I were you, I wouldn't scorn luck. Because understand this: I have a war to win, and no sacrifice is too big. So pray, Crow." I seize the bamboo doors. "Pray that your lordess is lucky enough to survive all my strategies to come."

Moonlight floods the room, illuminating the wet robes I changed out of earlier, piled in the corner. I should change out of these robes as well, but first I wait for Crow.

He doesn't enter.

I close the doors. Wait some more.

Crow remains outside.

I pace to the bed, sit—shoot up when I remember whose bed it is.

My hands curl shut.

Not human? Not a problem. I prefer being a god. *Not strategy?* I'll show Crow strategy.

But whatever I'm feeling burns through me quick. When

I defected to Miasma, Crow didn't bat an eye. He understood me. He was the only person in the realm who did. But today, he looked at me like I was a stranger.

Like we weren't the same.

I'm at the doors before I realize what I'm doing. *What* am *I doing?* I should *cherish* this reprieve, my first in weeks. I turn away—then freeze.

What if he's gone?

What if he's seeking out another body?

Shck. The doors open, my arms spread wide between them, and for a breath, I'm just relieved to see him, still here as a spirit.

Then the silence bears down. Just days ago, Crow might have asked me if I needed something, insouciant and flippant.

Now he stares at me, his eyes matte and lifeless.

I slam the doors shut. *Of course he's still here.* He's bound to me. Earlier? Was a fluke. The pirate's body must have caused it; the monks *did* torture his qì for months. The rattle of bamboo quiets, and I shiver. *Change into dry robes.*

Get some sleep.

But I don't move. I stand there, against the door.

Words lump in my throat.

I never would have really hurt Cicada. I just wanted Ren to save her.

Never? Crow would probably say. *Is that a promise?*

Yes.

Why lie, Zephyr? asks my mind-Crow, and I swallow.

You lied too. You never told me about Cricket.

Omission is not lying.

What was she really like?

Why don't you find out? You're in my room. Go on, have a look through it.

No. Why am I even talking to you? Leave me.

Mind-Crow obeys before I can withdraw the order.

Moonlight shifts across the floor in the passing minutes. Maybe hours. At last, I step away, my robes no longer dripping, just sodden. Teeth chattering, I walk to the desk and sit.

I open a drawer.

In it are a bundle of handkerchiefs, neatly folded.

I glance to the doors; Crow is still outside them.

I look back to the handkerchiefs.

I pull one out, embroidered with magnolias.

I already knew Cricket was a girl of many talents, but it's another matter to feel it, each stitch neat under my fingertips. This one handkerchief is nicer than the others of Crow's I've seen. *To remember me by*, Cricket said, but Crow didn't need mementos for that. He carried her in his heart. She's the person who never left for him.

An honor I once thought mine.

The handkerchief balls in my fist. Then I scoff. Even before I learned about Cricket, I'd dealt away our future. What use would our past have been?

I refold the handkerchief and place it back with the others, then open another drawer, gathering the necessary supplies. I light the candle, grind the ink, dab the brush.

I write, because the alternative is trying for sleep, and I don't want to face Crow in my dreams. I accomplished what I wanted. Crow's resentment? It's a small price.

I've already paid more to win.

But Crow doesn't have to make the same choices, and I write this for him. The night wears on. A cough begins deep in my lungs.

Blood flecks onto the paper.

‡ ‡ ‡

Crow doesn't speak to me the next day.

Or the next.

About time I had some peace and quiet. Coughing, I walk down the open gallery, stopping to look at the scene framed between two columns.

In the courtyard, Cicada moves through a parry while Ren watches. Her wrists are in chains, same as yesterday, when Cicada took her to the Southlands shipyards in what was ostensibly a show of might. But I was present. I heard the words exchanged, two allies discussing navy strength and infantry readiness. I don't need to be by Ren to know that she must now be giving Cicada pointers on how to wield her sword, Virtue.

Under everyone's noses, she's gone from being a hostage to wearing the guise of one.

See how my risk has paid off, I almost say to Crow, then remember we're not on speaking terms. A blessing we're not; two servants float down the gallery at that moment. They stop to bow at me, their lowered eyes peeking to the courtyard when I don't relieve them at once.

"I heard our queen owes the Xin lordess a life debt," one whispers to the other when I finally let them pass.

"But she's still a prisoner."

"I know. The grudges of royalty . . . how frightful."

Thanks to me, word of Ren's altruism that night has traveled. If Cicada has spies, it'd be foolish to assume Miasma doesn't. Why not use them? Stratagem Thirty-Three—Sow Lies in Enemy Fields—is best done with the enemy's own resources. If my diagram of Ren's disorderly camps wasn't credible enough for her, then let her spies send the reports.

Ren is being held hostage.

Their troops in the Marshlands remain divided.

It won't be long at all, now, before I lure the tiger from its lair.

‡ ‡ ‡

My other pieces move as the week goes on, starting with Sikou Hai. After he arrives at the Marshlands front lines with Ku, he writes to me in a lengthy treatise that, if intercepted, would detail the breakdown of negotiations with Cicada and Ren's kidnapping. But I'm the intended recipient, and I take out another sheet of paper, marked with the chess game that Cloud and I played. Only Sikou Hai has the copy, given to him by me at Taohui.

I lay the game over his letter, reading the words in the diagonals of white stones.

Ren. Captured. Part. Of. Your. Plans.

I knew he'd think this way. Good thing it now is.

Cloud. Last spotted. West.

Now this, I didn't predict. But I should have. Cloud hasn't abandoned Ren. She awaits her at our home base, is behind her, just like Ren imagined when she yelled *Cloud, now!*

I fold up the letter and burn it to be safe. Crow made the same calculation, when he wrote to Cicada. *Do not let down your guard. The head may have fallen, but the wind may not blow in the direction we thought.* He was smart to destroy the message, especially if his mail was being monitored like Plum's. But does he now regret not sending it?

Coughing, I clear my head of Crow's regrets and go to bed as he watches, silent. He disappears when I close my eyes, only to reappear across from me in the rowboat. Koi streak the water. The sun shines over the mountains on the horizon, and I ask Crow every question too shameful to voice in the light of day.

Do you regret knowing me?

Liking me, if you ever did?

If you really asked Cicada to spare me, why?

Through it all, Crow rows on without answering, until I realize *I'm* the spirit, invisible across from him.

‡ ‡ ‡

In the morning, my throat is sore, my head is hot, and Crow—

Is fainter.

Everything else is clear, which makes sense, because everything else is real. Only Crow is a spirit. Either I'm losing the power that allows me to see his qì—

Or his spirit is fading from this world, like Lotus's.

The former. It has to be the former. I stare at him, waiting for him to sharpen. When he doesn't, I wait for him to comment on the staring, but of course he stays silent. I hate him for it. *I assure you I'm here to stay*, he'd said before.

The irony if that turned out to be a lie too.

"Senge!" The name pierces my mind, as if it's been reiterated several times. I look up, and Cicada folds her arms in the doorway. "There you finally are."

"Forgive me. What were you saying?"

"I just decoded the latest reports from our spies in the North. Miasma has mobilized her troops. We can't yet tell their exact target, but it seems like they're aiming for—"

"The Marshlands," I say, and Cicada frowns.

"Are you extrapolating, or certain?"

"Certain." I'm the hand guiding Miasma's movements.

"What was the rest of the report?" I ask, keeping Crow in my peripheral vision. Fainter. Definitely fainter.

"There've been no more Xin rebels. Plum was demoted and is under Miasma's watch—"

"Plum is alive." Cicada's nod upends my world. My board. My pieces go rolling.

Falling.

Plum is alive. Alive.

She did not die.

A miracle? No. There's only one explanation: "Miasma treated her wounds."

"Three days after interrogating her."

"What caused the change in heart?"

"The report didn't say." Cicada peers at me. "Why? Is Plum a problem?"

Yes, but not one that makes sense to any advisor, general, or soldier. "No," I say, and start to cough.

"Do I need to call the physician?"

"No. Now that Miasma is on the move, we must respond. Go call the court. Go," I insist. After Cicada does, I pull on my robes and put my hair into a ponytail, a habit regained on the road. *Ally with the South.* We've done that, again. *Establish a stronghold in the West.* We've done that too.

March on the North.

The moment I've visualized day in, day out since devising the Rising Zephyr Objective has finally arrived, but I can't savor it, my mind too fragmented.

Crow is fading. Plum is alive.

Focus. Only Plum matters. I failed to end her, but it's not too late. I'll kill her as Crow, I think, before a new fit of coughing overtakes me. I clutch the desk for support until it passes, then wipe the blood from my mouth.

I won't let her survive as fate's chosen victor.

Outside, the day is tauntingly bright, the open corridors filled with advisors all streaming in the same direction. I let the flow pull me in. Miasma is the immediate threat, Plum the far-reaching one. How do I deal with the two of them? Together? Separately? Which first? My thoughts quicken, slowing only for a name, caught on a strand of wind.

"Qilin?"

I turn, and Ren's face smooths with disappointment.

"My offense," she says from between the two guards escorting her. "I mistook you for another from the back."

You didn't, some brazen part of me wants to say, because as I stare at my lordess, I realize what I have to do.

To deal with Plum, I must leave Ren.

I won't be able to march north with her.

"No offense taken," I say, nodding at the guards to proceed. They lead Ren past me, and I breathe out, shoulders settling, more coughs emerging.

But then comes Tourmaline.

"I saw how you stood by that night." She falls into step beside me, chained but guardless. No guard, I imagine, wants that honor. "You let the pirate attack your lordess."

She's right. I did. If I *were* Crow, I'd live up to her insult of soulless. And Crow I will stay; I vowed at Taohui not to tell Tourmaline who I am, as a strategist. Now I reaffirm that decision, but as a friend.

It'd be selfish, to reunite with any of them—Tourmaline, Cloud, Ren—when I'll be saying goodbye again.

"Zephyr deserved better than you," Tourmaline says.

I walk on without replying, only coughing.

We file into Nightingale Pavilion.

"I'll get to the point," Cicada starts once we're convened. "Miasma has mobilized her troops—"

"Lordess—Queen, if I may—" An advisor clears his throat and glances to Ren. "Should we really be discussing this in front of our hostage?"

"Ah, yes," Cicada says. "You reminded me."

She descends the dais and strides down the walk, unsheathing the sword concealed in her skirts. Advisors flinch; eyes dart to the table, still here, that Cicada cut when Zephyr and Crow last visited as Miasma's delegates. Sunlight glints off the table's three remaining corners as Cicada stops before Ren, who holds out her hands, pulling the chains tight.

Virtue slices through them.

Cicada turns to the advisor. "She's our ally."

"As our queen was saying," I pick up while the court flounders, grasping for an anchor. I'll cast them one. "Miasma has mobilized her troops. Her aim is the Marshlands. Our troops already there will defend against her attack as a united front. Unbeknownst to her, however, we'll also have our own offensives, starting with one out of the South."

The court murmurs. *An offensive out of the South.* The South is known for its defense, not its offense.

Precisely why Miasma won't expect it. "And another prong out of the West," I finish, eliciting a collective breath.

"West and South offensives?"

"Yes. While the empire is preoccupied with the Marshlands, our Southern and Western prongs will target the capital. Secure Xin Bao, and we win."

Advisors confer with each other. It's true in theory—capturing the leader is the most basic of all stratagems, but—

"The terrain out of the West is ill-suited for an offensive," one pipes up.

"It'll be difficult," says Ren, diplomatic.

"It will," I assent. "But it can be done."

It must be done. The court mutters. *A three-front war.* They'll think I'm being overcautious, covering all my territorial bases. What they don't realize is that the Western prong's true objective will not be the capital.

I have my own demon to slay, out West.

Plum.

I will right my wrong of not ending you first.

"I will go west," I announce, "and join up with forces from Xin City in the Xianlei Gorge. Sikou Hai and November will face Miasma in the Marshlands. Ren and Cicada will lead the charge out from the South." That's the safest prong. Ren must make it North unharmed. *I entrust her to you, Tourmaline.* My gaze sweeps over the sun-dappled court. "Speak now, or hold your objections."

No words come.

Then Tourmaline steps forward. "Who will lead the forces out of Xin City?"

"Your queen's swornsister. Cloud." As I say so, I look to Ren. She doesn't want to speak lesser of Cloud, but she also isn't so prideful as to swallow her reservations.

"Respectfully," she demurs, "I don't know if Cloud still stands with me."

"She does," Cicada counters before I can. "Stone may split," she goes on, "but sisterhood never will."

Ren meets her gaze, then glances to Tourmaline. Something in the warrior's expression must vouch for Cloud, because Ren at last nods and Cicada lifts her chin.

"Let the order be sent to all parties."

"We march at the week's end," I finish.

The court doesn't argue, awed by the maneuver's magnitude. Only I can see its rough edges. With more time, I could have refined it, but *Plum. Crow.* I glance to him again and can't tell if he's fainter than this morning. *Not my concern.* Success is within my grasp so long as I can end Plum, my one variable—

Of two.

"This is it, isn't it?" Cicada joins me as the others leave, and I glance to her, the girl who wants Xin Bao dead. But after is after. Like Ren, I must also believe in the sincerity of the alliance.

"Yes." By tomorrow, I'll be on the road. If all goes well—if Ren secures Xin Bao and Miasma is defeated and I end Plum—I might not see Cicada again. Ever. She doesn't know that, but she does know that this is our last day together before the war is won.

What would Crow do or say, if this was farewell for now?

I have a guess. It's a risk, but I'll risk it to be convincing. "Can you take me to her?"

A pause, as fragile as the breeze that meanders in.

Cicada starts walking.

I follow her, to a courtyard complex like all the others. Only the placard on the door marks it as an ancestral hall. We stop at the threshold, and in the dim beyond, I see name plaques gleaming on the altar, with the most recent deaths at the front. Cicada's grandmother, then mother, then sister.

Leaders who lived and died for their kingdom.

"I'm sorry." Cicada's voice is quiet.

"I am too. I wish I'd been there." My throat twinges at the

words. I know how it felt to be shown Ren's and Cloud's fates from a realm away. Crow must have felt worse, trapped in the North and hearing about Cricket's death after it had already happened.

My pain right now is but a fraction of his.

I take a breath, and walk in.

Before the plaques of the deceased are the usual offerings of incense and peaches.

Less usual is the chessboard, inscribed with Cricket's name.

This time, I wish my throat didn't twinge.

"Before you go . . ." Beside me, Cicada stares at the board with a complicated expression. "Can we play a game?"

Playing is a risk, bigger than finishing Crow's sentences or asking to see Cricket's memorial.

But as I said, all strategy is risk. "Get the board."

I've seen Crow play just once. His opponent was Miasma. *It's dangerous to think you've won when you've actually lost*, he'd told her. Only now does it strike me that he could have been talking about me. I thought I'd outsmarted him, but he'd outsmarted *me*.

Now I sit across from Cicada. A part of me wishes I could be sitting across from him. It's my only admittable regret—that I never challenged Crow to a single game of chess—and I snuff it out as I lift the lid to my pot of stones.

White.

Cicada doesn't initiate a swap. *Just like Cloud*, I think almost fondly before sharpening my thoughts. Crow lost on purpose to Miasma, but Cicada is his true lordess.

SOUND THE GONG ‡ 233

I won't go easy on her.

We play our openings. Midgame. Late. Stones fill the board. Black and white, staking out their territory.

I win by eleven points.

I clear my stones. When I'm done, I look up to find Cicada's head bowed, the stones on her side untouched.

Tears drip onto them.

Rat-livers. Was I wrong? Could it be that Crow also had a habit of losing on purpose to Cicada? How distasteful, if so. "Chanmei . . ." I start, trailing off as she lifts her head.

"Thank you, for playing me as you would have her."

"O-of course."

Cicada's head bows again; she wipes at her eyes with the heels of her hands. "You know, for those few weeks after I heard you—" She swallows. *Were steamed.* "I really thought I'd lost you too."

Too.

Outside the sun shines, painting the floor in light. Birds trill. The board scrapes, as I push it away. I scooch forward, put my arms around Cicada, and hold her.

Her tears seep into my shoulder.

Over hers, I see Crow, even more faded in the sun. My gaze shifts downward. Looking at him would make my next words gloating, and I've gloated enough. In this moment, I want to be sincere—as sincere as one can be while wearing another's skin.

"Chanmei, ah," I say, stroking her hair. "Remember something: I'm not that easy to kill."

四十

YOUR OLD COLLEAGUE

Dearest Plum,

Forgive the handwriting. I never quite recovered from the loss of that finger. To the rest of the realm, it seems I've lost more—my life, to start. Is it true?

Why don't you come and find out?

Before you deem this a hoax, let me say a few words. I know you, Plum. Perhaps you saw my body, horridly blackened. But you, unlike the others, didn't believe it was the doing of ghosts. You have a head of common sense. You've survived this long because of it.

But your life in the last few months can't possibly have been pleasant. I'll go as far as to guess your days are a torturous dance of watching your every step. Why?

Why, indeed, should you face more scrutiny for my sins?

I'll tell you why: You and I are forever intertwined in Miasma's mind. For what was that dream our Mi-Mi had again? Three crows on a plum branch. Why else would we appear in her unconscious mind, if not as a portent? And she was right to have suspicions. I validated them.

In her eyes, it's just a matter of time before you follow my descent.

And so though sense has served you well until now, you must choose your next move wisely. You can bide your time as you have and wait for Miasma to find an excuse to kill you, or you could turn the tide of her favor before it ebbs entirely.

Confront me, Plum, and end me for our lordess.

Of course, there's always a third option: You could kill her before she kills you. You would make a good regent. Imagine—the empire at your fingertips. Do you harbor those ambitions?

There's no need to answer now. Tell me in person.

I await you in the Xianlei Gorge.

Your Old Colleague

四十一

INTO THE GORGE

I *await you, Plum.*

Of course, if it were up to Plum, she wouldn't come. Not for a letter.

But Miasma will open it first just like she does for all of Plum's correspondence, and every detail will haunt her. Plum wishes to kill her. Plum told Crow about her dreams.

Crow, a dead person, wrote the words.

Depending on Plum's standing, Miasma will either order an execution or a test of loyalty. If the latter, Plum will be sent to the Xianlei Gorge, bait used to draw out bait, and she won't come alone. Soldiers will accompany her, on standby to kill both her and Crow. By the empire's hands, or mine, Plum will die. Her time starts dwindling the second I post the letter. It'll take two weeks for it to travel to Plum, then ten days for her to travel the seventeen hundred lǐ to the Xianlei Gorge.

I must cover twice the distance, riding behind our front lines in the Marshlands.

And I will. Never mind that my longest journey as Crow

almost killed me. I was steamed, slashed by bandits. Now I just have a lingering cold. It's nothing, really—

I hack through the first four nights in a row.

"Same old," I tell the soldiers summoned to my tent by the ruckus. "Same old."

I try to cough quieter afterward, to no avail.

"Lie on your left side."

I don't reply, or move. I don't know what I'm waiting for until Crow says, "Or cough up a lung. Whichever you please." Then I realize it's just to hear his voice again after so many days of silence.

"Why should I trust you?" I strain to see him in the dark, my snap diminished as a whisper. I have the tent to myself, but better still if the soldiers didn't think I was sick in the head as well.

"It's my body," Crow says flatly.

"That's trying to kill me."

"Just do as I say."

Huffing, I roll left.

The cough subsides.

Half a shí chén later, it's back with a vengeance.

Brilliant advice, I think witheringly to Crow as I crawl over to my bundled belongings and fish for the medicine balls Cicada packed for me. *They're good for you*, she said.

She neglected to mention that they taste like dung.

"I wouldn't recommend them," Crow says *after* I spit them out. I glare in his general direction, gagging, which leads to more coughing. *Hells.*

I leave my tent before I rouse the others again. The night

envelops me, clammy like clay. Beside us rushes the Mica; we're just southwest of Bikong. Halfway there.

Don't you dare give up on me now, I think to Crow's body, coughing freely once I'm at the river. Convenient that we're near one; when I release my mouth, my palm is splotched with blood.

Ugh. "How did you let yourself get to this state?" I mutter, crouching to rinse it off.

"You caught the cold."

"You pushed me into the lake."

"You didn't change out of your robes afterward."

"You—!" My finger shakes, pointed at Crow, then stills. Is it the moonlight, or has he faded more?

Who cares? Not me. I jab my finger again. "You work too hard!"

"Didn't you? Aren't you now?" Crow says, voice soft as I'm gripped by another coughing fit. "Who else would know my troubles as well as you, burdened by Xin Ren?"

"So you admit—" cough "—Cicada is—" cough "—a burden." *Cough-cough.*

"No more than any Southlands ruler would be, by virtue of our position."

"Oh yes," I gasp out. "You're so burdened by your fertile land." But even as I say so, I can build Crow's case. The South is resource rich; they attract pirates. The land has known stability; its people have more to lose. Their queen wants sovereignty, but a continent united is the surest path to peace, if previous dynasties are any evidence.

Regrettably, I do know Crow's troubles. We're the same,

something I've always relished, but now, all I can see is Crow's face at the top of the steamer, so composed, so unresistant. He was more than ready to sacrifice himself for his kingdom, just like his first lordess.

I want to tell him he'd be a fool to follow in her footsteps.

Instead I say, "Trade away too much of your health now, and you won't live to enjoy any of your successes."

"I don't seem to be living already."

I look to him; his eyes aren't angry. I remove my hand from the water. Stand.

Crow remains beside me.

I'm not forgiven. Not for putting Cicada's life in danger, or for stealing Crow's body.

I won't be in this lifetime.

But as the river rushes on, carrying snowmelt from the Northern mountains, I wonder if it's possible, in the time I have left, for us to coexist. Like now. By the water.

This quiet within us.

"What if," I start, "I told you that you could have your body back, after Ren wins the war?"

"Is that a promise?"

"A hypothetical. What would you do, after?"

The river burbles.

"I don't know," Crow says after a painfully long moment.

"Why did you alert me to the tea?"

"I don't know."

"Why did you ask Cicada to spare me?"

"You were interesting," Crow says plainly, his answer throwing me. I was expecting another *I don't know*. I could live with an *I don't know*. "You say I work too hard, and I thought so too. Then I met you and saw just how much a person could live to work."

It should be a compliment, but it doesn't feel like one. A draft rises from the river, blowing goose bumps over my skin.

Nothing escapes Crow's notice. "May I suggest a cloak?"

"I'm already sick."

"Take it from me that it's possible to get sicker."

"So?"

"I'd rather not listen to you cough until dawn." Then Crow shifts away from me. The chill reduces by a marginal amount, but it's the gesture that warms my face. Before he can notice that too, I turn from him and the river.

It's a crime that he can still act so considerate.

"And what will *you* do after the war?" Crow asks, following as I stride away.

"What does it matter to you?"

"Why wouldn't it? You are my sun, my air, no?"

I snort as Crow uses the words I put in his mouth. "Perhaps I'll teach chess. Or the zither. Perhaps I'll be one of those old crones who plays both in some tavern, the next time we cross paths."

"Perhaps," Crow says, and it's a beautiful word.

Then my guard rises. *He's being too nice.* The last time he was, he lied about Cicada's diminutive. I walk faster, back to the camp. The horses whicker at me—nostrils flaring when Crow skirts too close. "There now," I murmur to a mare while glaring at Crow. The mare nuzzles my palm, and my chest tightens. Rice Cake would never. I hope he's safe, fed, happy. He's lucky to be away from the war. Here, he'd be saddled with the equipment and grain funneled to us from Sikou Hai's and Ku's front lines. Each wagon is as precious as an army itself, and my lungs feel better as I count them. Maybe, now, I can finally sleep. I pass the last wagon.

And turn back to it.

I'm tired. I imagined it.

But then—again—the wagon's burlap covering moves.

Slowly, I approach. *Wild animal. Ghost.* When the burlap moves next, I rule out ghosts. Spirits can't influence the physical world to such an extent. I reach for the covering with one hand, my other going to the knife at my broadbelt.

Only then does Crow speak up. "She won't hurt you."

She.

I yank off the covering.

"K—" My fake cough quickly turns real. As I hack, Ku sits up. Grain spills off the wagon, raining onto the ground.

"Xiao—qiu?" I finally manage. How long has Crow known without telling me? Long enough, seeing as these wagons arrived two days ago. Good to know he's still the bane of my existence. "Does Cicada know you're here?"

Ku doesn't speak, as if the answer is obvious. She hasn't changed in this regard. Where someone else might use three words, Ku will use one or none. She jumps down—another rainfall of grain—and a familiar anger brews in me. How has she eaten? How has she slept? What is she *thinking*?

"You need a helper," she says before I can begin.

No. It's not safe.

But I'm not her sister. I never was, and she always knew it. The child she was died with Qilin. The real Qilin. I was the impostor.

Just like now.

I'm sorry, I think, as I slip into the persona of Crow, her mentor. *I'm sorry, Ku.*

November.

"Listen to me, Xiaoqiu." She stares at me, and I sigh as I imagine Crow might before capitulating to his disciple. "When we reach the Xianlei Gorge, we'll reencounter Cloud."

"I don't like her."

"I don't either. But we must put on an act, like you did when I came to visit South with—" *Zephyr.* "—Miasma's delegation. I'll wear the mask and you must act like I'm not Crow."

I hold her gaze until she nods.

"Come now. You must be cold."

I lead her to my tent, where Ku immediately curls up in the corner. I watch her drift off to sleep, then look up at Crow. What has Ku told him of me, if anything at all? I want to ask, but the moment we had by the river is gone. I'm back to the camp, back to tricking everyone. That includes Ku. Cicada is the only person I haven't stolen from her, and suddenly, I remember Crow's words from before.

And November? Ku? He'd stared at me, derision filling his eyes when I failed to realize that by harming Cicada, I'd also be harming Ku.

But how good *is* Cicada for Ku? She defended Ku before the Southlands advisors, but she also entrusts too much to her, sending her to Ren on her own, then to the Marshlands. She won't hesitate to use her, just like she used Crow as a spy in the North.

As for me? Even if I care about Ku, I won't hesitate to end her lordess if my hand is forced.

Heavens willing, it won't be.

‡ ‡ ‡

Past the river, the floodplain dries up. Limestone deposits form ravines.

Soon, we're riding through defiles so narrow, only a single soldier can fit through at once.

Out the other end, we face a series of hills, interlocked like waves and frothed with trees.

The Xianlei Gorge.

South of here is the Westlands.

Northeast is the capital, which Ren will soon reach with Cicada.

And just ahead is Cloud. I retrieve the clay mask from my belongings and put it on, becoming the masked advisor Cloud saw beside Cicada in Taohui. Otherwise, she'd kill me first and ask questions later.

"Southern chaperones!" she greets when we reach her encampment. "Just what I wanted!"

Nice to see you too, Cloud. Truly. I'm glad she looks well.

"We're only here to assist," I say, facing her horse to horse as my troops stream around us.

Cloud eyes my mask with open distrust. "More like get in the way."

Only in the way of fate. "It's my recommendation that you relocate your soldiers."

Currently, Cloud has all her forces camped atop the highest hill. I almost broke out in hives when I saw the setup. If I hadn't witnessed Cloud's fated death, I'd believe she was digging her own grave.

"Why should I?" Cloud challenges. "Everyone knows to take the high ground."

"When you have the element of surprise. But that?" I jerk my chin at the hill. "You'll be besieged in less than a day."

"Let them try. My soldiers can break out of anything."

"Can they?" My mask is hot, I'm tired and sick, and damn it, why won't Cloud *listen*? "I suppose they did help you escape Bikong."

I've gone too far; I know it even before Blue Serpent swings to my neck. "Say that again."

I keep silent.

"Say it!"

"Water." Ku's voice, behind me. She rides up and says, "There's no water on the hill. They'll cut you from your supply when they surround you."

"You." Cloud frowns. "You're Zephyr's sister."

"Three days," Ku goes on, giving no indication she's heard Cloud. "Less, maybe, before your troops go down the hill to escape death by thirst. They'll slaughter you then."

It's true, all true. I just wish Ku had broken it to Cloud a bit more . . . delicately, considering her blade's location. Slowly, Cloud lowers Blue Serpent from my neck—

Shing!

—and swings it out leftward.

"Move camp!"

As soldiers rush to carry the order to the hill, Cloud urges her massive mare toward me. Mine stomps the ground, uneasy, as they close in.

"Let me be clear: I'm listening to her, not you." Cloud trots past me. Behind me. "I don't care if you're the most senior advisor of the Southern Court; I don't trust people who hide their faces." She rides up my other side, her mare's tail swishing into my thigh. "Mention Bikong again, and not even your strategist can save you. You got that?"

I nod, keeping my eyes forward as Cloud rides off, sunlight winking off her crescent blade as if in promise.

"Beast." My gaze digresses to Ku. She too stares at the warrior. She worries for Crow in a way she never did for Zephyr. I should be sore, but instead I smile. *Beast.* Cloud would laugh at the weak insult.

"Go with Cloud," I tell Ku. "She listens to you."

And Ku listens, somewhat, to Crow. Her lips pinch, but she rides after the warrior. As she does, Crow asks "Why don't you tell Cloud who you really are?" He hovers beside me, unperturbed as soldiers march through him. I try not to focus on how faint he is; at least his voice is still clear, unfaded, as he says, "It'd make things easier to tell her. Unless she hated you as Zephyr."

You're not far off the mark.

"But that doesn't seem quite right, given her anger at Taohui over Zephyr's death. So why the secrets?"

Guess away, Crow. I watch as Ku catches up to Cloud, her figure small compared to the warrior's, but even Cloud's shrinks as she rides on, leaving me where I am.

My hold tightens on the reins.

You'll take care of Ren just fine without me, won't you, Cloud?

I turn my horse around.

You'll all be just fine once I clinch our victory.

‡ ‡ ‡

As Cloud moves her troops off the hill, I ride up it and assess the rolling geography, the ravines and defiles like the ones we squeezed through, imposing and ancient.

It looks like a landscape sculpted by a god.

Maybe Nadir was once here. Something in the air reminds me of her. My heart aches with longing, then anger. She tried to wipe my memories.

She's not my sister.

"What are you looking for?" asks Crow as I scan the land with renewed focus. "Maybe I can help."

"You, helping."

"Who saved you again from the bandits?"

"You just didn't want your body to burn."

"So my services are not altruistic." Crow's shoulders lift, his shrug elegant. "I help you when it helps me."

"Why would our campaign here help you?"

"Maybe I want to end the senior registrar too."

That gives me pause. Crow *did* watch me write the letter to Plum word by word. He knew I was luring Plum West, but for what? I was under no obligation to tell him, and evidently, he didn't need to be told.

"It's not personal," he goes on, and I look to him, his form so terribly translucent in the sun. "But I always did think that she'd be a force to be reckoned with down the road."

Crow hasn't had the benefit of reading the fates, and yet he's deduced the concealed enemy. He's the strategist for me to beat—except I've already beaten him. We're not really on this hill together. "What makes you think so?" I ask, trying for indifference even as I imagine what could have been, had I condemned Plum from the start.

"She has that rare and troublesome ability to endure."

"Better than even you?"

"She's done it longer than me, that's for certain," says Crow, cavalier, and I swallow, dropping my gaze back to the land.

Remorse is craven.

Remorse is useless.

I will not be its hostage.

Truthfully, I don't know what I'm looking for. To wield a weapon, you must move with it, maximize its nature and not fight it. This is especially true for wielding terrain. My eyes roam over the ravines and valleys, riven with shadows.

One shadow, in particular, is contoured like a calabash gourd.

I steer my horse down our hill.

"Where are you going?" Cloud hollers after me as I pass her line of moving soldiers.

"To survey the vicinity."

"We have scouts for that!"

Ignoring her, I ride in the direction of the shadow, arriving at the mouth of a gorge. And what a gorge it is—cliffsides taller than even Bikong's walls, entrance so wide that a rider wouldn't know they've entered a gorge at all until they reach the narrow middle. From there, the gorge flares into a second, smaller segment, rounded out by a dead end. At the terminus, I glance to the cliffsides. A ledge snakes up to the top. It's narrow, and after a tight turn—"Whoa," I ease my horse—I summit the cliff. I look back down at the gorge I traveled through and empty my mind of everything but its unique shape.

A stratagem rushes in.

"Burning House," says Ku, riding up beside me.

"My thought exactly."

Like a house, the gorge has limited exits. Set it alight, and Plum will be as good as dead once led in. Cloud's scouts put the middle-aged woman, along with an empire legion, at seven hundred lǐ away two days ago. That gives *us* just two days to execute my vision. We'll have to work without sleep. Fine by me. Not like I was getting much anyway. Through the night, under "November's orders," I oversee the soldiers, striding through the gorge as logs are carried in and trenches dug, coughing loudly whenever I see a yawn.

"You!" barks Cloud, and I turn to see her storming down the gorge. Have I overdone the coughing? No—Cloud has only met Crow twice, and never during a flare-up. She closes in—swerving as I spit out a mouthful of blood.

"Stop that!" she yells as I wipe the bottom of my mask. "You're hurting morale, and my people need sleep if they're to fight."

"Finish the work here," says Ku, joining my side, "and they won't need to fight."

Cloud's eyes narrow. Like most warriors, she prefers to battle it out in the open. She leaves the gorge, but reenters an hour later atop her mare. "All of you, to bed!"

Before I can protest, fresh troops flood in from Cloud's rear, replacing the ones leaving.

She rides in after them, assessing our progress. At the dead end, she turns to me and Ku. "A trap," she says, a notch between her brows, and I remember the time Cloud released Miasma from one of mine. *Master Shencius forbids killing by way of snare*, she'd said loftily, and I'd wanted to kill *her* by snare.

But Cloud is not the Cloud from before. War remakes everyone. "You can't expect to annihilate an entire legion this way," she says to me and Ku, and I correct her.

"Not after the legion. Just the leader."

"How do you plan on luring the senior registrar this far?"

"With me."

"You."

"Yes."

"And she's going to be so concerned with you that she won't notice all of this?" Cloud waves a hand at the hay we've lashed to the sides of the gorge.

"She will." Ku and I speak in tandem, deepening Cloud's frown.

"What's one elderly Southern advisor to the senior registrar? Wait. Don't tell me—an old flame."

Cloud guffaws while I smart at "elderly" and Ku says, "He's my mentor."

"So your *mentor* is going to start over there"—Cloud jabs her glaive at the gorge's entrance, coin-sized from where we stand—"and lead their leader all the way to over *here* as bait."

Of course. Who else? It's my stratagem—

"No," says Ku. "I will lead the registrar through the first bulge."

"What? No! It's—"

"My idea," Ku says over me, and I look to Cloud. Surely she'll think Ku is too weak.

But Cloud doesn't protest, and come morning, Ku's mind is unchanged. When a scout puts Plum at five lǐ away, she seeks out Cloud.

"Station yourself and your soldiers on the cliffs, above where the gorge narrows before the second bulge." Ku then faces me. "You go with her."

"What's your plan for leading Plum through the first bulge?" I press.

"Formations."

I wait for Ku to say more.

No words follow.

"What did you expect?" Crow asks me. "She's your sister. Why explain the stratagem to us lowly bystanders?"

I can't reply to Crow in front of Ku, not until I ride away. And I ride away. I know my once-sister. Wars are easier to win than arguments with her.

"Did you just insult your disciple?" I ask Crow once we're out of earshot.

"No. I don't ascribe to that school of mentorship. I assume you do? See," says Crow when I glower. "Now that's an insult. She might take after you, but I never said that was a flaw."

"We're not actually related."

"You still shaped her."

Shaped? Even my ego knows better. I slap the reins and trot up the gorge side, joining Cloud's soldiers hidden among the foliage above the second, smaller bulge. Should Plum look up, she won't see us.

Come on. Anticipation crowds out the air in my lungs. I've read the beats right so far—read that Plum would come, and with an army. Below, Ku's soldiers fill the first bulge. Ku rides out at their front, and for once, I can understand her state of mind perfectly well.

Come on.

Our banners ripple in the breeze. Everything else is still, the tall cliffs like sentinels.

Sound reaches us first, that of armor, hooves, and weapons, amplified by the ravine. A glint of lamellar becomes a shimmering sea of thousands; enemy soldiers flow into the fatter segment of the gorge, and joy flows into me. The more troops Miasma's diverted here, the fewer Ren and Cicada will meet at the capital.

But then the ranks fill in completely.

Still no Plum.

Have I miscalculated? At the thought, Cloud's voice rakes through my head. *When did you become such a defeatist?*

When I died twice, Cloud. You should try it sometime.

Then an undulation goes through the ranks. Shields reflect the sun as they move, revealing a rider in purple.

Plum rides out and stops a hundred strides from Ku. "Declare yourself."

"November, Cicada's strategist."

"Move aside, child."

Ku stays put. "Are you Plum?"

"Who else could I be?"

"I've never seen you before. Prove that you are Plum with your knowledge of formations."

"This is no game, child," snaps the senior registrar.

"Prove that you aren't an impostor here to bait out my mentor."

"Have him come out and confirm my identity."

Ku doesn't speak or move.

From my vantage point, I can't see Plum's expression, but I can imagine her exasperation. Formations are the equivalent of a chess match on the field, strength decided without blood needing to be spilled. Ren didn't have enough trained soldiers for me to deploy, when I still lived as Zephyr. Now we have the numbers, but does Ku have the skill? Does she know the flag and drum signals? The trifold, tenfold permutations?

Down below, Plum shifts on her horse. There's no blood cost to formations, she must be thinking, just time. She's come this far. Might as well.

"Awl!" she orders, and her lines devolve into noise and shape-lessness, before a formation emerges with a sharpened front and narrow obliques. The last shield thuds into place.

The gorge falls silent.

Ku's order is too quiet for me to hear, but I watch her troops array in a reverse image of Plum's; middle sinking into a V, obliques dense and thick. *Flying Geese.*

The correct response to Awl.

Plum calls out a permutation; the sides of her troops extend, as if they're going to meet Ku's. How will Ku answer?

Permutation Five, I think, and it unfolds, Ku having already called it.

On and on this goes. Plum questions. Ku answers. "You taught her this?" I ask Crow.

"I did."

You did well.

"She always wanted to be better than you," Crow says, and it's the first time he's acknowledged Ku ever speaking of me—the first time *anyone* has. Self-consciously, I adjust my mask.

"At what?"

"Chess, be it in the field or on the board."

"I never played her."

"She watched you."

"I never—"

Played at all, at the orphanage. But then, faintly, a memory pulses. A toy merchant had caught Ku stealing; I, too slow, was seized in her place and about to be hauled off to the magistrates when I'd seen the chessboard in the stall. Though I'd never played—had only watched some street-side games—I'd challenged the merchant. Win, and I'd clear my name.

I didn't win. The merchant had stared at me across the stones on the board, and I'd run. He didn't chase. Why? I'd lost, but did he see who I *could* be, and not who I was? Had I broken whatever concept he held of me as an orphan, like Ku now breaks my concept of her? Because she is no longer Qilin's dependent or sister. She is November, the Southlands strategist, and down in the gorge, she's been slowly drawing Plum's soldiers deeper, the forward movement masked by her formations.

Without realizing it, Plum has neared the second segment.

"Clear this final formation," Ku says to Plum, "and you may pass through to find what you seek."

At her flag signal, shields form concentric circles. A maze materializes out of our soldiers; Plum looks to hers, behind her. None move forward. They're here to monitor her, not protect her.

Whatever Plum did for Miasma to spare her life, it's still not enough to recover the favor she lost.

But this test of loyalty is, and the prospect of passing it must be what draws Plum forward. Alone, she enters the pathways formed by Ku's soldiers, and for a moment I wish I were among them. I'd kill Plum then and there, happy to violate the most sacred rule of formations—that they should remain bloodless. Then I tame my heart. Plum will die, and so will a number of empire soldiers while we're at it.

This is Ku's moment. She is the strategist.

While Plum works through the maze, I ride down the cliff. I still my horse behind Ku's final lines, and wait.

Plum rides out—and shortens her reins. My lonesome self on a horse faces her, and I'm quickly outnumbered as her soldiers thunder in behind her.

"Declare yourself!" Plum calls.

I think of Lotus, announcing herself by name. I see Cloud dueling Leopard in front of Bikong, a legend in the making. I used to be like them. Not a warrior, but every hair on my head, every feather in my fan, every outplay and outwit belonged to the Rising Zephyr.

I could be no one else.

Now I am simply no one. My deeds won't be attached to my name after all is said and done.

That's fine, so long as I win.

You lose, Plum. My hand rises to my mask.

I tilt it up.

四十二

UNMASKED

*M*ask, tilted up.

Wind skims my cheeks, swirling dust across the expanse between us. The ravine, tall on either side of us. The ribbon of blue sky, arrowing above.

Cry of a hawk.

I can almost feel Plum's heart stop. Her face has gone bloodless. She should be grateful. If I were atop this horse as Qilin? Then I'd really be a ghost risen to haunt her.

As it is, I warned her. She's come to the end of a nearly two thousand lǐ journey only to face the unthinkable she sought to debunk. Her mouth gapes, and I know the feeling. The mind shuts down, leaving only the scent of prey and muscle instinct.

Plum trots her horse forward. I trot mine back.

We repeat this dance twice.

Take a good look, Plum. I lower my mask. *I am the one you hunt to prove your loyalty.*

Don't let me get away now.

I wheel my horse around and dig in my heels.

"After him!"

I pound through the gorge, limestone ablur. Past a crag, I raise my arm. From atop the cliff, Cloud's soldiers pull on the ropes. Fences snap out of where we've buried them in the dirt, closing behind Plum's riders. Deeper in, I raise my arm again. Boulders crash down. Horses whinny in panic. Rocks smash into earth behind me, then pots. Jugs of oil break, splattering onto the dried brush we've lashed to the sides of the cliff.

Final phase. Arrows soar downward, streaking fire. I speed toward the narrow ledge of stone carving up the gorge. *I'll reach it before the brush catches.* When fire and wind are our weapons, a breath is the difference between life and death. Plum and her crew will be trapped—

Everything flies in reverse. The sky. The hawk.

For a split second, I'm just as airborne.

I hit the ground and roll over and over from the force. Grit in my teeth. Against my face.

My face, fully unmasked to Cloud. The thought lances through my mind, brighter than the pain. I lurch to my feet. *My mask—my mask—*

—rests concave side up, several chǐ away.

I scramble for it—fingers closing around the clay. Back on my face. I limp toward my horse. In the few seconds I've lost, the fire is everywhere. I started it, but I can't control it. Can't contain it. It has a will of its own. The wind blows, and fire rips through the gorge. My horse rears as I reach for the reins. She's terrified, naturally. There's the fire—

And there's Crow.

I didn't think twice of being thrown off the saddle, but now I realize I fell for a reason.

Now, finally, I notice Crow.

He passes through my horse, weaving in and out of the animal like a needle, spooking it with his chill.

He did this.

Behind me, the fire is growing. Its heat presses into my back like a giant hand. *Move.*

But I can't. Crow stills in his administrations, and we stare at each other through the smoke. I can feel his intentions as if they were scraped into my skin. The fall didn't kill me, but the fire will. Rather than try and fail to secure his body again, he would destroy it all, just to protect Cicada. This is his final play.

I admire him for it, for a perverse moment.

Then I see Cloud. I see Cloud, and all feelings of admiration evaporate, along with all thoughts of Crow, as she and her horse ride down the ledge, into the flames.

"Get back—!"

"Remove your mask."

No—I put it on quick. She didn't see. Couldn't have.

"I said remove it!" Cloud advances, swinging down from her horse. I back up—but there's nowhere to go. Fire behind me—and Cloud in front. She seizes me by the collar.

Tell her. I have to tell her—I'm Zephyr.

"Release him!"

At first, I can't tell whose voice it is, or where it comes from. The roar of the flames and the screams of the soldiers addle my senses, their panic my panic. Is it Ku? *No.* Ku would come from behind and this person—rides down the ledge before me, urging their horse to leap over the fire. They land in the gorge, and Crow freezes as I stare.

How—what—Cicada? Is that really her? She should be east. Why—doesn't matter. *It's Crow's lordess*, I tell myself as she rushes toward us. Not mine.

But then another shout cuts through the screams and strikes me like an arrow to the back.

"Cloud!"

And though fire surrounds us, my blood turns to ice as I see the rider behind Cicada.

四十五

THE WEEPING GOD

*B*ehind Cicada—

Is Ren, followed by Tourmaline. Cicada, Ren, Tourmaline. They should be over a thousand lǐ away. They should be leading the charge out of the South.

Not West.

Before my eyes, the three ride down into the inferno, one after another.

Cicada closes in first, and Crow's spirit stares on in horror as the Southlands lordess dismounts. My horror matches his as Ren again calls for Cloud. *"Gao Yun! To me, now!"*

And Cloud—her fists don't release me, but her gaze does. Her eyes jerk to Ren, then back to me, and I want to scream. *Listen to Ren! Protect her, your—*

Her grip hardens around my collar.

—swornsister—

Backward I'm shoved, bottom meeting dust. Cicada is instantly beside me; I barely register her presence. All I can see is Cloud as she makes her way to Ren.

Hurry. Get Ren out! I mentally urge Cloud as Ren calls for Cicada. "*Come to us!*"

The wind blows before Cicada can answer. Fire roars over the ledge that everyone rode down.

Our one escape, almost engulfed.

I pull Cicada to her feet. *We can still make it.* I tug her after me, toward Ren, Cloud, Tourmaline. Someone shouts. Something shatters on the ground. Clay shards, from a wine pot we launched. Fire must have dissolved the gorge-side shrub it was caught on. Wine jumps to flame, and I yank Cicada back, her body thudding into my bruised one, as a searing wall cuts us off from the others.

"*Leave!*" I shout at them. The air quivers, warped by heat. Choked by smoke. Crow's body won't survive this. *So what? So long as it's also killing Plum.* I cling to the thought as Cicada reaches for me; I pull her in, cloak lifted around her like a wing.

"*Nov—*" Cicada coughs. "*—vember—*" More coughing.

"*Isn't here,*" I cough back. She's in the first bulge, and thank heavens for that. Cicada nods, coughing too hard for words. I soon join her. Ash and blood fill my mouth. I raise my eyes to the sky, smoke-black except for a single, clear circle. Is it the Masked Mother, watching my end? For even if the fire doesn't kill me, if I kill Plum—if I succeed—it might be time—to pay—

Only you? I can hear her voice in my mind. *They'll pay first, with their lives.*

They will die, in this fire of your making.

Cicada, yes, but Cloud, Tourmaline, and Ren are closer to the ledge. They still have a chance—

They won't take it. Remember who you serve.

Xin Ren.

My lordess. My queen. She saved Cicada.

She wouldn't abandon her in a time of need.

I sink to my knees.

I did everything.

Everything.

I was *ready* to pay the price.

But now?

My eyes slam shut.

Why? In the darkness, I see light. The pink, everlasting light of the heavens. Endless jugs of wine. A dare gone wrong. *Why not?* I'd thought then, as I flatulated over the edge of the sky. I was a god. But I never felt alive, until I came down to this world. Among the humans, every match mattered. *I* mattered. But now, because of the humans I serve—now, because Ren might die even if I kill Plum—

Why? I squeeze my eyes shut harder, tears pricking at the corners.

Why didn't any of you listen to me? Why must you all be so— human?

The tears spill, against my will. So many tears on my cheeks. Too many.

My eyes open.

Rain thunders down, as if the heavens are weeping.

Or a god. Even without my powers, I'd know this qì any- where. *Nadir.* She's all around me.

As her qì douses me, I become her.

We're young, like the mortal world below, a land of rolling mountains and raging rivers, empty of life, until we create it. We pinch the humans out of clay.

We fall in love with one of our creations, a scholar.

He plays us a song on the zither—and I'm jarred apart from Nadir. This ballad—I know it. I played it to Crow. It's the story of a deity—Nadir, I now realize—and a human. A love story—until their child grows up to be a demon who devours his father before shattering heaven, pieces of sky falling and rupturing the earth.

The ballad ends there, but Nadir's memory goes on—to her destroying her own child, patching the heavens, then facing the same choice I did: For her sins, she can be banished, reincarnated, and join the humans she longed to be with.

Or she can stay. I watch her as she walks the terraces around Aurora Nest, searching for a reason to remain. I'm not in her mind, but I can feel her heart, the cold, horrible certainty that she will never love as deeply again. Maybe she *should* go. Dewdrop would miss her, but Dewdrop can take care of herself . . .

Nadir stops. A cloud glows in the lake by our home. She looks at the cloud, and a jolt goes through me as I recognize the qì. The cloud is me, in my primordial form.

The memories next blur—Nadir drinking the Elixir of Forgetting.

Every mortal memory of hers vanishing.

Nadir, I think, dumbfounded, blinking rapidly against the

264 ‡ JOAN HE

rain. No wonder the land here is so familiar. The falling heavens made this gorge, named after the divine tears a god shed for her child. Now she weeps for her sister, lost as well. Because by sending the rain, Nadir has saved Ren, Cloud, and my hopes by extension. They live. I can still avert the tragedy of their fates, kill Plum, help Ren free Xin Bao. But succeed, and I'll pay the ultimate price. Nadir surely knows. That's why she drugged the tea. She didn't want me to sacrifice everything for these humans like she almost did, even if she doesn't remember it.

The heavens continue to pour. I raise a hand, palm filling with water. The wall of fire recedes, and I see Cloud, Ren, Tourmaline. Coughing and downed with their mounts. Still in the gorge. In another minute, their bodies would have perished, leaving their souls to journey to the Obelisk before returning to the mortal world, reincarnated as different people. Not my people.

It really could have ended here in the gorge.

But we're alive.

Alive.

Not without a price.

I stagger to my feet, squinting through the rain, to the rubble behind me, fires still going but quickly dying. Through swaths of black smoke, I see broken wood and broken bodies—

A flash of plum robes. A badly burned figure, hauling onto an equally badly burned horse. Before I can shout, both take off— not toward Ku's troops, back at the entrance, but forward. Past Tourmaline, Cloud, and Ren.

Up the ledge and over the cliff.

‡ ‡ ‡

We're in no shape to give chase, and Plum gets away.

We might still defeat Miasma, but Plum lives.

Her soldiers aren't so lucky. As the rain thins, their moans fill the gorge. A hundred, thousand mangled voices beg for deliverance from their suffering, and Ren answers each, hastening the inevitable with her sword while Cicada looks on, face sallow. She demolished the Fen pirates, but that must have felt like retribution. The Fen slaughtered civilians. They were the villains.

But rarely is war like a game of chess, divided into black and white, and as the tang of iron overwhelms the smoke and ash, Cicada turns her back to the scene. I start for her, stilling as she shouts, "You! Warrior!" to Cloud, who's helping Tourmaline up.

"Why did you attack my advisor?" Cicada demands, and I brace my bedraggled self as Cloud faces us. If she accuses me of being Crow, it'll put Ren on the spot—

"No reason. I just felt like it."

Did I hear right?

Did Cloud . . . lie?

Cloud's reply doesn't placate Cicada. Quite the opposite. She starts for the warrior, and I snatch her sleeve. "It's done. We won the battle."

"She attacked—"

"I'll punish Cloud myself." Ren walks over, sword slicked red.

"Punish me? Again?" Cloud scoffs. "I'm not the one who's thousands of li from where they should be." Well said. "You want an explanation?" she asks Cicada. "Then here's one: I mistook him"—she gestures brusquely at me—"for someone else. What are *your* explanations?"

Yes, what *are* their explanations?

"You, Cloud," Ren says. "I came for you."

"What—"

"I didn't want us to part on the note we did." Ren's gaze burns into Cloud's, a thousand words passing in the silence. "It was ill-advised. Forgive me." She doesn't look to me, the strategist whose plan she ruined, or toward Ku's troops as they join us. Her eyes implore Cloud, and just Cloud. It's a moment I'm not a part of. I look away, and find Cicada staring at me, her eyes preemptively defiant.

And you? I could ask. *Why did you come?*

But I don't. I already know.

She came for Crow, same as Ren came for Cloud.

Instead of following the objectives I gave them, they followed their hearts.

What they don't understand is that I designed this final match to *protect* their loved ones. Because in the time it took Ren and Cicada to travel here from the South, they could have already reached the capital and secured Xin Bao. Instead, they came west. What if Miasma detected their movements? What if she diverts her forces from the Marshlands?

Did any of you consider that? No. They didn't, and they still don't. No one comes to me, asking of our next play. Just as well, because I have no answers. It's one thing to change course midgame, another to move troops across the continent. What's more, I still don't have my powers. I can't use the weather against Miasma, should she come.

Today, Ren and everyone survived, but tomorrow their mistake might still cost them.

We ride out of the gorge and make camp.

Without taking my leave, I retire to my tent.

Exhaustion washes over me the second I sit.

I'm tired.

So tired.

I just want to sleep. Not here, in my stained bedroll, but in my cloud bed, where Nadir might stroke my hair and where I want for nothing . . .

And nothing is wanted from me . . .

My eyes fall shut.

When they next open, a bee is hovering before my nose.

"Dewdrop . . ." I swallow. "Nadir . . . when she chose to stay . . . was it really for me?"

The bee bobs up and down. A nod.

"I didn't know. I didn't know about her past."

You deserved to. Bee morphs into child, and Dewdrop sits next to me on the bedroll. *I wanted you to know. But it was Nadir's to tell, even if she's forgotten it all.*

"I understand." I say nothing else for a moment. We just sit. "Aren't you going to persuade me to stop fighting for them and come home?"

You're not just doing it for them, Zephyr. I see that now. You like being around the humans, because among them, you feel like a god. The games you win here must feel different from those above. But it won't always be like that. Lose in heaven, and you can always win again. But lose here . . .

And it'll end on a loss for good, like it almost did today. The worst of it is that it wasn't even my fault. I'd set my pieces—

And then my pieces moved without me.

It's not too late to return, Dewdrop thinks to me. *Nadir and I, we asked the Masked Mother. She said you can annul your deal and come back to the heavens. All you need to do—*

"Is drink the elixir and forget them."

Dewdrop nods. *Yes. All you need to do is think of the humans and the deal you made, and drink. Drink, and you'll forget what is on your mind in that moment.* She slides off the bed and sets a bottle on the table in the middle of my tent. I stand.

"You're leaving?"

Yes. Dewdrop smiles at me, her toddler face dimpling. *This doesn't have to be goodbye forever.* She turns into a bee.

"Wait. Don't—"

I wake with a gasp, hand outstretched.

—Go.

My hand closes.

Lowers.

Just a dream.

Or was it? I still have no powers, but my qì feels more replenished. *A final gift*, I can almost hear Dewdrop say, and though I know she's gone, I still search the tent. There's Crow, who's less faint, and on the table . . .

Is a green bottle.

My fingers close over it.

A soldier enters. "General Cloud requests a meeting."

"Send her in," I hear myself say, voice scratched by smoke, then pocket the bottle.

Moments later, my tent flaps burst open. Cloud befalls me like a storm. Her arms tackle mine to my sides, and I yelp. I'm being attacked. I'm being crushed. I'm being—

Hugged. By Cloud.

Her throat rumbles over my head. "Am I the last to know again, *Zephyr*?"

The name hits me like cold water.

"No," I manage. "Ren thinks I'm Crow."

"Tourmaline?"

"Also doesn't know."

"Then who *does*?" Her arms tighten, as if to squeeze out the answer.

"Sikou Hai," I gasp.

Cloud releases me.

Her fist connects with my stomach.

I bend over, now gasping *and* cursing. "What—what was *that* for?"

"For not telling me *first*."

"When could I have told you?"

"Plenty of times, starting in Taohui."

"I was in a coffin!"

"And I grabbed you! Your mouth was right by my ear! Did it not occur to you to whisper, *Oh, it's me, Zephyr*?"

"I needed you to act believable." I dust myself off and straighten—coming face-to-face with Blue Serpent.

"Using me, just like when you defected. What am I to you, a chess piece?"

"We're all chess pieces to the heavens."

Cloud lowers the blade, eyes narrowed. I know I sound defeated, but how else can I sound? How, when Plum lives? When everyone is still charging into their fated deaths?

"Why?" Cloud demands, and I stiffen.

"Why what?"

"Why did you try so hard to get beheaded by Miasma?"

"It would have been you otherwise."

To that, Cloud doesn't seem to know what to say.

Neither do I, for a second. "You're Ren's swornsister. You dying was not an option."

"Severing your neck—*Lotus's*—wasn't an option either."

"I know. I'm sorry." My words feel inadequate. "I know you wanted to look for her." An impossible task, but that's spilled wine. "But she's gone. You have to let her go, Cloud. And the rest of it. Let go of avenging me—"

"Avenge *you*? Don't make me barf."

There we go. That's the Cloud I know.

"What gave it away?" I ask after a pause.

"When Ren rode into the gorge." Cloud looks aside, as if returning to the memory. "I saw your gaze through the mask." Her eyes rise to mine. "I knew then that you'd come back for her."

I did. I came back for Ren. But Dewdrop was right; I also came back for myself. As a god, I could make Crow pay for what he did to us. But the moment I was kneeling by him in the steamer, I felt emptier than ever.

Is that what succeeding will be like?

No. Vengeance is the poison. If I hadn't been so hell-bent on vengeance, I'd have gotten rid of Plum instead of Crow. Today, we almost died for it. Ren was wise to forget the score with Cicada. Cloud should too. "Don't be angry at Ren," I say to her, and Cloud *hmphs*.

"Easier said than done."

Stubborn warrior. But Cloud's also had her share of brilliant moments, like the time she ordered Ren to live and lead at Lotus's bedside—the first time I realized Cloud wasn't the simple warrior I thought her. "You once told Ren to move on," I now say to her. You reminded her of the vow she made to the people."

I know you can see the bigger picture.

But Cloud doesn't look uplifted. "Well, I was wrong." She glances to her glaive, pointed to the ground. "I could only say those things because I didn't actually believe Lotus was gone."

Silence falls. For me, Lotus died with Qilin in Pumice Pass, but I know that's not so for Cloud. She sniffs, swipes roughly at her eyes, and I raise a hand, tentative, about to pat her on the back when she asks, "Do I want to know how you stole this body?" A clear change of subject.

I go with it. "It's gruesome."

"What do you think I haven't seen?"

"I steamed him."

"Gods, Zephyr."

"I warned you."

Cloud shakes her head. "The things we do for Ren," she says, and I grow solemn again.

"Don't tell her who I really am. Her, or any of them."

I brace for an argument, but Cloud sighs. "Fine. You tell her when you're ready to, then."

That's never, but for Cloud, I nod. "You should leave my tent before they think you're murdering me."

"You should be so lucky. I wouldn't stain Blue—"

"—Serpent with the blood of a rodent?" My turn to quirk a brow, and Cloud scowls.

"Peacock. Not a rodent. Peacock, or whatever it was that Lotus called you."

The air cools, as if there's a third presence here with us. And there is.

Only I know it's not Lotus's.

"It was Peacock," I finally say.

Cloud snorts. "Fitting." She picks up her glaive and makes to leave, halfway out the tent when she turns back to me. "Hey."

I look to her, the star-studded night just beyond her broad shoulders.

"I'm sorry you had to steam him. I know how you felt about him."

For a long time after she goes, I don't move. Sounds from outside permeate the tent. Conversations. Laughter—louder, as I push through the flaps.

I walk through the camp, see Ren. Tourmaline. She sits down

beside Cloud by the bonfire, and I quell the urge to join them. I'm Crow in this game. If there's anyone I should be going to, it's Cicada. But I can't. For just one night, I don't want to pretend.

I walk quicker, to the very edge of camp.

The Mica River gleams ahead. It starts from the north, flowing through the hills here, then down south, carving out the Westlands eastern border. But it feels very far away, both Ren's base and Aurora Nest.

I can't choose both.

The bottle grows heavy in my pocket. My hand dips to it, a gesture that awakens another memory—of stealing the bottle from *his* pocket—and I pull myself together. I may be weary, but it's only fair that I address him.

"Speak. I'm listening."

My voice meets the night, dark and unresponsive.

"About what?" Crow finally says. "These supposed feelings of yours you did a terrible job of hiding?"

"No, *Crow*. About what happened in the gorge."

"There's nothing to say. I tried to kill you. I failed. I suppose you want to ask if I'm happy I failed." I wait for Crow to go on. "She was never supposed to be there."

His voice is quieter as he refers to Cicada. Everything he's done is for her, and as much as I want to rub salt into the wound that she almost died because of *his* actions, I can't. He's already been punished. We faced the same terror in the gorge—except Crow, unlike me, has already lost a lordess. How does one survive that sort of failure? How did Crow live on, however shabbily, without the luxury of forgetting?

"And what do you have to say, Zephyr? Or did you just want to listen to my voice?"

I inhale. *Focus.* "Ren wasn't supposed to be in the gorge either." But then my mind frays to the bottle again. *What would you do, Crow, in my position?*

If the people we serve are determined to lose, then isn't what we do meaningless?

"You failed and I failed," I say in the end. I face him, eyes tracing his form in the moonlight. "Let's call it a draw."

"A draw." Crow chuckles, no warmth to the sound. "Whatever gave you the impression I'd be content with a draw?"

"It's that or defeat. Take your pick," I say as someone approaches.

That someone would be Ku. "Xiaoqiu," I greet, too drained to be startled as she lifts my sleeve to her nose.

"You smell like smoke."

"It'll come out."

"You weren't in your tent."

"I needed some air. I'll come back soon."

Ku stares at me. Not moving. Waiting for me, I realize, to go with her.

Crow's chill follows us back to camp.

In the tent, I start to cough. *Ugh.* Even my restored qì is no match for Crow's consumption. Or is it the ash and smoke I inhaled?

Ku holds out a handkerchief. "Will you leave again?" she asks as I accept it.

"For the North? No."

"Will you leave, ever?"

"No."

"You lie. You're older."

Only by four years or so, which Ku makes sound like decades.

"I will live a long and healthy life," I say as glibly as Crow would, and Ku frowns.

"Cicada?"

"She won't die before you either."

"You didn't think about dying in the gorge." Ku's tone doesn't change, but I suddenly see the little girl lying beside Qilin's corpse, muttering *come back* to her spirit.

"No." The front of my tent ripples. "The thought of it never even crossed our minds. Right, Chanmei?" I ask Cicada as she enters. "I'm just telling Xiaoqiu here that we're all going to grow old together."

Cicada raises a brow. "You included?"

"Of—"

Cough.

"Come," Cicada says to Ku, taking her by the hand. "Senge needs his sleep." She glares at me as they leave, mouthing, *Take your medicine!*

I will! I mouth back.

I don't. I lie down, but don't sleep. Everyone else does. The camp goes quiet.

Quiet as death.

It was all I knew, as an orphan, and I never feared it. Not for myself. But today . . . My chest hurts, and not with consumption, as I think of Ku's questions, of Cloud's tight hug, of Ren's choice to come to Xianlei just to make amends with her swornsister, as if she might not get another chance.

Every chance could be the last for these humans.

It's different, I'd said to Nadir, when comparing our relationships.

Relationships are different when they're not meant to last forever.

But I could help them last a little longer.

They just need to listen to me.

My hand throbs around the bottle; I force myself to unclench it.

"Can I give you some advice, Crow?"

No reply.

"Don't kill yourself or anyone else in your effort to stop me. It's not worth the trouble, or the risk. I promise you this: I won't hurt Cicada if she doesn't hurt Ren."

"Give me one good reason I should trust you, Zephyr."

Because . . .

Because I like you, Crow had said to me first. A lie, like all his others.

In contrast, the words in my heart are true. *Because I like you, but I suppose that's not a good reason. In this war, I know it wasn't enough to stop me. And now it's not enough to gain your trust. I dream of a life in which it was, but in this one—*

Trust me, because I will succeed.

‡ ‡ ‡

We make it all the way to the Mica before an empire legion finally intercepts us. They're fresh from the capital reserves, and not Miasma's Marshlands forces like I feared. Still, had Ren and Cicada followed my plans and marched out of the South, our soldiers wouldn't have encountered forces at all. Blood wouldn't pour like water when the fight breaks out.

Our victory wouldn't come at such a cost.

‡ ‡ ‡

Miasma, true to my original predictions, pushes hard into the Marshlands, reversing course when she realizes Ren and Cicada are coming out of the Xianlei Gorge. Had Ren and Cicada gone North as I'd ordered, they'd have been in the perfect position to outflank. Instead the task is left to Sikou Hai, who does his best to attack the retreat.

We decimated most of their forces, he writes. *But Miasma managed to escape back to the capital.*

Where she'll be awaiting us. We'll have lost the element of surprise.

The message crumples in my fist.

"Any sighting of Plum?" I ask the soldier who delivered it.

"No."

"Keep searching. I don't care if you have to go as far as the Sanzuwu Sea. You have to find her."

"Yes, sir."

‡ ‡ ‡

Our march eastward continues, our forces closing in on the capital. With Cicada's and Ren's troops united, we defeat each wave of palace reserves sent out to meet us. But our ranks of wounded also grow. Farmers lose their harvests to us and to the enemy.

This, I think at night when the coughing keeps me up, the taste of blood heavy in my mouth, is why our victory shouldn't have been dragged out. War is senseless. It's the cause of disease, famine, and the lone child awaiting us in one abandoned village.

"We have to bring her with us," Ren says, and Cicada, beside her, nods and dismounts. She goes to the child. "Where are your parents?"

Dead, I think before the child can say so. Orphans know fellow orphans. Orphans are who I once fought for—

But you are not one of them, whispers my heart.

In my pocket, the bottle seems to warm.

‡ ‡ ‡

The next night, eighty li from the capital, an ultimatum arrives at our camp.

Surrender now, or Xin Bao will die.

A cheap, dirty trick, but not unexpected. That Miasma stoops to it must mean she can feel us closing in and doesn't like her chances.

"It's a bluff," says Sikou Hai, whose troops have joined up with ours.

"You don't know for certain," Ren challenges.

"Miasma wouldn't." Three of us say it at the same time—Sikou Hai, Cicada, and myself.

Ren doesn't reply. She touches the pendant on her throat, and I recall Miasma's dream. They know each other better than most, but proximity is also the enemy of perspective.

"If Miasma kills her," Cicada says, "then that's one more justification we offer the realm when we kill Miasma."

If Miasma kills Xin Bao, she will have done Cicada a favor—and perhaps me as well. Then I wouldn't have to hurt Ku and Crow's lordess.

I'm of Sikou Hai's mind, though. A puppet is only useful alive, and in the end, Ren takes our counsel to do nothing but press onward.

But the next night, when we're just forty li from the capital, another message arrives.

> *I see you did not respond to my previous offer.*
> *Then I'll give you a new one.*
> *Come to the throne hall, tomorrow.*
> *Duel me, Ren. Just you and me.*
> *Whoever wins inherits the empire and empress.*

Ren folds this letter up after reading it. She turns to us, and I'm back in the gorge, watching her ride into the fire. I'm urging her to take the title of governor. I'm facing her disappointment for the coup against Xin Gong, and I'm on the mountain, trying to save our soldiers *and* the commoners, convincing myself that I can do it, I'm the *Rising Zephyr*, practically a god—

But even I'm not limitless, and that awful bone-weariness sweeps back through me as Ren says, "I'm going at dawn."

"*Ren!*" the others cry.

"None of you are to follow."

"This is a trap," Sikou Hai protests.

"I agree," says Cicada, and points her dart shooter, prompting Tourmaline to step in front of Ren and Cloud to bark, "What do you think you're doing?"

"Darting her before she goes riding into her death."

Cloud raises her glaive, but Ren places a hand on her shoulder. "Stand down, Cloud. You too, Tourmaline. She won't do it."

"Don't tempt me," mutters Cicada. But she doesn't shoot when Tourmaline and Cloud reluctantly part before Ren, who addresses the Southlands queen.

"We've gotten this far together. But from here on, I must go alone."

"Not alone," says Cloud. "We're coming with you."

Ren nods, but her eyes are shadowed.

Through it all, I stay silent.

"You have to stop Ren," Sikou Hai urges me later when we, as two allied advisors, are walking through the camp. He stumbles as the child we saved clings to his legs, having taken a liking to him. "Miasma would only ask for a duel if—Heavens, I think I stepped on her."

"Carry her."

"Carry—?"

I hoist the child up; Cicada wasn't lying about Crow's ulcers.

"Quick—bend down." I plop her onto Sikou Hai's shoulders and grunt, "I can't stop Ren. I'm Crow."

"Then give *me* an idea on how to stop her," Sikou Hai grunts back.

"Weren't you the one who wanted to respect Ren's wishes on executing the messenger?"

"This is a mistake of even greater proportions! Miasma would only ask for a duel if she didn't think she could defeat us army to army. We ought to ride into the capital with all our forces."

"I know." Oh, I know.

We come to an overlook, an impromptu tournament taking place in the clearing below. Word hasn't yet reached our soldiers of what their queen plans to do—in part, I understand, to spare them of more bloodshed.

But no one wins if Ren perishes in Miasma's trap.

"A mentor once taught me chess," I say to Sikou Hai as Aster defeats her opponent and calls for another. "We played hundreds of games, until I won. 'Good,' she said, 'now remember that people are the same; everyone has a role, a place. But you can't push them around like chess pieces. You have to inspire trust. Only then can you use them.'

"But what about the people we do this for?" Down below, cheers rise as Cloud steps in. "We do this all for Ren, but sometimes . . ."

I trail off.

Sometimes, Ren doesn't know what's good for her.

282 + JOAN HE

The silence on our overlook grows; below, Cloud defeats Aster and everyone roars.

"Master . . ."

"Sorry. I know that's not an answer."

Sikou Hai hefts the child on his shoulders. "We've defeated nearly all Miasma's forces, because she aimed at the Marshlands like you predicted. Even if Ren rides in alone . . . Well, it's not ideal, but there can't be *that* many soldiers . . ."

If I'm bad at comforting people, Sikou Hai is worse. Like disciple like mentor, I suppose.

"I'm sorry," I say again, facing him. "I haven't been a good mentor."

His mouth works, not sure what to do with my apology. Then his jaw locks. "So teach me more. You have a lifetime to."

A lifetime. My smile feels like a grimace. I didn't have a lifetime with my mentors . . .

. . . And maybe Sikou Hai doesn't have a lifetime with me. Glass meets my fingertips; unwittingly, my hand has drifted to my pocket. If I choose to leave him—if I choose to leave all of them—"I should give you a sobriquet."

Let that be my parting gift if Ren refuses to win.

"I don't want one," Sikou Hai says to my surprise.

"You're that attached to your birth name?"

"Not attached. Just obliged." Sikou Hai looks to the arena, where Tourmaline has stepped in to challenge Cloud. "The people you saw that night we played the zither? They're not my birth parents either. I was left at their door."

"Sikou Dun?"

"Was their trueborn son, before Xin Gong adopted us both."

I blink, digesting this. "That doesn't excuse how they treated you. Why keep their name?"

"They did give me a roof and a bed," Sikou Hai says dryly. "For that, I owe it to them to take their name into the next generation."

You owe them nothing, I want to say. But I'm just a worse person.

Or not human. I turn away from the hill before I can see the outcome of Cloud and Tourmaline's match. "Get some rest."

"What about Ren?"

"Let me think of a plan."

But my mind doesn't even try, and when I reach my tent, I don't go in.

The bottle is still clenched in my hand.

Drink, and you'll forget what is on your mind in that moment.

I look across the tents, to Ren's.

Do I owe her? I thought I did. Maybe I was obliged by fate. I've done my best for her. I really have. But if I can't win for Ren *because* of Ren . . .

Then perhaps it is better to forget.

No. It's better for *Ren* to forget. Pass her the elixir in a cup of tea while she's thinking about Miasma's ultimatum, and she'll forget all about it and Xin Bao. Then she'd have no problem rushing the empire with the full force of her troops, and we'd defeat Miasma as planned.

Anything to secure our win.

The only risk is if Miasma actually kills Xin Bao. But that's a small loss. Ren would have ruled behind the scenes either way. Why not rule in name? It may not be what Ren wants, but it's what she must face. She just can't see it yet.

I can make her.

Lightning flashes in the night. The wind rises, smelling of ozone.

It wraps around me, ice-cold.

My gaze lifts from Ren's tent and meets Crow's.

He knows what I'm thinking.

He stares at me, and I stare back. *You can't stop me.*

I know, say his eyes.

You shouldn't want *to stop me. Your lordess wants Xin Bao dead.*

I know. Together, we look to the bottle in my hand. As green as the tea he stopped me from drinking. Would he have stopped me again, knowing the consequences? Almost certainly not. But if there's the smallest chance—if I wasn't misreading the look in his eyes that night—then maybe. Maybe he would choose to save my memories, for the sake of our rivalry—

But not for someone who then turns around and drugs her lordess.

Slowly, I pop the bead stopper to the bottle. The bottle that I only have because of Dewdrop. All this time, she and Nadir have been trying to stop me. To save me. Now I finally know how they must have felt, watching me deal everything away for these humans. But that's my choice, and if I regret it, then so be it. I don't want to be saved from myself.

Ren wouldn't either.

I tip the bottle over; the elixir spills onto the dirt.

I watch it vanish without a trace.

Then I find a jug of wine from our supply wagons.

I saddle a horse and ride out alone, into the gathering storm.

‡ ‡ ‡

I stop at the highest hill.

Thirty-five lǐ farther is the capital.

If Ren must duel Miasma at the palace, the least I can do is scout it out in advance. Problem is, I wasn't able to see beyond ten lǐ at my strongest.

I've only been able to cover more distance as a spirit.

"What are you doing now, Zephyr?" Crow murmurs as I dismount.

I grab the jug of wine. "Something inadvisable." Probably. Who knows? Who knows if this has even been done before? No god would be foolish enough to try. In principle, though, a spirit is nothing more than a nebula of qì, and a nebula can be split. With half my spirit, I can scout out the capital while the other half of me stays in Crow.

I uncork the wine and gulp.

Crow's alcohol tolerance is laughable compared to Lotus's, and in no time, I feel myself loosening. I let the sensation gather, then hold fast to a part of my spirit. *Tear. Split.* But the force isn't enough, and I don't know how to increase it. *Tear! Split!*

As I struggle, the night flashes white. Thunder immediately follows, the bolts close by.

So close, they are practically above me.

There's one more way to expel a spirit—the same method Nadir used to expel both my qì and Lotus's at the Obelisk.

I'm sorry, Crow, I think as I sit and hold my hands, palms open, atop my knees.

This will hurt.

I channel the atmosphere above myself, reducing the pressure in the lower clouds. Energy rises, a charge building in the friction until the heavens can no longer hold it.

Lightning cracks down.

四十六

SISTERS OF BEFORE

*L*ightning cracks down.

It strikes a cloud.

From the energy, I form. Around me, I hear voices. The sound of some plucked instrument. A girl with snakes, a toddler, and a bee (the last two are the same entity, I come to learn) live in a white gazebo not that far away. Often, the girl will read beside me while the bee does somersaults through my vapor.

"Hello," I finally say one day. "Who are you?"

The girl puts down her scroll. "Nadir. Your older sister."

And I'm Dewdrop, *says the bee, her words vibrating through my particles.* I'm your slightly less old sister.

"Sisters. What are those?"

"Family."

"What is family?"

The girl and the bee look at each other.

"Come." The girl reaches down to me, and even though I have no body, I feel a desire for one. The wind blows through me, and

from the cloud, I rise, a hand emerging to grasp hers. "We'll show you."

‡ ‡ ‡

Dewdrop. Nadir. I'm sorry, I think as the lightning severs through me.

I won't be coming home.

A tear.

In my spirit.

Becomes complete.

Half of me soars away, sweeping through the capital, finding the legion in the barracks, forces that I already knew existed. My connection starts to disperse.

No. Not yet.

I force my spirit half into the palace, looking for mines, rigged doors, vats of poison, anything that resembles a trap—

My connection snaps. My vision, granted by the spirit half, falls away like ash. I'm back—to the hill, the storm, the wind whipping the treetops below.

What Miasma has in store during the duel itself, there's no way of knowing, but besides her remaining forces, I found no other ambushes. I need to get back and tell the others. I rise—and bend over, clutching my chest as it spasms.

Blood splashes onto the grass.

What have you done? scolds the voice in my head as more blood dribbles down my chin. *You could have used your spirit to look for Plum. What have you done?*

I—

Another spasm; another splash.

Red grass, fading to black.

‡ ‡ ‡

Blackness, as far as the eye can see.

The night is endless.

Is this mortal death? Is that what happened? I spin, searching for some semblance of direction.

"Somehow, you still manage to surprise me."

"Crow?" I whirl, and there he is—the only person standing in the dark. He walks forward, and I retreat. "What are you doing? Are you here to take back your body?"

"You mean the body you just got struck by lightning?" He stops before me, shaking his head, but I don't trust him. The whole point of splitting my spirit was to ensure that I would remain in Crow. Now that I've passed out, anything's fair game.

Foolish. Desperate. My internal voice is harsh, so unlike Crow's soft one as he asks, "Why, Zephyr? You know this is a bad plan." He reaches out to cup my cheek, and this must be some hallucination, because the real Crow would never touch me so tenderly, and his voice wouldn't be so caring when he says, "You could have died."

No, Crow, you could have died.

I'm a god, and it's because I'm a god that I've made you suffer so much.

"I'm sorry," I whisper, "for everything."

Crow smiles, then flickers.

"Crow?"

His spirit blows away before my eyes.

"*Crow!*"

‡ ‡ ‡

Crow. I jolt awake, his name on my tongue. Around me, the hills blur by, blue in the dawn. I'm on a horse, mask on my face, my body held in place by a pair of arms.

Cloud's arms. "Cloud . . . ?" Another rider gallops behind us, horse white and armor silver. "Tourmaline . . . ?"

"What did I tell you about riding off on your own, Zephyr?" the warrior shouts at me, stopping my heart.

I look back to Cloud, who shakes her head as if to say *Don't ask.* "Tourmaline caught me riding out to that hill to find you. I tried to make some excuse—but you know her, always putting two and two together." Cloud makes a half-exasperated, half-affectionate sound. "Something about me *not* bashing in your skull must have given it away."

"H-how did you know I was on the hill?" I stammer, and Cloud grimaces.

"Don't laugh—but I followed the wind."

The wind. Crow. He led Cloud to me. I crane my head, searching for him. "Stop wiggling," Cloud orders, but I have to find him. Has his spirit really scattered? *No.* He can't have left—

A new voice rises behind us, winnowed by the wind, but still recognizable as Cicada's.

"You! Warrior! Where are you taking my strategist?"

Cloud doesn't reply, only urges her mare faster.

"Slow down for her," I order.

"No."

"Do it, or else I'll tell Tourmaline you lost to me at chess."

"I should have left you for dead." But Cloud slows down, and when Cicada catches up, I say, "I passed out when I was scouting ahead. Cloud found me."

"Impressive that you reached us," Cloud shouts to Cicada.

"What, think Southerners can't ride?" Cicada shouts back.

"Well, you're going to have to ride faster." To me: "Ren left for the capital without us."

I knew she would, but my stomach sinks regardless.

"I should have darted her," snaps Cicada, kicking into a faster gallop.

"I did." My gaze slingshots to Tourmaline. "Her horse, last night," she clarifies. "It'll be slower."

"We'll catch up," Cloud promises, and my grip tightens on her arm. We have to.

And we do just before the capital, Miasma's final legion stationed outside the walls.

Riding to meet them is Ren.

"Ren!" Cloud hollers, and Ren whirls her mount. "You forgot something!"

We gallop up behind her.

"Cloud—Tourmaline—Cicada—" Ren's gaze flits from face to face, unable to settle on a single person to be disappointed in. "You shouldn't be here."

"*You* shouldn't have left without telling us," says Cloud.

"I—"

"Queen!"

We all whirl; Sikou Hai thunders up with a cohort of soldiers, and Ren's face goes grave. "Send them away," she orders, but Sikou Hai stands firm.

"Why? Miasma has *her* troops outside the walls. It's only fair that we have our own forces here to ensure she honors her word to duel you one-on-one."

"I agree with him," says Cloud.

"And I," says Cicada. "Have the troops stay."

A tendon jumps in Ren's jaw. She turns from us and, without a word, gallops to the wall, drawing short of the enemy soldiers.

Her horse rears, throwing her shadow long on the ground.

"I'm here, Miasma! Show yourself!"

"Xin Ren!" a bell-clear voice rings out; a eunuch, clad in empire scarlet, appears atop the battlements. "The prime ministress awaits you inside."

Ren gathers her reins. "Make way."

"Wait!" says Sikou Hai, riding up behind her.

"This is my decision."

"But—"

"What have we been fighting for, if not this?" Sikou Hai looks on in dismay, and Ren's gaze softens. "I appreciate everything you've done for me. You, and Qilin. But this all started six years ago when the empress asked for my help, and finally, I can help." Ren glances up to the eunuch on the walls. "If this is a trap, then I have failed. Death would not be the worst possible outcome."

"But—but the realm—" Sikou Hai looks to me, imploring

me to do something, but there's nothing left for me to do. I made my choice when I poured out the elixir.

I understand that I won't be here to protect Ren and everyone forever—that to be a strategist means to serve.

"Have the soldiers surrender their weapons!" Cicada calls out.

"Disarm!" is the eunuch's response.

Miasma's legion complies, swords and spears clanging onto the ground. Their ranks part, and our troops stream forward, lining the enemy corridor.

Ren rides through them.

Cloud starts to follow, but I mutter, "Take me to Sikou Hai first." We canter up before him, and I say, "Stay here. If all is well, we will give a signal."

"What signal?"

"You'll know it."

"And if not? When do I come to help?"

"Use your judgment. I trust you."

"Wait—"

Cloud rides away before he can finish—but not to Ren. To Tourmaline.

Her mare blocks the warrior's white one.

"You stay out here and protect our soldiers with Sikou Hai. Do it," Cloud orders when Tourmaline frowns and tries to bypass us. "For me." Then Cloud grabs the other warrior's fist and presses the knuckles, once and quick, to her lips. Tourmaline blinks, and Cloud lets go, face redder than all the times she's wanted to kill me and Crow. "And do it for Zephyr!" she shouts, pulling away on her mare. "It's the strategic thing!"

Bold of Cloud to invoke me. If I were still here as Zephyr, I'd order Cloud to stay behind too. But I know she won't let Ren go in alone, just as Ren says, "I'm going alone."

"No. The ultimatum said you'd *duel* Miasma alone," says Cloud.

"But we're coming with you," says Cicada.

"And I with you," I say to Cicada.

"No, Senge—"

"I've left my lordess once. Don't make me do it again."

My words rob Cicada of hers, like I knew they would. For a second, we're all locked in a contest of wills. Stalemated in silence. Then—

A groan.

Ahead of us, the doors open.

四十七

LONG MAY SHE LIVE

The doors open.
We follow Ren inside.

The city is empty. The streets are cleared.

Our hooves echo in the quiet.

Cloud hefts her glaive. *It's safe*, I'd tell her, but best to be vigilant. Shuttered storefronts line the streets, shadows lurking behind windows. When we pass a half-closed doorway, I catch a glimpse of eyes from the darkness. The civilians are here, just in hiding. Are they happy to see us? Or are we simply more warlords to them, like the countless others who've fought to control the capital before Miasma? Perhaps they fear the turbulence of the future, should we defeat *her*, but they needn't.

Ren won't let it happen.

Unchallenged, we're soon at the palace. A great wall surrounds it, at least two stories tall, bisected by a single set of doors.

These too are already open.

Before anyone can move, Cloud gallops through with me. I

already know her fated death won't spring out from the eaves or fly down in the form of a hundred crossbows, but still. Warriors.

The coast clear, Cloud looks back at the others; Ren shakes her head while Cicada hisses, cursing Cloud for putting me in danger, I imagine, then following through herself.

We stop before the steps that ascend to the throne hall.

Ren breathes in.

She once walked these steps, as an official of the court under the previous tyrant. Perhaps she walked them beside Miasma, the tyrant of the present. It's been six years. Now we're here. We've ridden farther than the scrolls said, farther than the visions showed.

Fate will change.

In some ways, it already has.

Ren dismounts. She goes first. We walk up the steps after her. My muscles tremble. I stumble, and Cloud catches my left arm while Cicada catches my right; glares pass over my head, but they keep silent. A leaf drifts in the air as we climb; I look up to it, to the swooping eaves of the throne hall, lifted toward the sky like the snouts of dragons. Beyond the palace are the mountains and the origins of rivers. We're at the empire's helm. A draft surrounds me, and I shiver.

Crow? Is that you?

Please tell me if you're still here.

But no response comes, only the draft, and as we reach the top step, even that disappears.

The leaf settles on the marble of the pavilion.

Ren strides over it, then over the threshold.

"Ren, oh, Ren. How long has it been? You've grown thin."

The words are loud after so much silence.

"Where is she?" Ren asks, and Miasma rises from her cushion like a monk out of meditation. Behind her is the expanse of the throne hall—with no throne. No ghosts. Only a façade waits in the back, painted with mountains and rivers and flanked by two gongs.

"Impatience isn't like you." Miasma. My eyes go back to her. Her gaze is focused solely on Ren. If she notices me, Cicada, and Cloud, she pays us no mind.

"My patience for you long ran out," Ren says.

"Ah, the hatred." Miasma walks forward. "Did it ever make you dream of me, Ren? Did you ever dream of driving a blade into my neck? Because I've dreamed of the day I'd see you like this." She stops several steps away, the red bell chiming at her ear. "Sometimes, I worried you wouldn't make it."

"Where is the empress?"

"You betrayed me, Ren." Miasma speaks as if Ren never did. "We once fought on the same side. In the same army."

"You betrayed that army first by taking the empress hostage."

"Me? A betrayer? I'm the reason why your dear empress is alive at all. I'm the one who ended Gongsun Qian, Wang Boyang, and Xuan Cao!" Miasma's voice booms. "As you spent your energies fighting me, I fought to protect this empire, which is still named Xin, I'll have you know. Look at who you've allied with. That girl, there?" Finally, Miasma acknowledges us. My mask feels sheer, but she only points at Cicada with her sheathed sword, her eyes still on Ren. "She's the one who really wants to kill Xin Bao and steal her throne."

"You don't speak for me," growls Cicada, but my attention is on Ren. Even if she suspected that was Cicada's goal, will it faze her to hear it spoken?

No—she, like Miasma, is of one mind. "Where is the empress?" she asks for a third time, and Miasma steps back.

"Defeat me, and I'll hand her to you like I promised. I'll give her to you fair and square."

"I'm not fighting you until you show me that she's alive."

"So pedantic." Miasma waves a hand, and two eunuchs emerge from the wings, each going to one side of the façade. They pull, and the screen splits down the middle, revealing our empress.

Xin Bao, fifth of her line, descendant of the great Xin Bang who defeated the legendary warrior Gaixia to establish the Xin Dynasty. She sits in her throne, made of gilt. Her robes are red and flowing, her headdress towering, the beads curtained over her eyes. One bead moves—a red bell, same as Miasma's. It tinkles, jostled by a breath.

She lives.

She lives, but is tied. Ropes bind her arms to the throne's. Ren starts for her—and meets Miasma's still-sheathed sword. The rest of us freeze too, having moved with her.

"Uh-uh." Miasma wags her finger. "This is not how it'll work. Take a closer look at the empress you've journeyed so far for."

I squint.

Over Xin Bao's head, higher than even the headdress, is a bronze bowl suspended from a thin chain. At Miasma's signal, one of the eunuchs pushes the empress's throne forward, out from under the bowl. Miasma, meanwhile, walks toward Ren.

Cloud's fist audibly tightens around her glaive as the prime ministress stops three strides from our lordess.

She places a foot down, slow and deliberate.

Thwunk. Liquid splatters. My eyes flash to the bowl, now overturned.

"Under these floorboards is a series of levers," Miasma explains with great pleasure. "Should anyone step on one, the bowl will flip, and the oil within—hot this time—will pour down. You will fry our empress here—long may she live.

"So be good now." Miasma beckons Ren forward, and Ren alone. Ren walks in, eyes trained on the bowl as it's refilled. The oil is lit, the bowl hoisted up the chain, the empress wheeled back under its shadow. "Sit, and watch the show."

Ren unsheathes. "Stay where you are," she says to us, "no matter what happens." Her eyes never leave Miasma.

Cloud and I are silent. We've traveled thousands of lǐ with our lordess; we know better than to argue with her at this juncture.

Only Cicada is a stranger. "Wait," she says before I can tell her not to bother. Ren turns—catching her second sword by the hilt as Cicada throws it.

Virtue and Integrity, finally reunited.

"Defeat her," Cicada says. Miasma chuckles, but Ren nods. She turns back to the prime ministress, and I know this is the moment Ren has lived for, day after day. Facing Miasma in a battle to end all battles, so that no one else—not one more soldier or civilian—dies in her name.

How can we take this away from her?

But how can we bear watching her be taken away from us?

We must. *I* must, even as Ren's every step toward Miasma unravels me as if we're connected by a string. I plant my feet to the ground. I poured the elixir out knowing the risks. Ren is my lordess, but above that—Ren is her own person.

Her life is not a game I can win for her.

She stops across from Miasma, ten strides left between them.

"What are you waiting for? An invitation?" Miasma opens her arms. "Come at me, Ren."

We're far, but not so far that I can't see the rise of Ren's chest as she takes a breath. And another step.

Miasma stands where she is, smiling, sword still sheathed even when Ren's next step is quicker than the last. Three more steps.

She dashes.

Miasma sidesteps, ducks, Ren's swords swiping at where her head was. Her sword remains in its scabbard and my teeth grit, but Ren is patient. The bell at Miasma's ear tinkles as she jumps around, before finally stilling before the throne. I don't see her unsheathe so much as I hear it: a shrill of steel, then a *clang*, her blade brought up to block Ren's. She staggers backward almost playfully.

"Missed me, didn't you?"

Ren doesn't speak, just presses in, two swords to Miasma's one, Miasma's blade under hers—then between as Ren changes hold. She jerks and Miasma's blade would go flying if Miasma didn't spin with the torque, toward Ren. They break apart.

And meet again.

"Remember what you said to me?" Miasma asks, pressing into Ren. "'Names don't mean anything—'"

Arc of steel.

"But you lied." *Clang.* "Everything you've done—" *Clang.* "—and continue to do—" *Clang.* "Hasn't been for the people."
Clang clang clang.

"It's been for your good name." Miasma shoves, and Ren whirls back and crouches, one hand and knee to the ground. "Not talkative, are we? Then I'll make you talk."

Miasma springs forward and Ren pushes off. Blood flecks, someone cut. Miasma. Still she lunges, the tip of her sword nicking Ren's brow. Blood streams down, and I choke on a breath as Miasma moves in while Ren is blinded. Ren raises her sword as if on instinct, blocking Miasma's blow, but not her foot. It slams Ren's chest and the silence holding us breaks.

"Ren!"

She lands, swords spinning across the floor.

Miasma walks in, and I grab the back of Cloud's cloak just as it pulls taut. She glares at me; I glare back. I've sparred with Ren more recently than Cloud.

I know this is not the end.

Miasma swings and Ren rolls, out of the blade's path. I let go of Cloud. "Beside you," she hisses, and beside me—is Cicada, walking toward the forbidden floorboards.

Her eyes on the empress.

Should anyone step on one, the bowl will flip . . .

Stop. But say it, and I'll be like all her advisors. Cicada will only want it more.

If she stops, it must be by her own accord.

As she walks, I notice something in her grip.

The poison dart shooter.

She stills, stands, and eyes Miasma and Ren, who are now tangled on the ground. Fist to mouth, arm around neck, the upper hand gained and lost. My stomach turns with them. Shoot Ren, and Cicada could call it an accident. Then I stop worrying about Cicada, because Miasma is on top, a dagger suddenly in her fist. Ren stops it hairs from her face, grip shaking. Grip opening. The dagger plunges into the floor, Ren's face turned away, Miasma rooted—then pinned belly-down, Ren's hand wrapped around her lopsided ponytail. With her free hand, Ren draws another dagger from the hidden stash in Miasma's broadbelt.

She shoves the blade under Miasma's chin. "I win."

Two words, breath laden.

"No, Ren." Miasma grins, then grabs Ren's hand, dagger and all. "You may have gotten stronger, but you're—"

She bucks her head back and pulls the dagger up, over her face.

"—still too soft."

The blade skims through the base of her ponytail, leaving Ren with a stump of hair as Miasma twists around, freed, the tip of her nose sheared off. A fresh dagger flashes into her hand.

It all happens at once.

Cloud leaps over the floorboards as the dagger goes into

Ren's gut and Cicada fires a poison dart. It hits Miasma—in the armguard. She plucks it out, somersaults, and slams it into Cloud's jaw as the warrior bears down on her.

Cloud crumples.

Miasma rises and grins at Cicada. "Thank you, ally."

Cicada breathes hard through her teeth. "Our alliance is over."

"Your aim could have fooled me. And now for breaking the rules I set so clearly . . ."

She bolts at us. Cicada fires—dart in ceiling as Miasma seizes her wrist. She takes the dart shooter and the next thing I know, a dart is in my arm.

We hit the ground, Cicada and myself.

Boots stop by my body, already numb.

Miasma squats.

She slides my mask up.

"Hello, Crow. Thank you for sharing the physician's notes. Who would have known that her medicines would work so well in treating my migraines?" Miasma sighs. "I killed her too hastily, didn't I? I thought I'd spare Plum and give her a chance to redeem herself. A shame she couldn't, seeing that you made it out of the Xianlei Gorge. Ah, well, I suppose I'll execute you soon enough. For now"—she turns my head to the side, so that my eyes face the throne hall—"please enjoy their finales before your personal one."

My body might be frozen, but my mind isn't.

By using the notes against Crow, I inadvertently saved Plum and delayed Miasma's death.

My failure, and Ren will pay for it.

Miasma lugs her across the hall.

"Which would you like to be pinned with? Virtue or Integrity? No preference?" Miasma stabs Integrity through Ren's hand and Ren grunts, the sound more awful than the scream she swallows for us. I taste blood in my own mouth as Miasma nails the sword to the wall, then turns. Cloud is still a heap before the throne.

Miasma walks to the warrior and gazes down at her.

"Twice, I've captured you. Twice, I've set you free. Do you want to know the real reason why?" She looks over her shoulder, back at Ren. "She was never there to watch you die."

"Mimeng—"

A rasp from Ren. *Mimeng.* It's the name I heard in Miasma's mind, a name from another time. Will Ren beg for Cloud's life? I would, if only I could speak. If only I could do anything but lie on the floor, powerless, as Ren says, "Do you know why the heavens will never favor you? Not because of your name. Because—of what's inside. Your own bloodthirst made you irredeemable. The people—will never love you because of—it."

Silence.

"Do you think they love you?" Miasma says. "No. They love your 'Xin' and the continuation of this dynasty it represents. They follow you out of fear of change. It's anything but love."

Then Miasma turns her back on Ren, facing Cloud again.

"You said you'd serve me only in my dreams." *Get up*, I think to Cloud. *Get up! Be the warrior that I know you are!* But Cloud is as motionless as we are, and Miasma smiles. "Maybe you'll consider serving me in the afterlife.

"Goodbye, Cloud." She raises her sword, tip poised above Cloud's shoulder blades. "I thought of a poem just for this occasion. Would you like to hear it?"

Get! Up!

But still Cloud doesn't move, and I go cold with despair.

Or . . . is it the cold of Crow?

What should I do?

What *can* I do?

Miasma's voice warbles out, beginning her poem. "*The length of a life—*"

Across the room, Ren pulls the sword out of her hand. She staggers away from the wall, pooling blood, and I wish I could shut my eyes. *It's hopeless.* She can't save Cloud. Beside me Cicada strains to move. *It's useless.* I saw how long the pirate was incapacitated by the poison . . .

Cicada's poison. She'd have tolerance—

—or an antidote.

Something pricks my skin.

Too slowly, feeling trickles back through my limbs.

"*—whether long or short—*" Miasma recites on.

Twenty paces from her, Ren lurches to a stop, her face glistening with exertion, the cut above her brow stark.

"*Depends not on the will of the skies.*"

Miasma is taking too long. *Why?*

Ren raises her sword, her eyes closing against the blood dripping into them.

"One who sleeps well and is well-nourished—"

Crow's voice fills my mind. *Not everyone is a chess piece, Zephyr—*

—Least of all the people we serve.

For me, that's Ren.

For Ren that's—

No. My vocal cords strain to move, but any sound that I make is drowned out by Miasma's voice as Ren charges.

"Will outlive the tortoise—"

The distance, closed.

The sword, thrusted.

Blade through chest.

四十八

TWO SUNS

*B*lade *through chest.*

Sunlight fills the room, golden, and it's like I'm back in heaven, the scene before me just another one of the Masked Mother's reenactments. That's not Miasma. That's not Ren.

That's not our empress, standing between them, Ren's sword through her chest.

Blood drips in the silence.

Then laughter gushes. Miasma's. Ren releases the hilt, as if burned, leaving Xin Bao with the blade in her. An image so wrong, but it can't be undone. Pulling it out would kill her—

Faster. Kill her faster. The empress is dying. Beyond saving. The floor tilts beneath me, and Cicada beats me to her senses. A dart flies; down goes the prime ministress. She laughs on, her delight overcoming even the poison, which must be working through her veins at the same time ours is counteracted. Sensation floods my chest—then pain, as I realize what this means for Ren. She's frozen. Utterly frozen. A bell tinkles—Xin Bao's, as she sways—and Ren finally moves, catching our empress.

She lays her on the ground.

The last of the poison leaves me; I stagger to my feet and cross the floorboards, eyes trained on the throne.

Nothing happens. The bowl of oil doesn't flip. The demonstration before must have been staged. How naturally we assumed that it'd be in Miasma's character to concoct this sadistic punishment.

She deceived us.

Xin Bao did too.

"Don't touch her," Ren growls when I kneel by the empress and push up one of her sleeves. I stop, but Ren has also seen. The truth is on Xin Bao's arms.

They're unmarked.

She was not bound. Never bound. Even if she was, she freed herself.

She chose to stand between death and Miasma.

"Why?" Ren croaks. "Did she threaten you?"

"You're so good, Aunt Ren."

Xin Bao's voice is high-pitched. Girlish. It's my first time hearing it in person. My first time seeing the empress in person.

I don't know what I expected, or what to feel.

Can't feel anything but numb.

"You really are so . . . good. Six years, you fought for me. For one decree. I hear . . . not once . . . did you covet . . ."

Xin Bao's eyes roll to the throne.

". . . my seat." Her voice is already fading. Ren reaches for her hand, then seems to notice the blood dripping from her own.

Her outstretched fingers close, her fist crimson as the empress whispers, "I'm weak. The people know it ... but they'd see it even more with you beside me. You ... are a better me. A better Xin." A tremble of breath. "They'd have no need for me."

"Baomei—" The diminutive slips out, intimate and accidental like the blood that Ren drips onto the empress anyway. "I would have never—if the people think—" She breaks off, forcibly composes herself. "We can't control what the people think. Nor does it matter what they think." I don't know if she believes it, but she says it for the empress. "Only what you think matters. Only you. You sent me that message, your decree. Why didn't you retract it, if this is what you wanted?"

Must you ask for more hurt, Ren? Because Xin Bao has already answered. Maybe she genuinely wanted to be saved, at first. But as the seasons changed, so did her feelings. The more people Ren rallied around her cause, the more Xin Bao's insecurities blossomed. Miasma was oppressive, but Miasma could never be a true empress. Ren could. Be it at Miasma's behest, or by her own will, Xin Bao let the decree stand, let a cry for help become a lure, a trap.

Should there ever come a day when Ren actually made it to this hall, Xin Bao would know that it was time to end Ren or be ended herself.

"Why didn't you?" Ren repeats, and Xin Bao blinks, eyes wet. Blood ekes past her lips.

"I'm ... sorry ... Aunt ... Ren ..."

My numbness shatters. How dare she address Ren with so much familiarity?

How dare she, after betraying the *one* person who has fought for her?

When Ren doesn't speak, doesn't reject or accept the apology, Xin Bao's gaze rolls away from her and up to the ceiling, to the gold, cobalt, and vermilion beams of a man-made heaven. "In the next life . . . I don't want to be . . . born an empress."

She stares until she sees no more.

"What will you do now, Ren?" Miasma again. She lies beside Cloud, paralyzed all but for her tongue and mouth. "What, oh what, will you do? I know what. You'll run away from the people. You'll leave the throne empty, and this land will suffer another decade of fighting, all because you won't be able to live with yourself."

Miasma laughs—and falls quiet after Cicada shoots her with a second dart, the paralysis finally taking full effect.

Ren. I want to go to her, but can't as Crow. I could have asked Miasma about Plum's whereabouts, but can't do that now either. I can only watch as Cicada puts another dart to her shooter and aims it at Cloud, sending a stir through Ren.

"Cicada—"

"It's the antidote," the Southlands queen says, and fires.

Seconds later, Cloud groans. Moves, slowly, onto her knees.

She shuffles, toward Ren, still kneeling as well.

She presses her forehead to the floor before our lordess.

"Kill me, Ren." I stop breathing, my heart splitting as Cloud says, "I made you do this. If not to save me, our empress wouldn't—"

"Stop, Cloud."

"And Lotus—she also died to save me—"

"*Cloud.*" Ren clutches Cloud's bowed head. "You didn't make me do anything. Do you understand? I did this alone, and I'd do it again for anyone I consider family. That's you, Cloud." Cloud's shoulders shake with sobs, and I look away, eyes burning. Cloud is family, but Xin Bao was family too. We all know Ren wouldn't have hesitated to sacrifice herself for the empress; we all feel her grief as she comforts Cloud through it. "And Lotus, Cloud? She'd peel both our hides if she saw you in the afterlife. She'd want you to live, and live well."

Cloud's sobs heave huge and ugly, and Ren's head turns to the side, her brow furrowed, eyes shut, tears confined. Slowly, she removes her hands from Cloud. She moves back to Xin Bao, closes the girl's eyes, and pulls out her sword. She stands, and I find myself standing too, wanting to support her as she sways. *Help her, Cloud!*

But Cloud's head remains bowed.

Shaking, bleeding, Ren faces Cicada. "Let's end this."

Her sword drips, bathed in blood like Ren herself.

You promised.

This time, I hear the voice as if it's really in my head.

Crow? Are you here?

Whether or not he is, I did promise him. Cicada didn't hurt Ren, and I owe it to Crow to protect his lordess from hurt as well, even if I don't know how. I step toward Ren, stopping as she throws her sword. It lands between her and Cicada, streaking blood onto the wood.

The gesture is her answer. Weaponless, wounded, Ren concedes.

Cicada is free to take whatever she wants, be it the sword or the throne. Ren has no desire for either.

"Ren...," rasps Cloud, drawn up by the *clang*. She stares at her swornsister while I stare at the sword, then the lordess I serve. I chose her over my god-sisters. Happiness—I want that for her. But will this make Ren happy? Or will she come to regret her choice?

"Miasma was right about something," Cicada finally says after a pause. "If you leave the throne empty, more wars will erupt as others seek to claim it. The people will know no peace."

"There's you."

The words fall from Ren's lips. So easy, so quick.

Silence resounds in their wake.

Cicada's gaze surveys the throne hall. "I always dreamed of standing here. A dream greater than my sister dared. I've traded things and people to get this far." She glances to me. "I don't want to trade more." She looks to Ren. "This journey made me realize I have no interest in living in the North. It's too cold, and the people are crude. But you don't see them that way," she says as Ren's lips part. "So stay. Forget that you slayed the empress."

"And deceive the people."

"As if you haven't already. Are you really Ren the Righteous every second of the day? No, but that's how the people see you. All symbols are lies, and all rulers are symbols. That's what it is to rule. To be someone you're not. Kingdom over self. Fears hidden behind wants."

"What do you want for the South?"

"Sovereignty."

Gasps would be going through the court, if there were officials present.

Instead it's just Ren, her voice somber and quiet. "You're still young. You ask for sovereignty now, but in a few years, you might want more." Her eyes lower to her own bloodstained hands. "You might change."

"You might too," Cicada says without hesitation. "If you become a tyrant, I'll expose you. I'll tell everyone it was you who killed Xin Bao, not Miasma."

"Miasma didn't—"

"She did," insists Cicada, "and after your coronation, you'll execute her for it."

I hear the decree as it might spread through the realm.

Xin Ren, our worthy empress, putting down the tyrant who slayed Xin Bao.

The Ren I know wouldn't agree to this lie—or would she? For the soldiers, the orphans, the masses uprooted by our warpath, she would. But even if her reason is noble, will she be able to bear the guilt? I don't know. I want to discount Miasma's words, but they stay, echoing through my skull as Ren rasps, "War is no good for the people. I hope we can agree on this."

"Agreed." Cicada puts her dart shooter away. "Let's prove that this heaven can have more than one sun."

She holds out her hand, an invitation.

Ren doesn't take it. "I'd like a moment."

"Of course." Cicada glances to me, and even though it's the last thing I want to do, I follow her. Over the threshold, out of the throne hall, onto the pavilion. Cicada descends the steps. I linger on the topmost one.

I look over my shoulder.

The open wall frames them so perfectly, the scene between the columns like a painting, one that I've carried in my head this entire journey. Miasma, defeated. Cloud, still here.

Ren, at Xin Bao's side.

She kneels in the empress's blood, spread out larger than the scarlet imperial robes, and stares at Xin Bao like she doesn't know what to make of her, this goal that she's lived for, would have died for, only to have it die before her.

My legs weaken.

"Senge?" In the distance, I hear Cicada call for me.

The ground rises up as I collapse upon it.

What is this? If it's not the poison, then is it Crow's consumption? The consequences of being struck by lightning? This body finally retaliating after all the abuse it's taken? As I wonder, something glimmers in the sky above me. Two arches. The shapes of serpents. I hear her voice.

Time to pay.

No—it's too soon.

I didn't agree to this, three months ago . . . did I?

四十九

FATE AND PROPHECY

*T*hree months ago.

"Whatever the price, I'll pay it. Just send me back."

The Masked Mother had smiled, amused. "I'll be fair, then. For going back as a god, you will never be allowed to return to the heavens. And if you succeed in your aims, you'll never be allowed in the mortal realm either."

Banished from heaven. Banished from earth. I'd have nowhere to go.

Or to exist.

"That's correct, Zephyr: You will pay with your very existence. Succeed, and your spirit will be recalled to the Obelisk, but it will not undergo the cycle of reincarnation. It will be destroyed. You will have no chance of being yourself, a god, or someone else if you do change fate."

Change fate. Change fate. Change fate.

It was all that I could hear, and all that I wanted.

My only aim.

"How will I know I've changed fate—really changed fate?"

I'd asked the Masked Mother. I thought I'd changed Cloud's fate, when I took her place under Miasma's blade, but all I did was delay it. I couldn't rely on a goal so broad; I needed a concrete objective.

"What do you wish to fulfill?" asked the Masked Mother.

Make Ren empress. But it's not what Ren wanted, and I swallowed the words. "Unite the three kingdoms as we march north. Free Xin Bao from Miasma, and keep Plum and her descendants from the throne." *But is that enough?* "Wait, and free Xin Bao from anyone who seeks to control her." But freedom could mean death; language was finicky like that. "Can I write it out on a scroll?"

The Masked Mother had laughed. "Tell you what, Zephyr. When the time comes, you will only pay the ultimate price if you've accomplished what you want in your heart."

"In my heart?"

"Yes. If you're going to be dealing with mortal fates, then you should know this: The mortal heart wants what it wants."

Lightning had flashed, and thunder had shaken the heavens. But my heart was set.

I knew what I wanted.

I wanted what Ren wanted.

Now, lying on the ground, I curse. Was this what I wanted all along? Xin Bao dead? Could it be that my own heart betrayed me? Or has Plum died?

I hate that I have no way of knowing.

"Senge? Senge!" Footsteps, urgent, rushing over. I blink, bleary, as Cicada's face appears above mine.

Ren. I want it to be her, to have my true lordess by my side. I want—to say farewell to her. But it's too late. I made my choice. With the Masked Mother's terms, I knew I wouldn't be able to stay with Ren if I succeeded. Winning for her would be my goodbye, and as I strain to see Ren over the threshold, I almost convince myself that I've won in the way I envisioned. From this angle, I can't see the blood on the floor. Xin Bao could be sleeping, and Ren could be kneeling for no reason other than loyalty. A beautiful story. Legend.

Lie.

Already, I can feel Ren's nightmares. The dawns when she'll wake in cold sweat, remembering what it felt like to skewer her empress. I can feel her pain, if she stays as Cicada has suggested and rules. Mortals all die, sooner or later, but the guilt will kill her every day.

And I won't be there to help her.

But Cloud will. Tourmaline. Sikou Hai. And Cicada—she cares about Ku in her own way. She didn't kill Ren. She fought Miasma with us. She is young, like Ren said. Maybe she'll change. But maybe Ren will too. Every day they live is another day they can choose to change—if not destiny, then how they react to it. Live on in spite of it. Fate and prophecy—fulfilling either is just the beginning.

Only my time is ending.

Cloud . . . Out the corner of my eye, I see her rising, then Ren, Cicada's cries summoning them. *Cloud—keep the truth of my brief, meaningless return from our lordess. And comfort Tourmaline. Make sure she doesn't do something so foolish again. Live on, and live well. Lotus would want that, like Ren said, but I wish it for you too. I wish . . .* Tears blur my vision. I try to fight them, then stop. They carve down my cheeks as my eyes close.

I wish we could have all had a toast under the peach trees after Ren ascends the throne.

Forgive me for leaving too soon.

"Senge? Talk to me. What hurts? What's wrong?" Cicada wipes my face as the tears keep coming, her motions frantic.

For her, I blink them back with the last of my strength. "Sound the gong," I whisper to her. Sikou Hai will understand the signal, universal among armies.

Retreat.

We live to fight another day.

Then I release the body.

That's when I see him. Afloat in the air like me. He's here. He didn't disappear. We face each other, and I drink in the sight of him, the lines of his body clear. Then I notice the ghosts too, before the throne. I can see them again.

Maybe because I'm about to become one.

I want the last word with Crow before that happens. "Sorry that I couldn't save you the honor of ending me." I nod at the body, on the ground, its heart still beating. "Go on. Return to it."

Crow doesn't move. "Where are you going?"

Nowhere. There's nowhere left for me in heaven or on earth. That's the answer, and it scares me. I wish I could share my fear with Crow. I wish he could know all of me. Be with me. Hate me or love me.

Walk into this unknown with me.

But that's not possible. Even if it were, he wouldn't want to and I wouldn't make him.

I've tormented him enough.

"Somewhere where I don't have to stare at your face every day," I say, and then, before he can see my expression cave, I brush by him, one spirit passing another. To the world, we don't exist. We can't affect it. But as my sleeve grazes his, I shudder, my desire to stay a little longer so strong, it almost doesn't feel like a coincidence when a breeze stirs. Ahead of me, the leaf settled on the pavilion shivers and drifts, up and up and up, until it's sailing through the sky.

Whether I'm ready or not, I must join it.

"Was it worth it?" His voice accosts me from behind, and my heart lurches.

Maybe I'll tell you in another life, I want to say, but can't, too afraid my voice will crack. I keep walking, every step touching the ground a little less.

Eventually, I surrender myself to the lightness and float, soaring over the capital streets we passed, to see the troops we left outside the walls. I hear the gong, sounding out.

I see Cloud riding to tell everyone that we've won.

Was it worth it?

I've achieved the Rising Zephyr Objective, technically. And yet Ren bleeds, inside and out. Of her two swornsisters, only one stands with her. The empire is not united. Decades from now, this dynasty will fall and a new one will rise. None of that will be different.

But while we are here, we live. We love. We leave our marks.

Rain and wind may eventually erase them, but it won't erase the lǐ I walked with everyone.

Ren. Cloud. Lotus. Ku. Tourmaline. Sikou Hai. Crow—

My only regret is that I won't get to be your strategist, sister, friend, mentor, equal in another life.

The gong sounds and sounds, and I breathe in and out.

In and—

‡ ‡ ‡

Zephyr has gone.

I am fading too, the spirit half that she split off.

Soon, we will perish together, for we are one. We share the same emotions. The same heart.

I know what she couldn't see for herself:

Her heart never wanted for Xin Bao to die, but for Ren to rise.

I float before Ren, our queen and lordess.

I touch her shoulder.

"I'm sorry. I know it hurts. But you will heal," I murmur to her. "And when you do, I hope you see what the world sees: that you are worthy." My hand on her shoulder begins to fade. It's time. "Goodbye, Ren."

I don't expect her to hear me. She's mortal. I'm not her family. Cloud could only see me because of Lotus's qì.

But then Ren looks up, eyes glazed. "Qilin?"

She rises, unsteadily, from the empress, her gaze searching the hall, as if she caught my voice in the wind, and I smile.

I'd like to think that she can feel it, as I become wind myself.

STANZA FIVE

To the north, a queen
chose to stay
and revive a dynasty.

To the south, a cicada
returned home, blessed to have both
strategists survive the war.

To the west, two generals
rode, on orders of their new empress
to protect the peace.

And in the skies above—

The Scribe lifted the brush. All around them were blank scrolls, spread open, a dozen brushes writing upon paper as if compelled by an unseen force. That force, the Scribe knew, was none other than the mortal will itself. Sometimes, those fates would change as the heart changed. More often, the heart inks the path long before the body ever walks it.

Only the fates of gods were written by the heavens.

No one knew this secret but the Masked Mother, and as the Scribe set the brush down, they became her. The Masked Mother glanced toward the scroll at her fingertips, then to the pile under the table—half-burned god-fates rescued from the fire, awaiting restoration.

That Zephyr, creating so much work for her.

Still, it would not do to write an untruth in haste.

Because, you see, the Masked Mother knew another secret.

‡ ‡ ‡

"Mortal affairs are not to be meddled with."

From the backs of her serpents Qiao and Xiao, the Masked Mother addressed the gods assembled on the pink clouds below. Some took on humanoid forms, others those of beasts. Still others preferred to be streams of vapor. At their cores, however, they were all made of the same godly qì, purer than any mortal's.

Now one had departed their ranks forever.

"Zephyr is our latest example."

And Nadir had been the example prior. *Do no harm to the mortals*, the Masked Mother had declared to the masses in the aftermath of the demon-child's destruction. *And do no good.*

"In trying to rewrite human destinies, Zephyr destroyed her existence. Let her needless sacrifice be a lesson to you all."

The crowd shifted uneasily. The Masked Mother could hear their murmurs, read their deepest fears and wants. She understood every god under her charge better than they understood themselves. That included Zephyr and the occasional god like her who found the unending existence intolerable. But in the collective mortal existence, every outcome could still be outdone, undone, and redone.

Is that any less unending?

‡ ‡ ‡

After the speech, the Masked Mother returned to her palace, where one god knelt on the steps, another buzzing as a bee by her shoulder. Two gods come to plea clemency for Zephyr.

The Masked Mother stopped beside them. "You do realize

she's already paid the first price: Even if I spared her existence, she will never return to the heavens."

"I know," said Nadir. "I don't care. She deserves another life, even if it's not with us." Nadir's gaze flashed up, and the Masked Mother noted it was unusually fearless. "She couldn't have accomplished everything that was in her heart to warrant her spirit's destruction. I don't believe it."

An interesting argument. *Did you succeed at everything you desired, Zephyr?* mused the Masked Mother. Who really knew but Zephyr herself?

Either way, it didn't matter. For here was the second secret of the heavens:

Zephyr's spirit may have been recalled, but her destruction depended not on her success or failure. The fact of the matter was that gods couldn't die, because to die was to be reincarnated, and gods couldn't be reincarnated. The gods the Masked Mother had banished down the Obelisk?

They perished.

Only mortal qì could be transformed to live and die again, in another life.

At the end, who was Zephyr? Did she have enough mortal qì to call hers, and wholly hers, to withstand the Obelisk and be reincarnated?

Or would she vanish into the ether that begot her?

The Masked Mother entered her palace, where Zephyr's spirit was held in an urn.

She picked it up. "Why don't we find out?"

CODA
Crow

There's a reason why gods and humans shouldn't fall in love. Crow is the living testament.

He doesn't realize it immediately—the consequences of being possessed by a god, or of falling in love, an act he spends every waking moment denying. His heart? Belongs to Cricket. The dreams of *her* that plague him? Are closer to nightmares. The way he can't seem to listen to a zither song without seeing a flutter of white robes? That's just trauma.

(It's definitely trauma when he flinches back from a steamer of dumplings set before him at an inn, one day many years later.)

As for the times he thinks he hears her voice, usually when he's very tired or very sick, that's trauma too. Pray tell, why would he want to listen to her for another second when he spent months listening to her lie to the people he cared about while he could only suffer in silence?

Silence. She left him in a bitter sea of it, never answering his final question. If there's any reason Crow still hears her from time to time, it's because he wants that answer, and not because he wants *her*. But fine. Fine. He's happy to have the final word.

(He is. He convinces himself of this.)

Except he's wrong about that too.

‡ ‡ ‡

She left him a note.

Of course she did.

It goes like this:

Crow. Sen . . . What do I call you? Not Senge, since I'm most certainly older than you. Doesn't matter, does it now?

Must be a relief, to never have to hear my voice again.

I'm guessing, if you're reading this, that I've left this world. Yes, I knew this day would come. In order to return to earth after I died as Lotus, I made a deal with another deity, one that would end with the destruction of my spirit. Forgive me for not telling you sooner. Would you have spared some effort, if I had? I doubt it. You'd have had no reason to believe me. And so while I'm sorry, I have no regrets. It was entertaining, seeing you try to best me. Can I confess to that? Will you hate me more for it?

Too bad. Let me confess, because I will confess to nothing else. The nonsense you thought about my heart beating faster for you? It's still nonsense.

Go on, then, and live your silly little life. Teach ~~Ku~~ November every tactic you know. Compose more pretentious poetry with Cicada. Chase all the ladies and gentlemen (without poisoning them, if I may suggest). Forget me, if you can.

I won't be offended.

Oh and one more thing, Crow? Rest. Take yourself to a good physician. If I didn't kill you, why should the consumption?

Zephyr

It took Crow a week after returning to his body to find the note, flecked with dried blood, written at some point when he wasn't watching and slipped into his cloak's inner pocket.

It took him a lifetime to discover the second gift she'd oh-so-graciously left him.

No one noticed, at first, when he didn't age. He'd always looked a bit worse for wear compared to his peers. But now the opposite seemed to be happening, his youth growing more pronounced by the year, inviting comments from Cicada's suitors.

"What a young strategist you have," they'd say to the Southlands queen, glancing at him through their lashes, and Cicada and Crow would privately chuckle over the insinuation. There had never been anything between them, unlike Crow and Cricket. They were better as friends. As lordess or queen—whichever title Cicada preferred on a given day—and strategist.

But when the comments persisted, Cicada's laughs grew a little shorter, a little quieter.

Concern began to crease her eyes.

Finally, she summoned a monk to the Southern Court, who'd circled Crow, then taken his ice-cold hands and read the lines upon them. She'd concluded her assessment with a long sniff of his person, and grinned, golds and silvers in her teeth, and called him blessed. When Cicada asked her by what, she'd crowed, "Divinity! He's exchanged qì with a divine being."

Exchanged. Such a mild, ambiguous word. What had he and Zephyr exchanged? Hatred? Bodies? Saliva, on that night that Crow, no matter how he tries, can't stamp from his mind?

Which event was to blame?

He didn't ask the monk—he doubted she would know—and what did knowing help?

"Can it be undone?" he'd asked instead.

They'd tried to exorcise him, and that hadn't worked—a suspicion Crow held when he remained cold, his heartbeat quieter than normal, but that he couldn't confirm until years deeper into the future. By then, the anger itched Crow's heart like a badly knit scar. What gave Zephyr the right to leave him with not only that letter, but also this strange keepsake?

Forget her, she'd said.

How? Crow wanted to demand.

How?

‡ ‡ ‡

How do you forget someone who's carved themselves into your bones?

‡ ‡ ‡

He's lived long enough to see history play out.

Xin Ren, to her credit, secured sixteen years of peace, enough for a generation of children to grow up without knowing war and famine. But eventually, just as Miasma predicted, Ren left the throne for longer and longer stretches, though not to an untrusted advisor.

Her most trusted advisor, Sikou Hai, had a good head on his shoulders—except on one matter. Sikou Hai worshipped Zephyr. *That* made for interesting conversation, seeing that the person Sikou Hai revered as a god really was one, but not any that Crow admired. Far from.

They became friends despite this fact (or was it because of it?). They'd play chess in the imperial gardens whenever Crow was in the palace on Cicada's behalf, and Crow would wonder what Zephyr had taught Sikou Hai. This was how he allowed himself to think of her—always in relation to something else, so that he could plausibly deny he wasn't thinking *about* her.

"How is the empress?" he'd ask Sikou Hai lightly, as the willow leaves drifted and they played their openings.

"Well," Sikou Hai would answer, then prattle on about some land reform that Xin Ren was passing, and everything *did* sound well, but Crow had also heard rumors of Xin Ren spending every morning in the royal cemetery, and in Sikou Hai's voice he'd hear the undercurrent of a *but*.

There was always a *but*.

Just like in Sikou Hai and Crow's relationship.

Aside from Sikou Hai, Crow had no one else to talk to about Zephyr, because as far as Cicada knew, Zephyr had died in the ambush, and November refused to speak of the strategist she'd once called sister. Only Sikou Hai understood what it felt like to be haunted by such a force of mind, and sometimes— sometimes—they discussed her. Even bonded over their respective near-deaths at her hand (with Crow inevitably making it a competition to win, for who else could claim to have been steamed *and* struck by lightning?).

But, it was precisely what brought them close that formed the final chasm between them. One fall, while playing chess, their fingers had brushed. And whereas before, even after the loss of his first love, Crow might have raised his eyes to the player across from him and enjoyed a moment of connection—or a night, for the body could move on before the heart—all he could wonder now was if *she* had ever touched Sikou Hai and if there might be a shred of *her* qì lingering on his skin.

She really had ruined everything for him.

‡ ‡ ‡

Several autumns after that chess game, Ren left the throne to attend the long-awaited wedding between her swornsister, Cloud, and General Tourmaline.

She did not come back.

By the time Crow traveled to the Westlands to see what had happened, Ren was nowhere to be found. Neither were Cloud and Tourmaline. There was a rumor in the air—something about an old war horse named Rice Cake last spotted in the Xianlei Gorge, which Cloud had taken as a sign to search for the third swornsister called Lotus. Three old warriors, in pursuit of a lost cause. Crow couldn't help but sigh and feel melancholic. *Was it worth it, Zephyr?*

To have sacrificed all that you did, just for everyone to chase after spirits and horses?

Try as he might, he still catches himself asking her even though she can't answer.

Cicada, in the year of Ren's departure, was no longer young herself, and as her age increased, so did her appetite for empire. As she rallied the Southlands armies—against Crow's advice, but all he could *do* was advise—the throne passed to Sikou Hai's adopted daughter, the child Cicada and Ren had rescued together. She was a friend, by all means, even if she ruled the land Cicada wanted. But time was a balm and a poison, a poison precisely because it was a balm, dulling the lessons learned. They went to war, as they had before, and people died, once more.

Sikou Hai's daughter won.

For its defeat, the South ceded its sovereignty, and Crow knelt before Cicada and beseeched to be retired from her ranks of strategists.

"Why?" his queen, friend—younger sister, for all intents and purposes—demanded. "Why are you punishing me? Why do you want me to say goodbye to two strategists in the span of a week?"

"I'm not leaving you. I'm just leaving the battlefield. I'll be waiting for you when you're ready to leave it too."

With every word, Crow's voice had gotten quieter. Wind had drifted into the court, sunshine too, and for a flash, Crow recalled the sunlight that'd glittered on November's blood, her body struck down by a stray arrow when Sikou Hai's daughter's troops had overrun the ford. Cicada hadn't cried. Not then. Not in front of the army following her. But after, through closed doors, Crow had heard her sobs. His own pain was a blistering, silent desert. He'd failed his lordess. Failed his disciple too.

But one of them still lived, and so long as she did, there was a chance for the girl she once was to resurface. With time, Crow believed, Cicada would find her own happiness.

And she did.

Everyone around Crow did, until only he remained.

‡ ‡ ‡

He's seen all the sights in the realm. Mastered every skill he's wanted to learn. He's lived with the consumption, for better or worse. Even the pain of Cricket's death, and the deeper pain of not being there to save her from it, healed in the passing decades, until the memory of her ached only when pressed, like a bruise.

All said, he has no reason to be unhappy.

But at the deathbed of Sikou Hai, and then later of Cicada, he always saw *her*, floating over his body on the ground, cast there like a molted shell. *Go on*, she'd said, *return to it*, and he knew he should do exactly that.

But he only had eyes for her.

As he held the hands of friends and loved ones before they passed, he thought of the fear he'd seen in Zephyr's eyes, as she too relinquished her existence. A fear she did not voice to him, but he felt it. He still feels it.

Despite everything, he wishes he could have assuaged it.

But would he have been able to?

After Cicada's death, he'd walked through the Southern Court, to the courtyards where he'd caught dragonflies with Cricket and November and Cicada, to the watchtowers where

Cicada had challenged Crow to a poetry duel and Cricket had been the judge, and even to the lake, where the X in the stone steps appeared as sharp as if it'd been struck yesterday.

Finally, he'd stopped in the ancestral hall, where Cicada's plaque stood beside Cricket's. He'd taken down the chessboard, set out the stones, re-created the game Zephyr once played against his queen, move for move, and he'd cried. He'd cried the most he had in his life, and then he'd done something he hadn't since he was truly a teenager—he drank a whole jug of wine.

He might never know the fear that Cicada and Sikou Hai felt, or the bravery it took for Zephyr to walk into the sky. Or was it cowardice? Because sometimes, Crow loathes this world, left with nothing and no one for him. He'd rather leave it.

When he'd woken up groggy, he thought he saw a girl in white robes. *Her.* She'd come back to haunt him. He blinked, and the mirage fled.

How pathetic was this, to be haunted by memories, and not even by a real ghost.

He hated her, he thought, swearing off alcohol for the rest of his life, however long it lasted.

He hated her.

But time healed even the hate.

And left something worse in its wake.

‡ ‡ ‡

Not love. He's known love. It's warm and sweet, pure and simple. Memories of Cricket, however imbued with loss, still make him smile. But thinking of her? It hurts.

It hurts.

If this is love, he'd rather be poisoned.

⹋ ⹋ ⹋

After a long winter, spring is finally in the air. A new empress has ascended the throne: Sikou Hai's great-granddaughter.

The great-great-granddaughter of Plum.

Crow only found out after everyone else had left. Alone and with all the time in the world, he'd wandered, and finally let himself remember. Willingly. Peacefully. He let every one of his and Zephyr's interactions into his mind without trying to suppress them or his reactions, as he remembered the kiss, the duets, the many (too many) lǐ they'd ridden, until he recalled the letter she'd written to Plum. As much as Crow had regarded the senior registrar as a formidable force, Zephyr had gone to such great lengths to remove her. Perhaps she knew something he did not, as a god.

So he'd dug.

And though Plum had never been seen again after the gorge, all of them left a history, no matter how buried. And Plum had tried to bury hers: the son she'd had, when she was still young and finding her footing in court.

The son she'd given up. Sikou Hai.

Had Zephyr somehow known the dynasty would fall to one of Plum's progeny? Except it also wasn't her progeny. Sikou Hai was bound to Plum by blood, but not his adopted daughter, granddaughter, or the great-granddaughter on the throne now.

Then again, does family have to be blood? So much of Crow's never was. To him, the new empress might as well be Plum's progeny.

Would Zephyr agree? He mulls over this as he strolls the capital streets, soldiers marching past to celebrate the coronation. And had it all been worth it? If she'd wanted to keep Plum *and* her descendants from the throne, she'd failed.

Still, if you were here, would it help to see your disciple's heirs running the realm?

What is he thinking? Zephyr, happy with failure of any sort?

Smiling ruefully, he passes by a tavern. The sound of zither music floats out from within, a song tickling the air.

His step slows.

The song rises. A ballad. Same as the one that Zephyr played for him many years ago (he'd requested it, in jest, to be played again at his funeral). He still remembers her phrasings, her technique, the strings she left open, the notes she deemed important.

This player shares her interpretation.

He stops outside the tavern. He dares not look in. Hope is just the precursor to disappointment. And he knows disappointment. He's woken from so many dreams of her (yes, they're just dreams now, not nightmares). He's scared to hope.

Scared of more hurt.

Then fear turns to anger. For over a hundred years, he's been tortured by not having an answer to his question. She owes him closure. She owes him, he thinks, recalling the words from her letter, the first she ever wrote him, as a soft breeze swirls past him.

May we meet in another life.
It must be her. It has to be.
It can't be a coincidence.
Crow takes a breath.
And walks in.

AUTHOR'S NOTE

Three Kingdoms, the novel reimagined across *Strike the Zither* and *Sound the Gong*, is a work of historical fiction.

It is also a tragedy.

The heroes don't win. Nor do the villains. It may come as a shock to the first-time reader to see our hero Liu Bei[1] and his swornbrothers killed off with hundreds of pages to go; Cao Cao[2] succumbing to a brain tumor not long after; and Sima Yi[3], the

---

1 Xin Ren's inspiration

2 Miasma's inspiration

3 Plum's inspiration, withheld until now because fans of the classic will know that Sima Yi's descendants ultimately reunite the three kingdoms under the Jin Dynasty. Out of respect for those fans, I decided against saving this historied outcome as a reveal for the end.

dark horse, battling Jiangwei[4], Zhuge Liang's[5] protégé, because Zhuge Liang himself has died due to overwork.[6]

As for when this downturn starts, the inflection point can be traced back to Guan Yu's defeat at Fancheng[7], leading to the South's betrayal[8], Liu Bei's failed campaign of vengeance ending at Baidi[9], and the cataclysmic loss of Jingzhou.[10, 11]

Just as the inspiration behind *Strike the Zither* sprung from

---

4 One of Sikou Hai's inspirations. The other is Zhang Song, as mentioned in *Strike the Zither*. The third inspiration, which I can finally reveal, is an amalgamation of Sima Yi and his sons.

5 Zephyr's primary inspiration

6 On Liu Bei's deathbed, Zhuge Liang promises to serve his son, who is infamously incompetent; fearing usurpation, he recalls the strategist mid-march north. This costs Zhuge Liang a decisive victory and draws out his campaign against the empire, contributing to his eventual death by exhaustion.

7 Renamed to Bikong/碧空 (blue, cloudless sky) to denote the place where Guan Yu, Cloud's inspiration, would have lost, leading to his death.

8 The South kills Guan Yu in their first act of betrayal. In *Strike the Zither*, the betrayal takes place earlier with Crow's facilitation; had Zhou Yu, Crow's inspiration, lived longer, he also would have surely advised *against* killing Guan Yu.

9 Renamed to Taohui/桃灰 (peach ash) to denote the place where Liu Bei passes, thereby fulfilling his Peach Garden Oath to live and die as one with his sworn-brothers. Like many other details in *Sound the Gong*, the exact manner of death has been changed while preserving the essence of Liu Bei's broken heart.

10 The Marshlands in my duology. See footnote 24 for more.

11 Character vices play into this series of disasters. Guan Yu loses because of his pride, Zhang Fei (Lotus's inspiration) because of his temper, and Liu Bei because of his dedication to his swornbrothers—not a vice, in modernity; but Chinese scholars of old might have disagreed, since by Confucian hierarchies the brotherhood should not have superseded the lord-and-vassal relationship. Zhuge Liang likely would have concurred and added that Liu Bei's role as a brother should not have superseded his role as an eventual emperor.

a *what if* of mine—what if Zhuge Liang wasn't just *like* a god—
the inspiration behind the duology's arc sprung from my biggest
what if as a reader: What if Zhuge Liang *had* been able to prevent Guan Yu's defeat at Fancheng?[12] What would it take? What
would it change?

Would the characters still meet their fated ends?

‡ ‡ ‡

I had the pleasure of covering even more source material[13] in this
sequel, as you'll see in the selected points of convergence below.
While not exhaustive, I hope they can serve as trailheads for the
reader looking to venture deeper into *Three Kingdoms*.

The repeated attempts to appoint Liu Bei as king ran on for
several pages in the classic. Though compressed in *Sound the Gong*,
I tried to capture the scene's almost-Sisyphean spirit.[14]

Guan Yu playing chess while undergoing arm surgery is
another iconic scene that I intended to preserve regardless of its

---

12 Likewise, what if the alliance with the South could be genuine, instead of one
of convenience?

13 The first-half events in *Strike the Zither* are more popularized in the West
thanks to *Red Cliff* and Zhuge Liang's legendary arrow-borrowing scheme. But
Strike the Zither ends around the point of Liu Bei solidifying his Westlands base,
leaving the even bigger battles of Jingzhou, Xiaoting, and Zhuge Liang's Northern Expeditions to be covered in *Sound the Gong*.

14 Yes, Zhang Fei (Lotus) does have an outburst at his lord (sans cockroaches).
His frustration is an outlet for the readers', seeing as neither us nor him are the
paradigms of Confucian mores. The properness of titles is repeatedly empha-
sized throughout the classic; Cao Cao (Miasma) purposefully never calls himself
"emperor," and even his son Cao Pi seeks the last Han emperor's "permission"
(pressures his abdication) before taking the throne.

believability by modern standards, as well as Hua Tuo's[15] medical prowess.

Zhuge Liang's empty fort victory, on the other hand, is a well-known scene that I've adjusted to give other characters more credit. Rather than have Sima Yi retreat from Zhuge Liang playing a zither atop an empty fort out of genuine fear—just one of many examples where the novel deified Zhuge Liang through outsized reactions to his feats[16]—I chose a different explanation much like other *Three Kingdoms* media have.[17]

As mentioned, our heroes die prematurely; the South indeed tries to scapegoat a corpse[18] responsible for Guan Yu's death while suing for peace, but this fails to appease Liu Bei, who is on the verge of defeating the South before the young Southern strategist Lu Xun thinks to burn his camps. Other details, from brocade pouches containing written instructions

---

15 The physician in *Sound the Gong*. The bone-scraping is canon, as is his assessment of Cao Cao's brain tumor (likely done via pulse diagnosis) and his execution thereafter.

16 In another instance, Sima Yi mistakes a wooden effigy of Zhuge Liang for the real person *despite* hedging (correctly) that Zhuge Liang has already died. Rather than have a wooden effigy of anyone appear, I chose to bring a real corpse back to haunt Plum, in the form of Zephyr as Crow.

17 *The Advisor's Alliance* reinterprets Sima Yi accepting "defeat" at the fort as an act of self-preservation; he knows the fort is empty, but he also knows that if he defeats Zhuge Liang too early, he will no longer be indispensable to the empire's court. This *Three Kingdoms* C-drama refreshingly focuses on Cao Cao's strategists and advisors, and adapts Cao Cao asking Sima Yi to interpret his dream. Other Cao Cao moments featured in *Sound the Gong* are his red flag, white flag test, and his "ability" to kill assassins in his sleep.

18 Lu Meng is responsible for killing Guan Yu.

to stones sliced with Xs,[19] are likewise seeded throughout for the discerning fan.

In the gorge, Sima Yi *does* escape Zhuge Liang's fiery trap because of some well-timed rain, an intentional deus ex machina[20] that spurs Zhuge Liang to bemoan "man devises, but heaven decides" (人算不如天算).[21]

A notable change, of course, concerns the timeline. Since the war between our main players does not span decades in *Sound the Gong*, matters of succession play a minimal role in my plot.[22] In sharing the Marshlands with the South, Zephyr is able to construct a three-prong final attack instead of being restricted to the West, which proves to be a challenge for Zhuge Liang given the inhospitality of the terrain to both their soldiers and their supply lines. Even so, his success isn't an entirely forgone conclusion in the classic, until Zhuge Liang meets his own turning point with

---

19 In an illuminating example of how Sun Quan (Cicada's inspiration) and Liu Bei's partnership was always self-serving, each man strikes the stone as a gesture of their alliance while thinking to himself that if the stone splits under his sword, it's a sign he will prevail over the other.

20 The "deus" in *Sound the Gong*, Nadir, is a loose recombination of Nuwa and the White Snake from Chinese mythology.

21 Other famous lines that I owe to the classic are Miasma's "betray the world" line which comes from Cao Cao ("宁教我负天下人, 休教天下人负我") and Crow's "Why did the world have to make a you when there was already a me?" (from Zhou Yu's dying words "既生瑜, 何生亮?"), a line that encapsulates their rivalry perfectly.

22 Sima Yi and his heirs being represented across Plum and Sikou Hai are the exception (deservedly so, since they are the only heirs who prevail). I made this choice based on my own reading experience; after spending more than half a novel invested in the main players, it was harder to root for their sons. Other readers may feel differently, and all the heirs remain preserved in *Three Kingdoms* for those curious.

the loss of Jieting.[23] Here, he fails for the same reason he failed to stop Guan Yu from losing Fancheng: It's not possible for him to be everywhere at once. If it were—if he *were* able to push everyone like a chess piece—then he may have prevented both Fancheng and Jieting.

But had Zhuge Liang succeeded in helping Liu Bei to Emperor Liu Xian's side, it's unclear what Liu Bei would have done at the final crossroad.[24]

Throughout both *Strike the Zither* and *Sound the Gong*, I've strived to pay homage to Liu Bei, the figure behind Ren, while also resolving my frustration with the novel's white-gloved treatment of him.[25] My reimagined characters do not enjoy the same protected status of the classic's heroes; they win, but unlike their inspirations, they must pay character-tarnishing prices for those wins. This applies to Zephyr, who

---

23 His subordinate Ma Su positions all his troops atop a hill, allowing the enemy to cut off his access to water.

24 The emperor is not a main player in the classic, and even though everyone in Liu Bei's camp claims to be fighting for the emperor, it is understood that everyone is actually fighting for Liu Bei. *Three Kingdoms* clearly sets up Liu Bei as deserving of the title *emperor* on two fronts—his surname and his virtue. As a foil, Cao Cao (Miasma) lacks both (whether or not he *should* be less deserving because of his surname is beyond the scope of the classic, let alone my book). But it's precisely because of Liu Bei's virtue that he struggles with his legitimacy. Now, had Emperor Liu Xian not abdicated to Cao Cao's son, and had Liu Bei actually united the three kingdoms, the classic likely would have absolved Liu Bei of any direct responsibility for "replacing" the emperor through careful narrative framing. You see such framing around Liu Bei's refusal to return Jingzhou / the Marshlands to the South, an arguably dishonorable act that is distanced from his lordship and shouldered instead by his strategist.

25 See above footnote.

is never meant to fit into the role of hero; but it also applies to Ren, whose ending with Xin Bao is my way of preserving Liu Bei's costly choice to be a swornbrother.

Even with these wins, however, it's hard to say if history would have undergone a drastic change. The opening lines of *Three Kingdoms*, after all, claim that nothing is everlasting.[26] Not the united empire. Not the divided empire. Not the wins and losses of our characters. But the legends they create *are*. In this light, Liu Bei's tragedy is perhaps not a tragedy at all. His brotherhood will always be remembered, and while Zhuge Liang failed too, his loyalty to Liu Bei is the element from the novel that has stayed with me the most. As such, I've tried my best to preserve this relationship while also taking perhaps my greatest liberty yet:

In a striking example of the classic's Confucian spirit, Zhuge Liang is always one step removed from Liu Bei's found family, ever conscious of his role as a strategist and as a vassal. His loyalty to Liu Bei, for example, transcends personal motivations such as love—romantic, platonic, or familial. Understandably, the idea that one might labor tirelessly for another person or cause for no reason other than adherence to a philosophy can be difficult to comprehend through a modern lens. A proxy explanation would be that it's simply a loyalty fated, an explanation explored in the twist of *Strike the Zither*.

But as my story continues, Zephyr's fight to overcome fate forces her to confront the people around her more so than

---

26 The coda with Crow is my homage to the spirit of the opening lines (and the theme of the *Three Kingdoms* as a whole): "The empire, long divided, must unite; long united, must divide. Thus it has ever been."

Zhuge Liang ever did. She chafes against the obvious pitfalls of the camp members she's trying to win for and, in the painful process, she comes to see that they contain multitudes as well. She learns to let go, and finally is seen in turn. Like Zhuge Liang, Zephyr is a god—albeit more literally. She has a home in heaven.

But in my reimagining, she also finds a home on earth.

ACKNOWLEDGMENTS

Ask me if any of my characters are based on people I know, and my gut answer will be "no." But that's not entirely true for my main characters. They aren't me, but they each begin from some facet of me, be it a fear, a trait, or a want. In Zephyr's case, her drive to succeed no matter the cost is one I can deeply relate to. That's why I chuckle a bit at the thought of Zephyr learning a lesson that I still haven't fully internalized: Life is lived in the journey, not at the destination.

In my defense, it's hard to embrace all the ups and downs and sudden dead ends of the author's journey. But no matter how long the path runs or where it goes, I'll always cherish the stretch I've walked alongside my editor, Jen Besser. Jen, it's a highlight of my career—and of my life (let me be a little Zephyr here)—to have had your faith and guidance in my work. Thank you for fulfilling my yearslong dream of being able to complete Zephyr's story and for pushing this series to heights I wouldn't have reached on my own.

There's one person who's been with me on this journey for a

long, long time. William, you've lived with me through the highs and the lows. No one knows my struggles as intimately as you, and all the uncertainty of tomorrows aside, I doubt anyone else will.

Sequels are intimidating, but I'm blessed to have role models who've conquered mountains like sequels—and bigger—before me. Hafsah, thank you for the pep talks and advice. I'm glad we're still here and climbing. Thank you to my mom, who let me word-vomit all my beats to her, chapter by chapter, and to my dad, who encouraged these phone calls and remains my 靠山. And a million thank-yous to Heather, first-ever reader of the complete draft, who has known since 2018 the bad things in store for Crow and has suffered through too many lobster emojis. I can't imagine where I'd be without you, friend.

I'm eternally grateful for Luisa Beguiristaín, who shepherds my books across the finish line with the utmost grace, even when I start stumbling. Thank you for always keeping me back from the cliff. Thank you as well to June and Cory for all the emotional support while I'm in the depths of the deadline tunnels, and to Jamie, Onyoo, and Hesina's Imperial Court for being the light at the end of them.

Once again, I'm indebted to Anna Frohmann, whose map I referred to constantly to make sure Zephyr and I were on the right path. To Kuri Huang, whose perfect rendition of Crow motivated me to do him justice, and to Aurora Parlagreco, who—pinch me—has designed all of my books so far. For another Aurora cover and interior, I hope this journey is a long one.

A very special thank-you to Tida Kietsungden, whose

dedication shines through in her illustrations of the characters. I'm so happy that we could collaborate again on the sequel.

Time is precious in any passion, and I'm humbled to have secured the time of Xiao Tong and Suto for their incredible commissions. The same goes for the members of Online Go Forum who generously pointed me toward example games played in the ancient Chinese tradition. Any mistakes are mine alone.

The truth about sequels is that they can only reach as many people who've found the first book, and I have many to thank for spreading the word about *Strike the Zither*, starting with you, the reader of these acknowledgments. Thank you for not only reading *Strike the Zither*, but for picking up *Sound the Gong*. I'm sorry for any pain, but I hope it was worth it. (If you need healing, may I point you to the bonus short story on my website?) Thank you to the authors who took valuable time to read and blurb the first book, to the team at Books Forward, to the indie booksellers, with a shoutout to Ann Branson for the Indie Next blurb, and to the entire Macmillan team, not limited to but including Kelsey Marrujo, Teresa Ferraiolo, Kristen Luby, Jackie Dever, Sarah Gompper, Jennifer Healey, John Nora, Natalia Becerra, Kathy Dawson, Katy Miller, and Veronica Ambrose. Thank you to Nancy Wu for bringing the voices of these characters to life, and to my foreign publishers who have helped Zephyr travel the world. And of course, thank you to my agency Folio and agent, John Cusick, for making all journeys, domestic and international, possible.

Last but certainly not least, I must thank Dr. Moss Roberts. Like many kids of the diaspora, language has always been a pressure point for me, and learning to read and write Chinese has been an uphill battle since my days of memorizing characters after school at the kitchen table. It remains a battle to retain literacy gains between a work and life overshadowed by English. The truth of the matter is, I wouldn't have been able to take the first step with this duology without Dr. Roberts' work. His translation bridged the gulf between my desire to read *Three Kingdoms* and my ability to, and I highly recommend it.